THE DRAGONS OF THE NIGHT
Darrell Schweitzer

We fight the dragons of the night in our despair.
—A madman.

The son overtook his father on a darkened plain amid some ancient stones. There was no moon. The boy could see the man moving against the brilliant stars, and he could see the stones. The boy wore old clothes and was barefoot and rode on a plough horse. The man was walking, and garbed for a journey, with heavy boots on his feet and a staff in his hand and a pack on his back, and there might have been a cooking pot on his head. It was hard to tell in the dark. But his old sword definitely hung at his side, clacking against his breastplate as he walked.

"Father, come home," the boy said.

"I can't. I have to go."

"Mother is weeping."

"She'll get over it. She understands. I have to go fight the dragons of the night."

"No, she doesn't."

"That's too bad then." The man rapped his knuckles against the piece of metal strapped to his chest. The boy recognized that thing now. It had been hung on the wall of their house for as long as he could remember, an almost shapeless slab of tarnished scrap. Sometimes his mother chopped vegetables on it, when his father was not around, as this were a substitute for the last words in some long-running argument.

The boy slid off his horse. For an instant he thought that there was someone else there, a third person, but, no, it was a trick of the darkness, of shadows. He took his father by the hand, but his father shook him off.

"Please," said the boy.

"Suppose a high-flying hawk drops down out of the sky for a time, to settle and make a nest, and raise nestlings in safety. That's how it is. Now I must return to the sky. To battles. To what I am sworn to."

"Father, this is crazy talk."

The boy, who had been leading his horse by the bridle, let go of it and ran in front of his father. But the man sat down among the ancient stones, in the dark, and said, "Maybe so, but you need to hear more of it."

The boy sat on a stone opposite, and then, he was certain for just an instant, a ghost in black armor, mounted on a ghostly steed came charging at them. The boy let out a cry and raised his hand to ward it off, but the man did not react, and it burst over them like a wave, only the boy felt nothing more than a puff of cold wind, and then the ghost was gone and a moment later he wasn't sure he had seen anything at all.

"Your mother heard the horns blowing, in the distance, late at night, as did I. For a long time she insisted it was a dream. 'Are we both dreaming the same dream?' says I. 'It must be,' says she. But it was not. Do not think, my son, that this does not hurt me, that my heart is not torn, that I do not love her still like a hero out of some wonderful old story...only the stories are less than entirely wonderful if you have to live them. Heroic strife is not all fun and games. There is a lot of pain. And now, I am summoned back to it all, and I must go."

Gradually it seemed to the boy that ghosts gathered all around them now, among the ancient stones, huddled thick as a herd of sheep, and sighing softly, though it could have been the wind, and the ghosts themselves could have been some illusion caused by a limitation of the eyes. If he looked at them directly, they weren't there. Out of the corners of his eyes, they seemed grotesque, with faces like dogs.

"But it's—"

"All just a story?" said his father.

"Something like that."

The boy looked down at his dirty feet, which he could not see in the dark, but that was better than gazing into his father's eyes, which even by starlight seemed filled with some frightening intensity.

"You will have to understand this as you get older," the father said. "Maybe your mother never will, but I think she already does. She just cannot bring herself to admit it."

"What? That you are running away?" the boy said angrily.

Now the father's voice became very calm, and somewhat terrible, and commanding. "Not *away*. No, never away. *Toward*. I am the hawk that fell out of the sky. Maybe for a while I fancied I could live among the chickens. Maybe I deluded myself. So, for a time I did, but the dreams came again, and I knew it was not so."

Then the boy himself heard, faint and far away, a horn blowing, though it could well have been herders in some distant field signaling one another, or a watchman in a town marking the hour of the night. But somehow he didn't think so. He was afraid it was not so. He felt fear and sorrow rising within him. He struggled to hold back tears.

"If you're a hawk," he said, "which am I? One more of the chickens to go in the soup at supper time?"

Weirdbook

VOL. 2, NO. 15 **ISSUE 45**

Features

Short Stories

Poetry

Artwork

FROM THE EDITOR'S TOWER

How time flies! This is the relaunched *Weirbook's* eighth year of publication. We have had fifteen regular numbered issue, plus three annuals.

We have a wonderful line-up, as usual, and I'm sure that all of you will enjoy this cavalcade of fantastical wonders.

This time we have stories by such fine authors as Adrian Cole, L.F. Falconer, John R. Fultz, Sharon Cullars, Marlane Quade Cook, Franklyn Searight, Laura Blackwell and John C. Hocking (among many others). These folks represent the best in modern weird fiction, fantasy, neo-pulp, and horror.

Looking to the future, this year's themed annual will be "vampires." I just now started ready the submissions, and I can tell you that we have a winner on our hands.

I do have one serious question. Does anyone know what happened to esteemed poet Frederick J. Mayer? He dropped out of sight back in late 2019 (before the pandemic). No one has heard from him since then. Fredrick has been a regular part of this magazine for years, and his friends miss him and are deeply concerned. Please contact me at weirdaether@t-online.de if you have any information.

And, on a sad note, *Weirdbook* contributor Molly Noel Moss passed away in December. This issue is dedicated in her memory.

I hope that all of you reading this find yourselves, and your loved ones, in a healthy, happy and sane state of mind and body. Let's all hope and pray that 2022 is a better year than the past two. At the time of writing this, I don't think that a few prayers for peace would do any harm, either.

Take care, and God bless.

—Doug Draa, Editor

Staff

PUBLISHER & EXECUTIVE EDITOR

John Gregory Betancourt

EDITOR

Doug Draa

CONSULTING EDITOR

W. Paul Ganley

WILDSIDE PRESS SUBSCRIPTION SERVICES

Sam Hogan

PRODUCTION TEAM

Sam Hogan
Karl Würf

His father took hold of him and raised him up.

"What do you think?"

"I think you are a crazy old man with a pot on his head," said the boy.

"Is this a pot?" His father took off his helmet and gave it to him, and the boy realized, less with surprise than with dread, that it was not a pot at all, but a finely crafted war-helm, with cheek flaps and a kind of visor that lowered over the upper half of the face. He could tell by touch, though, that it was somewhat rusty. He toyed with one of the hinged flaps, which creaked.

His father took the helmet back and put it on.

They stood atop a fallen stone and looked to the east, where the sky was beginning to lighten. Something was moving on the plain before them, like a vast, silent army, or the wind stirring the tall grass like a sea.

"Here is what you need to know," said the man. "I am a paladin. I am one of the champions of the Sky King, whose brilliantly polished mask men call the sun. In the beginning of the world—before the beginning actually—darkness fought against light, but it's a battle that nobody can win, ever, because the gods themselves are fighting their own shadows, for they stood in the light and cast those shadows, and were afraid of what had come from themselves. They are fighting their own dreams, their night-mares, which, being the dreams and nightmares of gods, took on monstrous and solid shapes, and would have torn apart the world, and devoured all of creation—not just mankind, which was newly made then, but everything, the sky, the moon, the stars—and unless eternal champions battled these monsters, these dragons of the night, forever. The gods call to themselves champions, the greatest of men, or the maddest, who yearn for glory, who follow impossible dreams, and get swallowed up in them, even as you might be sucked up into a whirlwind if you don't have the good sense to get out of the way."

"These are stories, Father. I've heard them all my life."

"All quests and rescues and great deeds. Your mother never liked sto-ries of that sort."

"No, she didn't."

"Your mother knew, and was afraid to tell anyone, that once upon a time one of the characters inexplicably fell out of the story, onto the earth, and he was in those days a mysterious and charming young man, who be-guiled her, and she married him, and began to grow old with him, and she hoped that she could go on doing so, to the end of her days, and he hoped for it too, but then she, and he too, heard the horns of summoning, and they both knew it could not be so."

"This is crazy talk, Father."

"Absolute lunacy, I quite agree."

"Then come back home."

"I can't. Sorry."

Even as they spoke the run rose in the sky, and the boy's eyes were dazzled, and he could never account for what he saw. Maybe it was a kind of dream in which there fled before the brightening rays every sort of monster: great serpents, and giants, and, indeed, dragons breathing out white, cloudy vapor, beasts with clattering armor and gleaming spikes and claws and wings that stretched to cover the sky. These rushed over the man and the boy like a storm tide, and it may have been the wind of their passing, or just a sudden gust, that nearly knocked the two of them off the fallen stone they stood on.

And the horns blew, loudly now. Or it might have been thunder. Maybe a storm was coming up this morning, though for now the sun was very bright.

And the boy saw, in the brilliant light, that his father was not a seedy and slightly ridiculous old man with a pot on his head and a scrap of old metal strapped to his chest, but a knight, in full war-armor, with a spear in his hand, quite magnificent in his golden-trimmed war helmet. The visor was up, and his face was still visible, and it was still the same face, but somehow harder, firmer, less worn by time, though the eyes looked very old and the beard was as gray as it had ever been.

The horns blew like thunder, and the earth shook from a thousand times a thousand hoofbeats, and in the glare of the risen sun he saw the polished, burning mask of the Sky King, and he saw the King's champions all around him, buffeting him harder and harder as they leapt over and flowed around the standing stones like a fiery torrent; and the eyes of the Sky King opened behind the mask, and the voice was more terrible and more beautiful than any he had ever heard or could ever describe, but he couldn't make out what it said.

His eyes ran with tears. But somehow, dazzled and stunned and deafened though he was, he was still able to make out, as if he gazed into a raging furnace, moving shapes, and in an instant he saw his father snatched up and hauled onto a gleaming horse and vanish in the mass of golden warriors. At the same instant something sent the boy tumbling backwards into mud. But he got up on all fours and screamed for his father, and his father called back to him once, but it was just a cry and nothing more, not even a farewell or a command to go back home or anything.

That must have been the end right there. What seemed to happen next couldn't have happened, outside of delirium, or some kind of seizure. Nevertheless, with great effort, as if leaning against a hot, terrible wind, the boy got to his feet and groped his way back to his plough horse, which stamped nervously, not quite able to perceive what he thought he had, but still afraid out of dumb instinct.

He boy mounted. He kicked the horse's sides with his bare heels and got it to lurch forward in a lumbering gallop. He pursued. He rode into the light and somehow could see again. He rode with that incredible army with the Sky King at his side and the dragons of night retreating before him. All around the champions swarmed, and the gods themselves, some of them not at all human in their form, half-beasts, or living flames.

For a time he actually caught up with his father, and road beside him, and called out. His father raised his visor, and turned toward him, and the look on his face was hard to read, astonishment, then perhaps pride, perhaps sorrow.

The boy called out, "Father, I am a hawk and the son of a hawk!"

And his father replied, "Yes, you are."

"I want to come with you!"

"Then you are going to have to learn how to soar."

And the father seemed both proud and weeping.

"This is crazy talk," he said at last. "You heard it from an old man with a pot on his head."

They might have said between one another, but not much, because the boy's horse was a mortal horse and it soon fell behind. For a time he was merely blinded by the brilliant light, and when he could see again it was early evening, and he sat up stiffly, squishing in a muddy field. A storm had come up after all. The sky was dark and it was raining hard. His eyes were dazzled and it hurt to open them for more than a moment or two. He looked around and he saw his poor horse, dead beside him, its flesh steaming.

When he stumbled home, it was clear that something very strange had befallen him. His clothing was seared to tatters and he was sorely hurt. His eyesight was never very good after that, and sometimes he saw things that other people said weren't there. Sometimes glowing shapes floated before him in the darkness. Sometimes he spoke to them. People said he wasn't right in the head, that he'd been hit by lightning and it had addled him.

What had become of his father, no one could be sure. His mother finally said, in despair, just before she died, that he had been a mere tramp, a wandering madman, who had somehow beguiled her once upon a time, but then reverted to his old ways in the end and deserted her. He wept to hear her say that, for he knew she had lost the dream she and her husband had once shared.

But did he ever learn how to soar, that son of a hawk? Did he ever follow after? I know that he grew to become a man, because I am that man, but a man who doesn't see very well and talks to phantom lights and whose ears ring with sounds no one else can hear and wanders around with a pot on his head and carries he piece of metal which he insists is a breastplate but everybody else thinks is a piece of old junk isn't likely to learn to soar. More often than not, he will use that pot as a begging bowl. He may amuse people with his funny stories. Let them laugh. Let them be amused. Let them even pity him. It is all part of the greater story, a striving as heroic and as desperate as any battle fought against the dragons of the night by gods and armored knights, a means to an end, even as he might somehow in his loneliness comfort a woman who is herself lonely, yet destined, and he will treat her with love and kindness and tell her stories; even as the two of them have a son; and he will tell the son stories, and the son shall be the completion of his quest and his victory over despair.

For his father did reveal something more at the very end, something he could not tell just anyone because it was a thing of dreams, not expressible in words of the waking world. But he could tell his own son, when the time came. It was a name, not his own name but one by which a new champion would be able to announce himself among the heroes and the gods. A true name.

What he came to understand in his madness was that this name was not mine, but something to be passed on to another, a gift and a burden, and a weapon against the dragons of the night.

LOVE AND SORCERY
John R. Fultz

It was a good day to die.

Like all warriors Naaiko accepted her own death before going into battle. Accepting death was the key to victory, an escape from the chains of self-preservation that spawned cowards, weaklings, and victims. To embrace death meant that she no longer feared to die. A warrior with no fear of death was the most effective and dangerous killer of men.

Naaiko planned to kill many men today.

The warband sat in a ring of silence about the Holy Flame, dreaming of death. Ongi passed the bowl of pigments from hand to hand. Practiced fingers scrawled warpaint on placid faces. Naaiko painted a black stripe across her eyes and another across her lips. The singing began as the shaman came dancing from his hut. The feathers and scales of spirit animals hung about his chest and arms. The skull of a ground lizard was his mask, strung with talismans and random jewels. The bleached skull of a man topped his walking staff.

The warband raised their eyes to the rising smoke. The stars glittered and the moon seethed a golden warmth. The bitter herbal fumes took hold of their hearts and honed their senses as they sang. Naaiko would need to kill twice as many enemies as her brother-warriors. If she did not excel on the Path of Blood, she would be shunned and forced to accept the Path of Motherhood, the path she had already rejected. Choice of paths was the right of every woman, but few of them chose the way of the spear and the sky-worms. Naaiko's choice set her apart, even from the other members of the warband. Many of them openly wished her to fail.

The shaman danced about the Divine Well, calling to the sky-worms as the warband's song reached its resolution. The warriors took up their spears, each weapon twice as tall as its bearer. In the cradle of their free arms they carried round shields of boiled hide and timber. Naaiko bore the shield of her grandfather, which the old man had sworn to her was blessed by ancient spells. She would soon test that claim.

The shaman sang alone now, his voice echoing across the Plaza of Stones.

They came rising from the deep well, quivering snaky bodies flapping venous wings of pink leather. The sound of their trilling filled Naaiko's ears. The beasts flew in great loops and circles, each one settling near to a waiting spearman. Naaiko stifled her natural repulsion as one of them came to ground at her side, wrapping its tail about her legs. She had expected a cold touch, but the slime coating the wormflesh was warm and sticky. The broad wings spread above her head, blotting out the moonlight. The eyeless worm's mouth opened near her cheek, a mass of concentric fangs dilating with excitement. She turned to face the fangs and spoke the sacred words without fear.

The worm slid between her knees, exactly as the others did with their chosen warriors. The slime bonded with the naked skin of shins and thighs. It would not prevent her falling due to violence, but it would save her from the shame of an accidental fall. Naaiko's brothers had explained all of this to her, yet still her stomach turned at the convulsing mass of wormflesh settling beneath her. Then the worm's wings flapped, and the wind stole her breath away.

She watched the dancing shaman grow tiny as the sky-worm carried her high. Outside the Plaza of Stones the slabs of the Fallen City leaned at crooked angles, agleam with moonlight and heavy with flowering moss. The ruins grew small beneath her, and soon the entire island revealed itself to her eyes. All of the hollows, vales, coves, and cliffs she knew so well took on a new relationship to each other, now that she saw the fractured island as a whole.

She clutched spear and shield, her legs squeezing tight about the sky-worm's middle. The wings pounded like thunder on either side of her. Blinking as the wind tore at her eyes, she counted thirty-seven worms supporting the warband, each one topped by a spearman hungry for glory. Almost all of these warriors were more experienced than Naaiko, except for the two youths Zali and Volod, her fellow first-timers. She grinned at Zali across the flapping swarm, and the boy grinned back. She could not tell where Volod was, but there was no more time for adjusting to flight, no more time to reflect on her bond with the sky-worm.

Now came the time for killing.

The dense green carpet of the island fell away, replaced by the darkness of the great chasm. On the far side of the island, across the yawning ravine, stood the second of the island's two mountains. The ruins of the Smited City lay about its base, built of the same glittering stones as the Fallen City. That side of the island was identical to her own side, except for the wicked beauty of the ruin. Unlike the Fallen City, which hid its splendor beneath the jungle canopies, the Smited City's remains stood proud and sparkling on the hip of a dead firemount.

Naaiko's view of the distant ruin was obscured by a fresh mass of sky-worms rising to meet her warband above the chasm. The hated Yonni,

Children of the Smited, rode on their own flapping beasts, called up from their own Divine Well. The shaman had sung many times his tale of how the Yonni stole the worm-magic from the ancestors of the Saachu. If not for that thievery, the Saachu would have long ago wiped out the Yonni and hammered the stones of the Smited City into a fine powder.

Naaiko gritted her teeth as the two flapping swarms converged. The war-cries of her brothers and cousins rose above the thunder of worm-wings. The Yonni advancing toward her were painted in foreign patterns, but otherwise identical to those who fought beside her. History whispered that the two tribes used to interbreed, back in the long days before the cities died. It only made sense that the men she would kill today looked exactly like her own kin. This was her last thought as the two tribes met above the chasm in a collision of flesh, flint, and bone.

In three cases, colliding worms wrapped themselves about each other, tangling the bodies of their riders in a simultaneous death-grip. They drifted slowly downward like convulsing, four-winged organisms, while the riders wrestled each other with elbows and knives. Most of the sky-worms did not collide, but soared into screeching circular orbits while their riders jabbed spears at each other. Naaiko's shield turned the first of the spears aimed at her throat, and she lunged forward to ensure her own weapon struck true. The spear's sharp head slid easily into her enemy's ribcage, but the trick was pulling it free before the dying man fell from his worm and took her weapon with it. He fell, bleeding and cursing, as she wrenched the spear free.

The riderless worm fled as another took its place. The Yonni outnumbered the Saachu tonight, but Naaiko had welcomed that. It meant more men for her to kill, more glory for her to steal, and therefore more freedom to follow her chosen path. Naaiko's four brothers rode in tonight's warband, as they had ridden in countless others over the years. If she did not claim enough kills in this fight, even her own brothers would not support her remaining with the warriors. Ukoi, the eldest and most vetted of them, had already declared that Naaiko's place was in the birthing hut. She had defied his will to ride the sky-worm. To prove herself to him was to prove herself to the entire tribe.

Her spear took down another Yonni rider as she shouted her own war-cry. The worms never stayed to quibble after their riders fell into the great chasm. They simply flew off and returned to the bottom of whichever Divine Well had spawned them. The ancient spell that shamans worked to bond them to warriors ended with each warrior's death. The chasm below was the boundary line between the island's two territories. Some called it the Well of Death, although it was not a well at all. Its length ran almost the entire width of the big island, and no living man could say how deep it extended into the earth. Since the Time of Fracturing, when the island had cracked itself in two, the chasm had divided the island like a great, toothless maw. Those who fell from their sky-worms, dead or merely wounded, disappeared into the dark belly of the gorge. A layer of grey mists shrouded the lower depths of the fissure, preserving the secrets of its rocky bottom. Perhaps it had no true bottom, but reached all the way to the blazing center of the world. There were many who believed it so.

Naakio watched her youngest brother take a Yonni spear to the belly, and the distraction of it caused her to miss her next spear-thrust. Her latest enemy's spear flashed forward, but not at her raised shield. It sank deep into the gasping throat of her sky-worm. She had not expected such an indirect attack, although it seemed an obvious strategy now. The worm spasmed beneath her gripping legs, and its wings faltered, pulling it from the impaling spear. Black ichor spurted from the beast's wound, and the enemy's spear flashed again, this time at Naaiko's head. It found her shield instead, punching through the grizzled hide and entangling her on the Yonni's weapon.

The dying worm ceased its flapping and fell away from her, its slimy flesh peeling away from her own skin with a sucking sound. Her panicked fists grabbed at the enemy spear as she dropped her own weapon. She would pull herself onto his mount, or fall to join her youngest brother in the Well of Death. The Yonni rider was too swift for her. He simply released the spear, and she plummeted toward the chasm, still grasping the stolen weapon like it had some power to carry her home. The dark fissure raced upward to swallow her. She closed her eyes and sang a final warsong. She smelled the sea, mingled with the reek of blood on the warm air, and once again she accepted her own death.

She landed far sooner than she expected, and on something far softer than she could have imagined. Her eyes flashed open, the sensation of falling not yet done with her, even as she lay flat on something that floated in mid-air. She had not even reached the lip of the chasm, but floated some distance above the island's highest treetops. The battle continued above her, wings thundering, worms screeching, men howling for life and death. Squirming shapes fell past her into the abyss. The fact that she did not fall now amazed and confused her.

She lay a flat surface, pliable yet firm. The lean figure of a young man stood over her. She blinked at his brown-skinned hand reaching toward her, as if she had stumbled over a root and a polite stranger wished only to help her up. His face was lean, slightly unshaven, and his eyes were spinning motes of rainbow colors. Living jewels that refused to confine their beauty to a single hue.

She took his hand, and he helped her to stand up next to him. His ragged cloak flapped in the night wind. She looked to her bare feet and saw a thick rug of great size, the firm softness that had stopped her fall. A rug that floated in the sky like a cloud.

"Are you all right?" asked the stranger. Somehow he spoke the island tongue perfectly. Naaiko had met a few foreign traders, but this man with the beautiful face and flashing eyes was no wrinkled sea merchant. He wore a robe of patchwork colors and a cloak to match. At one time his garments may have been rich and silky, but it seemed that years of powerful winds had blown his vestment to shreds. He seemed a wayward prince wrapped in glorious tatters.

Naaiko did not have a reply at first. She could only stare at his impossible eyes. When he finally blinked, she tore her gaze away to study the battle once again. Already the two warbands were disengaging, each side having lost more than half its numbers to the chasm. The last few men dropped into the deep darkness even as she watched. The beautiful stranger did not seem to hear them. His glimmering eyes studied only Naaiko. She felt the need to meet his attention with polite words at least.

"I…I should be dead," she said.

He laughed, a pleasant sound.

"Now that would be a tragedy," he said. "You're far too beautiful to die."

She examined the rug again, floating above the Well of Death on a soft wind, drifting slowly toward the far side of the fissure. "No," she said, looking at the Smited City's distant glow. "Do not take me to that side…" She pointed to her tribe's side of the breach. "Take me there."

"As you wish," said the stranger. The flying rug turned itself around at some unseen signal of his, and it rushed away from the chasm. The green jungle lay etched in shadows and moonlight. They floated above the highest canopy as the stranger sat himself down in a cross-legged fashion.

"Why did you save me?" she asked, still standing before him.

The stranger's eyebrows raised. "Should I have let you die?"

"Yes!" Naaiko said. "No. I'm sorry. I don't know what to say…"

"Please, sit down," he said. She did, laying the Yonni spear across her knees.

"Thank you," she said. "Living is preferable to dying. Even if one must live as an outcast."

"You do not seem to be an outcast," said the stranger.

"I may not be," she said. "I killed three men today…"

She almost said "before dying," but stopped herself.

"Who are you?"

"I thought you'd never ask," said the stranger. "Call me Magtone."

"I am Naaiko."

Magtone took her fingers gently in his and pressed his lips to her knuckles, at a spot where there was no discernable Yonni blood crusted.

"To be honest," he said. "I saved you because you are the most beautiful girl I have seen in ages. I hope you don't mind me saying so."

She smiled, despite herself. He was no warrior, no trader, there was not a counterpart to him in her island world. He was something new and altogether strange. She could not deny his attractive nature. Yet he must know her truth.

"I walk the Path of Blood," she said. "Not the Mother's Path."

Magtone blinked his blazing eyes at her, tilted his head as if uncertain.

"Can you stop doing that?" she asked.

"Doing what?"

"That thing with your eyes," she said. She could not help but stare at them.

"Oh, sorry," Magtone said. "Is this better?"

The swirling lights faded, replaced by two white eyeballs with golden pupils.

"Yes," she said. He was even more beautiful now, but at least she could look away.

"What exactly is the Blood Path?" he said. "I assume you speak of your enemies on the other side of this island. I have seen their crumbled city. A gorgeous ruin…and I've seen many a gorgeous ruin."

"The Smited City is beautiful, yes," she told him. "But it is a place of wickedness. You will see that the Fallen City is more beautiful by far. Take me there now. I will introduce you to my people. They will either praise me for tonight's work, or cast me out."

"Point the way," Magtone said. His flying rug followed her directions.

They flew toward her home as Magtone answered her blunt questions. "I am the last survivor of Doomed Karakutas," he said. "I carry with me all the secrets of its knowledge, its magic, its long history. I'm taking it across the world to Odaza, City of Walking Gods, where such wisdom can be set in sacred keeping."

"I think I understand," Naaiko said. "But I have never heard of either place."

Magtone nodded. The wind whipped knotted locks of hair about his shoulders.

"I had never heard tale of your Fallen or Smited Cities until passing over this island."

"How is it that you make this rug fly?" she asked.

"Although my primary vocation is that of a poet," he said, "I am also a wizard, as you may have guessed. Long story, but suffice to say that I have swallowed a massive dose of sorcery, and it has…changed me. Yet I do not make the carpet fly. It makes me fly."

He smiled at her again, and she found herself returning the gesture.

"What is a poet?" she said.

"Have they no word for it in your language?"

"Perhaps," she said. "What does a poet do?"

"A poet creates beauty and power from mere words," he said. "A poet sings visions of truth and wisdom to open the eyes of the world. A poet breathes miracles and speaks wonders…"

Naaiko considered his words as the rug soared above familiar jungle paths. The Fallen City rose from the undergrowth, a collection of broken ziggurats and shattered towers.

"We have a man like that," she said. "We call him shaman."

"I would like very much to meet this man," Magtone said. "I've been flying cross the Sea of Ages for more weeks than I can count, and this island is the first sign of humanity I've found."

"You travel alone?" she said. "You must be lonely…"

He looked at her in a curious way. It made her uncomfortable and excited at once.

Why did she say that? His only answer was another handsome smile.

The tribe had gathered in the Plaza of Stones to welcome the returning warband. The survivors passed a gourdful of liquor between themselves, telling of their deeds above the Well of Death, and mourning the loss of those who did not make it. Magtone's rug landed at the far edge of the plaza, where nobody even noticed it beyond the edge of the Holy Fire's light.

Naaiko walked from the darkness into the ring of light. Faces turned to her with eyes wide, mouths agape. Someone screamed her name, and her three living brothers rushed forward to embrace and congratulate her. They were certain that she too had died in the chasm, and some had even seen her fall. She told them right away that she had killed three Yonni before losing her sky-worm. They marveled at her bravery and skill, and their jubilation ignited her own. She was smiling as she introduced Magtone, the foreigner who had saved her life.

The warriors examined him with closed mouths and blinking eyes. They sniffed at his ragged cloak, which smelled of distant lands and nameless spices. The shaman came forward and the warriors fell back. Inside his bone mask, dark eyes narrowed with suspicion.

"This is no man," said the shaman. "It is a demon." He spat at Magtone's feet. "Leave us, demon!" He raised his staff and pointed in a random direction. The wives of the warriors and their curious children watched from a safe distance, mothers clutching the shoulders of the small ones.

Magtone only laughed and sang a few lines in his own language. Naaiko found it charming and pleasant, but the shaman obviously did not. He waved his staff again before Magtone's face and a bolt of green flame burst forth. Magtone ducked below the shooting flame, but it circled in the air like a living thing and struck him in the back. For a moment he writhed in the grip of the shaman's power, but Naaiko was amazed to see that the blast did not burn his flesh or clothing. She had seen the shaman's green flame burn men to blackened husks. Magtone only fell face-down, his body steaming with rainbow vapors, unconscious but unburnt. The warriors fell silent.

"I have not yet slain the demon," said the shaman, "but only put him to sleep. To lift his curse, we must throw him in the Divine Well. Let the sky-worms devour him."

Naaiko watched her cousins lift Magtone's body and carry him toward the round hole at the center of the plaza. She wanted to shout at them, to stand in front of the well and defend the stranger's goodness. But she barely knew him, so how certain could she be of his true nature? He was a thing of beauty, yes, but also a thing of mystery and danger. Even if she cried out to save him, they were not likely to listen. Despite this knowledge, she found herself pleading with her brothers.

"Wait!" she said, jogging alongside them toward the well. "Why would a demon save my life? Ask him yourself and you will see! The shaman lies!"

"Why would he lie?" asked an anxious warrior.

"Because he fears what is unknown," Naaiko said. The shaman stared at her from across the plaza, watching his orders put into action. Ukoi, her eldest brother, pushed Naaiko aside.

"You are a warrior now, Little Sister," he said. "You must act like one."

She stood silently as they dumped Magtone's limp body into the well.

Suddenly the rug of many colors darted from the edge of the plaza, as if to follow its owner into the earth. The shaman reached up and caught its edge, and now he wrestled with a wild, elemental thing. The rug leaped and flapped in his fist. Its fringed edges slapped him about the face, knocked his lizard-skull mask to the ground. He struggled to master the living fabric as a man struggles to pull a great fish out of the ocean. He sang another spell, and the rug fell as lifeless as its owner. The shaman did not toss it in the well. He folded it and locked it inside a wooden chest, a key of rusted iron hanging about his chest among a cluster of bone amulets. The chest he carried to his hut beneath the shattered southern wall. As dawn crept into the sky, the tribe dispersed to seek their lodges between the mossy slabs.

Naaiko's brothers honored her with a final round of drink before going off to find their wives and some well-earned sleep. Less than twenty men had survived tonight's battle. The others lay broken and pulped at the bottom of the great chasm. One of those lost was Dawal, the brother she had seen fall with her own eyes. It was not the way of warriors to dwell on those fallen in battle, but to celebrate their deaths as honorable. So her brothers commended Dawal and the fine quality of his death, then stumbled off to find sleep.

Magtone had saved her life, but had not been treated with honor. This seemed wrong to Naaiko, if to nobody else. The shaman glared at her from across the plaza, until she closed the flap of her lodge against the dawn. She lay on her bed of furs and soft hides, unable to sleep despite her weary limbs. Whenever she closed her eyes, she saw not the battle's events playing in her mind, but the rainbow eyes of Magtone flashing at her like unspoken dreams.

The only man who had ever called her beautiful.

The man to whom she owed her life.

She expelled a lungful of frustrated air, gathering up her knife and stolen spear. The shaman had disappeared into his own hut by the time she slipped over the edge of the Divine Well, spear strapped to her back, fingers grasping the roots of wildgrass that sprouted between the stones. As dawn turned into day, she slipped into the darkness of the well. Descending its length was blasphemy, but it was also incredibly easy thanks to the profuse wildgrass and the bricks that poked from the earth in uneven patterns. Once these well walls were set smooth, back when the Fallen City stood proud and high, bright as the sun with all its stones set level. Centuries of shifting earth had made it a rough hole infested with weeds.

She smelled the pungent dung of sky-worms and the scent of damp earth. The light of day became a pinpoint far above, and she reached a point where no more weeds or roots grew from the walls. From that point on down, the well was carved from volcanic rock. She climbed deeper, fingers and toes grasping the porous rock, slipping now and then, stopping to gather her breath, and always proceeding downward again.

Finally, she reached the bottom. A void of subterranean darkness swelled below her feet, and the cool air was humid. She clung to the wall with one hand, her other reaching into the pouch at her waist. She pulled out her dead mother's glowstone and spoke the sacred words she had inherited along with it. The jewel gleamed bright as a torch in her hand without producing any heat. She held it tightly inside her fist, rays of light spearing between her fingers. "Thank you, Mother," she whispered. It was the only inheritance her mother had provided. As for her father, she had inherited only his warrior spirit.

Black water sparkled below her perch. She had no way of knowing how deep it was, or what horrors might swim in its depths. But she had come this far, she had no choice. She let go and dropped into the dark water. It splashed and chilled her, but she sank only to her waist. The floor was muddy yet firm beneath her heels. She unsheathed her spear and waved the glowstone in a wide circle. The water glistened in all directions, and the glow revealed a rocky dome above. She stood at its center, directly beneath the open mouth of the Divine Well. Three cavernous tunnels led from the dome chamber in three separate directions, and there was no sign of Magtone alive or dead. She poked with the butt of her spear about the circumference of the watery chamber, but found nothing. No drowned body.

"He lives," she decided. A tiny flame kindled in her heart, mimicking the jewel in her fist. The poet-wizard must have come to his senses after the fall, and now he probably wandered among these tunnels looking for an exit. Naaiko had no idea if any such exit existed, but finding it was her only course of action as well. She could not reach the high well-mouth to climb out as she'd climbed in. So she must find another way or die down here. But first she would find Magtone, and ask his forgiveness for not saving him the way he had saved her.

"He lives," she promised herself in the dark.

She chose a tunnel at random, since one seemed as likely as another. It rose up out of the water so that she walked on dry earth now. The tunnel led to another, then another, and all of them reeking of sky-worm dung. It lay heavy as bat-droppings about the floors of each tunnel, yet there was no sign of the worms themselves. She found a great nursery chamber, where purple-veined eggs stood taller than her head. They lay in webbed clusters between pillars of unhewn rock. Still she found no sky-worms, only their empty nests scattered about the egg-chambers. Two more such chambers she discovered before realizing she was utterly lost.

By this time her eyes had grown used to the glow of luminescent lichens growing across walls and ceilings. The lichen-light served as well as the glowstone, so she spoke the sacred words again and dropped it back into its pouch. She passed glittering mounds of crystal protruding from the earthen walls, alive with nameless colors, but she only stumbled deeper into the labyrinth. She began to regret her foolish decision to try and save Magtone. For all she knew, he was already dead. She cursed herself for a fool. Warriors did not behave in such a manner. She should have listened to her cruel but wise eldest brother.

A tiny echo reached her ears, the first sound she had discovered in the catacombs. The echo grew louder and became a voice, singing softly somewhere in the tunnels. She followed the sound until she found Magtone sitting in the dark reciting verse to himself. She feared for a moment that he had gone mad. He turned his rainbow-glinting eyes toward her, and met her wide smile with his own.

"Naaiko?"

She rushed to him and wrapped her arms about his neck.

"I knew you lived! I knew you did! You are poet! You are wizard!"

She peppered his face with little kisses, and he laughed. His arms wrapped about her, and then he was no longer laughing. A sudden heat grew between them, banishing the darkness and burning away the chill of wetness. Their tongues danced together, and their fingers followed, an urgent festival of discovery and sensation. She had become a warrior last night. Today she would become a woman. She thought of nothing else in the consuming heat of the poet's touch.

Moans echoed through empty tunnels.

Let the sky-worms hear them. Let the deep earth witness their union.

Again she rose to heights dizzy and amazing, and again she plummeted into his saving grasp. The thrill of it dwarfed the thrill of soaring on the magic rug, or any thrill she had ever known. The fire between them vanquished fear itself from the face of the world. Eventually they lay exhausted, limbs wrapped about each other, bodies stained with mud and lichen.

Sleep came then, gentle and absent of worry.

"Wake up, Lovely One." Magtone's voice, quiet yet urgent.

It was too soon. She craved more sleep, days of sleep. Months, perhaps.

"We must find a way out of here," Magtone said. "Do you know the way?"

She shook her drowsy head.

"Your winged thingies live down here," he said. "Tell me, how is it such inhuman creatures serve your tribe and also the tribe of your enemies?"

"The shaman," she said. "His sorcery calls them forth, binds them to us, so we can ride them to war. The Yonni have their own shaman, although they stole the magic from us."

"Where are the sky-worms now?" he asked.

His eyes were still rainbows, but their colors were strange in the lichen half-light.

"I don't know," she said. "I found many of their eggs down here."

"So did I," he said. "Yet not a single worm. They must be somewhere… if we can find that route, perhaps it will lead us to the outside. I've been trying to summon my carpet for assistance, but it refuses to come."

"The shaman locked it in an ancient box."

"Well, that explains that." Magtone grimaced. "I'm not a violent man, but I'm having bad thoughts about that bone-faced fool."

"I will kill him for you," Naaiko said, "when we get out of here."

Magtone laughed, but she did not understand why.

They wandered through the maze of tunnels until they stumbled onto a lower, broader passage that seem to cut through the middle of the labyrinth. A distant gleam of orange light drew their eyes toward it. She no longer felt lost with Magtone at her side. Walking the length of the lower tunnel, they watched the light resolve into dancing crimson shades.

Beyond a wide opening, dark shapes squirmed through the luminous crimson. The sound of flapping wings rose and died in short bursts. The screeching of sky-worms echoed now and then through the dark.

"Looks like we've found our exit," Magtone said. He grabbed her hand and she wondered again why his touch thrilled her so. No man had ever caused such a reaction. But then, no man had ever saved her life. Or called her lovely. Or taken her maidenhood in the depths of the earth.

She did not know what to say, so she smiled her relief at him. They walked hand-in-hand into the red glow of a dozen flaming pits. The tunnel opened on a flat, rocky expanse littered with mounds of scattered bones. A steady heat pulsed here as the fire-pits erupted in random spurts of flame every few seconds. More sky-worms than Naaiko had ever seen crawled among bones, their heads dipped low to feed on fresh human carcasses. The torn and broken bodies of Saachu warriors lay mingled with the bodies of Yonni warriors. Every warrior that died in last night's battle lay down here, a red feast for the same sky-worms that had carried them to battle. Generations of such battles had filled the ravine with bones. The skulls of her brave ancestors lay in shattered heaps, indistinguishable from those of her enemies. Somewhere, the skull of her father and grandfather must lay among the refuse.

Magtone looked up at the soaring rock wall behind them. On the far side of the ravine, another wall rose to match it. A dull memory of daylight penetrated the canopy of smokes that shrouded the feeding ground.

"It seems we're at the bottom of a deep chasm," Magtone said.

"The Well of Death," she said. "I never thought to see this place."

"Lovely name," Magtone said. "Luckily the worms seem far too intent on feeding to bother us."

So this was the cost of the sky-worms' service. These beasts answered the shaman's call again and again, and so earned the right to feed on the flesh of the fallen. Somewhere among the bones her youngest brother's body fed the worms even now. How many centuries had this same scene been played out? Where was the honor of such a death? She studied against her will the splintered and torn bodies, the viscera ripped to shreds between lamprey mouths, the sky-worms crawling on their greasy bellies through the gore chewing, mindlessly chewing. The grinding chomp of bone and fang. The heaps of prized skulls that spoke of a deeper intelligence and primitive ritual. She turned away and vomited onto the filthy ground.

Magtone grabbed her shoulders, leading her back into the shadows of the tunnel. She shivered in his arms until her breathing returned to normal.

"My brother is out there somewhere," she said. "I saw him fall..."

"I am sorry," Magtone said. "But it's far too late to help him now."

"He died as a warrior," she said, wiping tears away.

"Yes," Magtone said. "So many choose that noble fate. Too many. Tell me, why do you make war with the people of the Smited City? I want to understand, but it all seems so...unnecessary. In Karakutas we had wars, but they were always fought in distant lands. Yet your war is here, where you cannot avoid its cost."

"I cannot explain it," Naaiko said. "It no longer makes any sense to me."

"Do you think your brothers will still ride the sky-worms when you tell them what you have seen here? Will anyone?"

"Why should I tell them?" she said. "If I do, they will know that I defied the shaman. Some will want to kill me for invading this holy space."

They sat in silence for a while, until the sound of worms chewing meat came drifting into the tunnel's mouth. "We need to climb," she said. "Now, while they're still feeding. If they turn on us, we'll never survive."

"Don't worry," Magtone said. "I'm hard to kill and impossible to digest. I have the power to drive them away if I need to. But without my carpet I cannot fly."

"Then climb," she said. "You can have your rug back after I kill the shaman."

Now she had another reason to keep that promise. She knew the shaman's pact with the sky-worms. His bloody secret. It swelled like bile in her throat. He had been feeding them warriors for generations.

She kissed Magtone once and turned to embrace the hot stone of the cliff face. She was glad to see wildgrass roots growing from the earth here. This would be a long climb, but not a hard one. "Follow me," she said, and Magtone climbed after her. Soon the sound of the feeding worms was lost beneath the wind blowing through the chasm. They climbed into the layer of smoky vapors, stopping to rest on a secure ledge.

"How deep is this chasm?" Magtone asked.

She looked at him and he laughed.

"Nevermind," he said. They nuzzled for a while on the ledge. He whispered the sweet words of his craft in her ear, but she did not understand most of them. She obtained snatches of meaning, isolated images of beauty and wonder, tidbits that made her hungry for more. More of his language, more of his thoughts, more of his touch and scent and the warmth of his strong arms. She wanted to lay with him again right then, perched above doom and horror, but the warrior inside said no. Magtone may be hard to kill, but she would die easily if she fell from this height.

"Climb," she said, and they did.

Sunset hung orange and crimson above the jungle as they crawled over the high lip of the chasm. The first living things to ever climb from the Well of Death, or so she presumed. The climb itself was a deed for the ages, but also a blasphemy that must remain her secret. Hers and his. She could not even let the Saachu know that Magtone was alive, or risk their scorn and punishment. She wondered if returning to the Fallen City was a good idea at all.

"You must leave," she said. "They will never accept you here. And I can never reveal the secrets I have learned."

"Nonsense," Magtone said. "You are a warrior and a free woman. You can do whatever you like. The world is much bigger than this broken island. Come with me to Odaza, where gods walk the streets alongside men and share their divine songs, where the world's finest wines flow like sparkling rivers."

"This is my home," Naaiko said, but even as she said it she wanted to say the opposite. "I cannot leave," she said instead.

"Why not? If you don't like Odaza, I'll simply bring you back. The thought of leaving you now pains me."

"I will be fine," she said.

"I know," he said. "But I'll be miserable."

He fell to his knee on the mossy ground, grabbed her hands. "There is not much beauty or greatness left in this world. We must take care with precious things when we find them. Keep them close to our hearts. That is where I want to keep you. Close to my heart."

Naaiko tore her hands away. "You speak pretty words," she said. Her heart beat wildly, and her limbs that should have been tired from climbing felt light as air. "Now is not the time for words."

"You're right," Magtone said, dusting himself. "It's time to go and get my carpet back."

"No," she said. "I'll get the box for you. Wait for me outside the Plaza of Stones."

"There's really no need—"

"Promise me," she said. "That you will do as I say."

Magtone paused. His eyes pulsed with clashing colors.

"All right," he said.

It took more than two hours of walking through the dark jungle to reach the Fallen City, but she knew the quickest and safest paths. No nocturnal predators accosted them, even when they stopped to drink at a stream where wild things hunted. Naaiko heard the growling of hungry jungle cats, but none of them came near. Perhaps the animals sensed the innate strangeness of Magtone. She had felt it ever since she first saw him.

Now she reveled in it, the oddity that was his distinct nature, the greatest thrill of her young life. The experience of meeting Magtone coincided with her triumph as a warrior. Yet these two events were hopelessly intertwined.

This must be what the elder ones called fate.

Magtone crouched in the undergrowth as she approached the ruins alone. She slipped through the shadows cast by the Holy Fire, which burned low this night. She avoided the eyes of the sentinels placed about the ruins, an easy feat since she knew where every one of them was stationed. She slipped across the Plaza of Stones and approached the shaman's hut. She sat before the closed flap and listened to his snoring. As quietly as possible, she pulled back the hide and slipped inside. She took the stone knife from her belt and crawled on fists and knees toward the sleeper. Only when she raised the blade above his wrinkled neck did she notice his open eyes. He wasn't sleeping at all.

As her knife plunged toward his neck, the shaman's fingers curled like claws and unleashed his green flame. The force of the bursting magic knocked her backward, into the woven wall of his hut. The fire singed her hair and burned both of her raised forearms from wrists to elbows. The burns were not deep, but the pain of them woke something animal and desperate inside her. She rolled to the side, avoiding a blow from the shaman's staff. The spot where it struck the furs beneath her burst into magical flame.

She fought the urge to scream, both from pain and from anger, and fell on him like a storm. The knife plunged and plunged again, catching him in the breastbone, slicing open his right bicep, then a diagonal slash across his thin belly. His blood poured, but his eyes raged with the anger of the green flame. She tumbled out the door of his hut as the flames leaped from his eyes to chase her. She took up the spear at the place where she had left it, and turned to meet the shaman's rushing body. His claws shot green bolts at her, even as he rushed too quickly to stop the spear-head from driving through his belly. The spear's shaft emerged dripping from his back, and he stood impaled, dripping green flames and red blood.

She did not wait for him to finish dying, but raced into his hut and grabbed the ancient box. When she came back to him, the green flames were gone and the plaza was filling with curious faces. Her fight had awoken the tribe, and now she stood above the body of a murdered man holding his property. All of these things were punishable by death.

She cast the wooden box to the ground, but it did not break. Enchanted wood, the shaman would have boasted. She found the iron key on his bloody breast and used it to open the box. Immediately the rug unfolded itself like a huge, gaudy flower. It soared across the plaza into the jungle, where Magtone was waiting for it.

Someone called Naaiko's name. The voice was dark with fury. She turned to see her eldest brother marching toward her with spear in hand. "Murderer! False warrior!" His look condemned her as much as his words. "Damn you, Sister! You should have died today at the Well of Death. Now I have to kill you myself!"

"Ukoi!" she called him by name, but it was too late. He rushed at her, thrusting his spear at her belly. The edge of its scalloped blade slashed across her midsection. A shallow wound, but only because his first strike was unsteady. He would not hesitate again. Perhaps he had always wanted to kill her.

"I cannot kill you," she said. "We have already lost a brother today."

She parried his spear with her own, but his greater strength knocked her across the flat stones. A ring of family and friends gathered to witness this latest murder.

"Stop!" she cried. "My brother!"

Ukoi's spear pierced the earth where she had lain a half-second earlier. He swept her legs as she tried to run, so she fell again, and he raised the spear for a killing strike. His watering eyes burned with misery and rage, but most of all she saw hate there. Raw and simmering hate, where familial love ought to reside. She would die never having asked him why he hated her so.

A streak of mingled colors shot through the morning light, impacting Ukoi's chest with a meaty thump. The flashing light turned toward the stars, carrying her brother with it into the air. She heard his voice bellowing and recognized Magtone on his speeding carpet, surrounded by a gleaming bubble of rainbow shards. Ukoi lay sprawled across the top of the bubble, his spear lost somewhere below, his body helpless before the velocity of Magtone's sorcery. The comet of many colors turned its course level with the earth, and Ukoi fell into the jungle on the far side of the ruins.

Magtone flew back to the Plaza of Stones, where Naakio stood waiting for him, spear-in-hand. The eyes of her remaining brothers stared from an uncomfortable distance. The rest of the village had awakened slower than the warriors, but she had become a spectacle for all of them. They pointed at the shaman's body and the man on the flying carpet as he descended to the ground beside Naaiko.

"You're hurt," Magtone said, examining her scalded arms.

"It's nothing," she said. "My brother's words hurt much worse."

Magtone looked across the gathering of confused and angry faces.

"Well, so much for keeping my continuing existence a secret," he said. He came to her then, unexpected, and wrapped his arms about her. He pulled her to his lips in full view of the Saachu and their dead shaman. The children in the crowd laughed as their parents rushed them back to their lodges. The warriors stood impassive for a moment, then turned their backs to her. A few of them went into the jungle to find the fallen Ukoi.

A new flame sparked to life inside her. She wanted to shout the truth about the sky-worms and their hideous feeding ground. She longed to make them understand that they were the tools of flesh-eating monsters, driven to war by the same creatures who preyed on them like hawks on mice. Yet the shaman's spell would not summon the sky-worms anymore. Not until a new shaman was raised up. That could take years. Until then, there would be no more pointless aerial battles above the Well of Death. She wanted to tell them everything, but decided that they did not deserve to know. Let the dead shaman take his awful secrets with him.

She watched them haul away the shaman's body and said nothing. They would not listen to her now anyway. She had proven herself a warrior, but she was still a woman. Still somehow less than her brothers by virtue of her sex. Perhaps it was the simple fact of her womanhood that made Ukoi hate her so. It was hard to know the thoughts that swam behind men's eyes.

She felt Magtone's arm slip about her shoulders and turned to meet his smile. Here were eyes she could understand, despite their oddness and their sorcerous glow. Here was the love she had never seen in a man's eyes.

"Will you fly with me?" Magtone asked.

"Yes," Naaiko said. "Take me away from here."

They embraced on the carpet as it spun them gently into the sky. A few of the tribe stood near to the Holy Flame and watched her leave, but she did not see the face of her brothers among them. The ruins of the Fallen City grew small, then the island itself grew tiny. The sea was a plain of golden light, and the cool wind soothed her stinging forearms.

They flew eastward across endless water. He sang to her in a language she understood more with each song. At night, resting on the airborne carpet, he whispered love poems in her ears, and tales of ancient wars in realms she had never dreamed existed. He told her again of Odaza, City of Walking Gods, which lay somewhere on the other side of the ocean. The last of the world's great cities, and the most splendid. His destination, and now hers, too.

Magtone painted pictures of Odaza with his words and his magic, although he had only seen its likeness in books where artists attempted to capture the impossible. His words tickled her mind as his fingers tickled her skin. His touch left her breathless and giddy, even more than his feats of magic. Sometimes she feared losing everything that was herself in the warmth of his embrace, and she pulled away from him to think for a while. But always she came back to his lips and his warm hands. His dazzling eyes.

"Just the other side of this great water," he said. "It won't be long now."

She sat with her head against his shoulder. At times she wondered if it were all a dream, and if she was lying alone at the bottom of the great chasm. Dying and dreaming. At other times she imagined Magtone had cast a spell on her, one she welcomed and yet scarcely believed.

"What is the difference between love and sorcery?" she asked.

Magtone shrugged. "That's no question," he said. "It's the kernel of a great poem…"

So they wrote it together on conjured parchment above the leaping and foaming sea.

THE WIZARD OF HALLOWEEN
Chad Hensley

Way deep within gigantic pumpkin patch
he sits on throne of broken upturn'd grave
stones decorated with glowing skulls that scratch
with shiny teeth and tiny hands that wave.

Two apple core-like hands and shriveled head
wear orange cape with spark'ling, black top hat.
Pieces of tattered suit whip tendril'd threads;
His necklace pulled-out teeth from stray black cats.

Thin ghosts flow like thick fog around his boots,
Giant albinic bat on shoulder perch.
His cloven-hoofed feet dance, calling recruits—
Red eyed, corn-candy skeletons that do search

For bonfire witch dust thrown into moonlight
Spring horn'd tentacles for Samhain birthright.

THE RECKONING
Sharon Cullars

Each night I smell the moist, peaty earth of the bog. The smell suffocates me in my dreams, fills my nostrils, pushes aside my air until I wake up gasping. In those moments, I'm not sure whether I'm actually dying. It often feels that way. In those moments, my body forgets to inhale and my hand reaches into the darkness, grasping for life.

Thankfully I sleep alone…for now. Over the years, I've chased away my few lovers with my dreams. Or rather, my nightmares. More accurately, my nocturnal memories. No matter how each relationship began during my wakeful life, each eventually perished in the night. Man for man sooner or later became spooked by the half awakened woman lying next to him, thrashing and wailing in the darkness. The drama was more than they bargained for no matter how good the sex was.

Each time I laid silently as they slunk out the door, out the room and eventually out of my life forever. I couldn't blame them though. I wished I could escape along with them. But I'm imprisoned in this life, chained to my memories. In the darkness.

Those lovers can't possibly understand how the child of my past haunts me.

And that my dreams are the child's desperate need for atonement. For what she did those many summers ago. At the edge of that moist Louisiana bog.

Tonight, I let the dream, the nightmare lead me. I don't try to fight it, not this time.

1985.

Annie pulls at the lax ribbon hanging from one of the many braids unraveling on her head. Annie's Gram calls them *plaits*. The elderly woman is the one who makes them but with her arthritis, the braids aren't nearly tight enough. They do not hold against the sweaty heat, the grit and wandering hands of a ten-year-old girl hanging upside down from a low but sturdy limb of the sickly, gnarled willow that has been on her family's land for decades.

"Catch it!" Annie demands as the ribbon finally escapes her frizzled hair.

I reach up and swipe the bit of material just before it lands to the mossy ground. The yellow silk is already soiled and the threads are loosening. But no matter. If Annie loses it, she's going to get a whupping. Her Gram is not one to waste even the barest of cloth, no matter how tattered.

Annie jumps down from the limb, laughing.

Is it the dream state or does Annie's laugh sound a bit tinny, a shade hollow? I'm split between the woman I am and the child I was. I stand off to the side, watching, observing the scene, marking the slight deviations this time. There is always something different.

For instance, Annie's jumper is plaid this time, a cross of black and yellow stripes. Like a jumbo bumblebee. Her shirt is torn at the shoulder. Definitely a whupping offense but I don't tell her. I don't think she knows though.

The woman I am studies my child self. The sun has darkened my warm brown skin to a burnt sienna. The whitish scar over my left brow has also darkened and is not nearly as noticeable. It is all that is left of an accident that killed off my father two years ago. My own tangled braids are knotted with cockaburrs and grass. Aunt Josie, my father's only sister, will complain tonight as she combs them out, tearing at my naps while muttering how young ladies "do not rumble around like unruly boys." Not that her admonitions keep me from running, catching balls or climbing trees and fences. I'm not a girl who appreciates Malibu Barbie. Not even with her pink convertible.

"Got it?" Annie asks as she reaches for the ribbon.

"Here." I hand her the ribbon. "Wouldn't want your Grams to beat your butt."

"Ha, ha. Like your aunt's not gonna whup your behind with all those cockaburrs stuck to your nappy head. Oh, oh. I think one of those burrs is crawling. Oh God, it's a giant bug!"

I let out an "eek" and swipe at my hair, doing pivots as I search the ground for a loosened critter. All the time Annie is laughing. The laugh is definitely tin. And brass.

"Fooled you fool!"

"That's not funny! You know I hate bugs in my hair!"

"How you gonna be scared of a little bug when you not even scared of a snake? Makes no sense."

"That's because bugs are creepy with all those legs."

"And snakes aren't creepy?" Annie asks with defiance.

"They don't have all them damn legs," I reason back, just as defiant.

"Girl, you know you're a fool."

"Stop calling me a fool."

"Then stop acting like one." And with the about face that children can so smoothly segue into Annie asks cheerfully, "You want to hang out by the old creek." And with a sneaky smile, "Catch a snake?"

My grown self watches my younger self go through several facial metamorphoses, all an attempt to disguise my sudden fear.

"I can't. It's getting dark."

"So what? It's summer. We can stay out later. At least I can. I don't know about you. Big ole baby."

"I'm not a baby!"

"Well that's how your aunt treats you, like an itty bitty baby."

She was right. Aunt Josie barely let me ten feet from the back porch. Thankfully, that ten feet included Annie's backyard. Further out, a distance away, was pure marshland surrounding a dirty creek. Things lived in that creek and hovered in the many willows that stood like old, grizzled men with scraggly beards. Annie knew I hated going there. Especially when it was getting dark. She knew that, which was why she suggested it in the first place.

I want to warn my younger self…except she can't hear me. Nor would she listen anyway. She's hardheaded.

So much might have turned out differently if I hadn't take Annie's dare. If I'd just gone home, back to my aunt's old shotgun house. The house had seemed so ugly to me then but with an adult's retrospect I now realize that it had been a place of warmth and tidiness, interlaced with an ever-present smell of ginger. Abandoned since Josie's death, it was nothing more than a fire trap now. But back then the exterior of the house had been painted a muddy green with yellow clapboards over the windows, pale green walls inside. In the small living area, two overstuffed brown wing-back chairs had been placed together in front of the large floor RCA where I watched cartoons in the morning while Aunt Josie made cornbread sausage waffles that she would slather in butter and Alaga syrup. I once asked why she didn't buy the Aunt Jemima brand and she gave me a withering look before saying with a snipped tone, "We don't use no slave products in this house." Which meant we also didn't use Uncle Ben rice either. I loved those waffles and wished I had the recipe now. I wished I had all of Aunt Josie's recipes but she'd passed away eight years ago and it hadn't occurred to me to ask her to write them down. I thought she'd live forever.

Back then on hot Saturday summer nights, the mayflies gathered outside the window screens while in the distance the crickets chirped endlessly. Drove my aunt crazy but I loved the sound as I lay on my stomach watching TV. Sometimes if my aunt was in a good mood, she let me watch old reruns of *The Love Boat*, all the time complaining that the show was too grown for a child.

It is after seven and dusk is already approaching. The division between day and night is so quick that one minute the whole sky blazes a deep orange with tendrils of white, blue and yellow woven through, and in the passing of that minute the sky has turned a murky blue that eventually morphs into a suffocating darkness only broken by the lights from the houses along the long road.

"So, you comin'?" Annie dares me again. She is standing fully upright now, which makes her tower over me by half an inch.

As I often do at this point in the dream, I yell to my twelve-year-old self, "Don't go!" forgetting that I have no power to stop what is going to happen. I can only watch helplessly, view it like a scene from a Saturday evening show. A horror show.

"OK, but only for a little while. We gonna need a flashlight and a bag."

"Yeah, let me go get Mama's," and Annie scampers off, races up the steps to her porch then disappears into the house. She's back within a minute holding the flashlight and a plastic Piggly Wiggly bag for the snake.

"Your mom say anything?" I ask. She shakes her head.

We start toward the darkening trees and after a few minutes in their depths she asks, her voice less cocky, "You gonna get in trouble?"

"No," I lie. Despite Annie's earlier assertion, Aunt Josie isn't one for whuppings. Her punishments are more painful. No television. No sweets. And definitely no going outside to play for weeks. After that, you wished for a whupping just to get the punishment over with. So you can at least have some apple cobbler and vanilla ice cream to soothe the hurt of your tanned hide.

"I mean if you're gonna get whupped, we can turn back."

That's when I realize that she's just as nervous as I am. That she is all bluff. She's hoping that I will be the one to back down. But I don't.

"Let's hurry up though. I don't want to get a bunch of mosquito bites."

The willows mock our courage as their looming silhouettes crowd around us on our lonely path to the bog. Even a half mile away we can smell the marsh gases. The odor is like something dying. In past excursions we often saw bodies along the banks of the bogs. Dried up shells of snakes and frogs as well as other things. In the light and the dark, we know how to stay clear of the bog, keeping the known path along the solid ground. Get too close and the mud could suck you under.

That's what happened to Mr. Lee, Layla's daddy.

After almost two years, nobody hardly talked about Mr. Lee anymore. There had been rumors though. Among the grown folk. And the young girls. Just whispers.

Layla and her momma had moved shortly after Mr. Lee disappeared.

Everyone knew how Mr. Lee liked young girls. How he went after them sometime.

How it got so bad that supposedly Layla and her friends had lured him to the marsh with the promises of things they shouldn't be promising.

Once Annie and I overheard one of the church mothers talking.

"That's how you do things. No guns, no knives. You just let nature take its course. They can't even get you in a court of law if nature is the end."

Layla had been several years older, one of the pretty girls that everyone gushed over. But as pretty as Layla had been, she never seemed happy. Always there had been a sadness around her eyes. But after her daddy disappeared, the sadness was replaced by something like fear. And relief.

It's normal to be afraid of things that move and make sounds in the dark. As we creep closer to the bog, I can hear the slithering among the bushes. Annie's flashlight provides a path leading us through the curtain of dark, interspersed with the milky glow of a new moon. A screen of nocturnal sounds surrounds us. The smell of the bog makes it harder to breathe now. And fear compresses my young chest.

My grown specter follows behind the girls. I feel everything that my younger self is experiencing. Right now, my mouth is dry and my breathing is hollow, raspy. I try to control it to stave off an asthma attack. I swallow against the dryness. And I follow Annie. Brave Annie who will never let fear stop her. I latch onto her bravery. With Annie, nothing will happen to us.

I was so wrong.

All we have to do is catch one snake. Then we'll have a bragging right to last us a while.

We'd caught snakes before, but always in the daytime. Never at night. This will be a first. Something only the brave dare do. Even the boys in the neighborhood couldn't boast of this thing we are doing.

I imagine holding the husk of the dead snake in front of Davin Coles who is always showing off his reptile catches. Of laughing at his expression as we divulge the details of our exploit.

Because girls are supposed to be scaredy. But not us. Definitely not Annie. Annie can whup any boy on the block, even those taller and meaner than her.

"Why you so quiet?" she asks me.

"You quiet too," I mouth back.

"I'm trying to listen out for a slider."

"So am I," I counter a little too glibly. I'm too aware of those things around me.

We've neared the edge of the bog. Plenty of snakes teeming here. Mostly crayfish snakes that don't have any poison. Then there are the hognosed kind. They'll bite, but their bite isn't any more lethal than a bee sting. Unless you're allergic to bee stings, then you're in trouble.

Annie's light catches movement and we see a water snake. Like other water snakes, this one has bands all around. To those who don't know how to tell, water snakes look like cottonmouths. But water snakes are more slender than cottonmouths and have flatter heads.

A water snake would be a good catch.

Annie hands me the flashlight as she prepares the bag to gather up the slider. It is slithering to the water so Annie has to move fast.

We're so focused on our individual duties we don't hear nothing until it is almost too late.

A sound that shouldn't be. The sound of muck separating. Of something emerging. But even then we're not paying attention.

My adult self screams to the two girls. But, of course, they can't hear me.

Annie holds up the bag triumphantly as the snake struggles against its confines. The light captures its shadow in its near transparent prison.

The mucky sound is louder now. I look out at the center of the bog. There's something standing there and it is moving toward us.

My young self stands and turns the light toward the moving figure.

The figure is tall, like a man and is covered in mud.

I scream. Both girl and woman.

Annie turns to see the figure as it reaches out. Even in shock, she doesn't let go of the bag. The snake must be suffocating but it is still thrashing.

I'm the one closest to the figure and fear has me trapped to the spot, the flashlight shaking, its light bouncing. A muddy hand grabs my arm, steadies the light.

I'll always remember the smell of the bog. I'll remember the cold feel of the hand through the warm muck. A hand of bones.

Cold bones that gather around my throat.

The young me tries to scream, drops the light.

It doesn't matter that the flashlight is no longer on his face. The moon shows me enough. Mud and bone define familiar features.

Many of the older kids who hung around the marsh often teased each other about Mr. Lee rising from the depths of the bog, his skeleton grabbing for any young girl that happened by. But that was just some tale told to scare the younger kids.

Until this moment, I'd thought it was just a story.

"Let nature take its course," the church mother had said.

Layla had led him here and somehow had gotten him in the bog where he'd sunk into its depths.

No one spoke of it. No one ever said murder.

But then no one had ever spoken of Mr. Lee's nastiness. But everyone had known. There'd always been those whispers.

I yelp as the bones begin to squeeze, as the bones call me "Layla."

Layla is long gone. She'd escaped.

But the stories say that any girl will do.

Mr. Lee's trying to drag me into the bog. My grown self reaches desperately for my younger self.

I can't touch her. But I scream at her.

A name. *Annie.*

And this is the part of the nightmare, the memory that I don't understand.

Because my younger self hears me somehow.

And she reaches for Annie, grabs her friend who had been standing frozen on the edge.

Even as the man bones began dragging me, I drag Annie along with me with my free hand. The other hand is pulling at the muddy fingers around my throat.

I yell again, inform my younger self what to say, what to do.

"I'm not Layla. She's Layla!" I lie to Mr. Lee, motioning my head at Annie. Brave Annie.

The bones stop their deathly squeeze and release my throat. Release me.

Because Mr. Lee believes my lie. Our lie.

Annie screams as the bones latch onto her, as Mr. Lee begins to drag her off. Brave Annie struggles and screams, but she is no match for a determined monster. Monster in life, monster in death. He slowly pulls her down into the depths of the marsh. His eternal victim.

Brave Annie. Who only wanted to capture a snake.

Her screams are cut off by the mud that encases her, by the bones that drag her down even further.

I awaken, my bed smelling of the bog.

It is the smell and dampness that scares off my lovers.

It is the scream of a girl who cannot escape death.

It is the cry of a girl who cannot escape her sin.

A sin that will eventually lead her back to that bog one fateful night. One night soon.

Where I will give my grown self over to the ghost of the girl Annie, who beckons me each night in my nocturnal memories, her bones reaching out for me. A beckoning, a reckoning.

Brave, brave Annie. I'm coming.

✗

EVERY BONE IN HIS BODY
Adrian Cole

The sensation of falling was overwhelming. His gut dropped away and he came awake, on the point of vomiting. Shaking almost uncontrollably, he switched on the bedside lamp. As he did so, something shifted beyond the foot of the bed, a crippled, uncomfortable retreat. His own shadow? Somewhere downstairs there was a sequence of thumps. Always the same. Every night for three weeks.

* * * *

When the nightmare finally quit on him, Hatherley woke up refreshed. Relieved. It was Autumn, but very warm, only a few clouds marring a blue sky, ideal for mowing or pruning the shrubs. Funny how things worked out, he thought. Melissa had been the gardener. Fussy and fastidious, determined to have the place immaculate, which she'd done. He'd never paid much attention and told her more than once to get a gardener.

Ironically, now she was gone, he worked on the garden himself. And, if he was honest, he enjoyed it. It wasn't Melissa's pristine, regimented place, instead reflecting a wild look, but that was fine. Since he'd taken early retirement, he'd had more time to indulge himself. Without Melissa he'd found life far less demanding financially. He'd invested wisely, using his knowledge as a financier in the City. It was certainly paying off now.

Today, pushing the old mower across the lawn, he felt the first twinge in his right hand fingers. It wasn't pain exactly, but it brought him up short. He flexed his hand, wondering if it was the first hint of something sinister—arthritis, maybe. He was fifty two, although he knew younger people than that suffered from it. Briefly something flowed up his arm to the elbow, pulsed like a small electrical charge, then was gone. He flexed his fingers again. Nothing.

Minutes later it was forgotten. He continued mowing, pausing to study the landscape beyond the garden. The land sloped away into forest: across the valley, the first tors of Dartmoor rose up, dominating the horizon. There were pockets of movement against the heather, off-white blobs where sheep grazed, spread out in sunshine. A single chimney stack poked up among the debris of its former buildings like a slender brick finger, a tribute to the Moor's industrial past when, like the more distant Cornwall, men had busily dug deep into the earth for its copper, tin and other metals. Something about that reflection made him shiver slightly, as if a cool breeze had sprung up. He flexed his hand once more, but it seemed normal.

Next day he shopped in the nearby village, a quiet place that probably hadn't changed in a hundred years, at least, not noticeably, save its road, where a coach and horses once splashed through en route to the larger southern urban areas. Hatherley never felt completely isolated out here on the Moor's skirts, but the environment was very insular and generally people kept to themselves. Of course, it had suited him ideally. Made things very easy.

Driving home, he felt a twinge of pain—yes, this time it was pain—in his right hand and up his arm. So much so that he pulled the car into the edge of the narrow lane and stopped. He swore. *Damn, that hurt!* His fingers curled up, cramped, pain shooting through them. His joints flared, the bones in his lower arm very painful, his elbow burning. He thought he was going to pass out, it was that bad. Slowly it subsided.

After ten minutes he drove on and reached the cottage without a repetition. The rest of the day passed without any further occurrences of the acute discomfort. He forgot about it.

The next morning he'd started washing up his few breakfast dishes, when the pain stabbed at him, so violently he reeled, clutching the sink with his free left hand. *Jeeze, it feels like it's broken!* his mind shouted. How could it have happened! How could anyone break their arm without being aware of it at the time?

Slowly the pain eased off, but this time not completely. A dull throb persisted, in his fingers, hand and arm, and worse, it had moved up towards his shoulder. He had no idea what it could be. He took a shower, hot water relieving the aches in his body: things eased a little. By the end of the day, he was almost pain free. His hand and arm moved flexibly, without grating. Obviously nothing was broken. He'd have understood it better if it had been muscular, but it had been his *bones* that ached like hell.

When it all began anew the next morning—he was sitting in a sun-splashed conservatory, casually skimming through the daily paper—he realized he'd have to speak to his doctor. Morton was a friend, as well as his GP, so he was able to get through to him personally.

* * * *

Morton's face screwed up in puzzlement as he carried out his examination. Hatherley felt embarrassed—the pains had disappeared altogether by the time the doctor arrived the following day.

"Nothing's broken," he said. "No fractures. You say it just comes on in waves? We'll have to get you x-rayed. It's a ten mile trip—I better drive you."

Hatherley was duly checked and treated, but again, no one could find anything wrong with him. They told him for a man of his age, he was in particularly good health. Heart, lungs, blood pressure, and so on. All in excellent condition. He was relieved to hear it, but frustrated.

Morton visited him that evening. "Take these," he said, handing over two packets of pills. "When the pain kicks in."

Hatherley grunted. "Are they placebos, Giles? Do you think I'm imagining this?"

"They're proper pain killers, chum. Don't take more than it says on the box. You *could* be imagining it. That's not impossible. This last year's been pretty difficult for you. It's only been a year since Melissa left you. This could be a delayed reaction. I'm not a psychologist—"

"Hell, Giles, I hardly think about her. Don't miss her at all."

"No, well, just take the pills. See how it goes."

Later, sipping a large malt whisky, Hatherley pondered the doctor's words. Was the pain psychosomatic? It was bloody real enough.

* * * *

The following morning he was okay—until he went downstairs. His left ankle twisted under him and he stumbled, gripping the banister. Both arm and leg shot through with pains like fire. He let out a shriek and sat back, half way up the stairs. It took him a long time to get downstairs, finally hopping on one leg. He made it to the kitchen, slumping at the table. The agony in his leg had reached upward to his groin: by now the whole of his right arm throbbed like murder.

It went on for an hour, slowly easing off. He made coffee and took some of the pain killers, tempted to ring Morton again. This was ridiculous. He'd never damaged a bone in his life before. Christ, he'd played a high standard of rugby until he was in his mid-twenties, a brutal, competitive game that had dealt him enough bruises to last a lifetime—but no breaks. It was true he didn't visit the gym these days, but out here in the country he did a lot of walking and climbing. He had an annual health check that always showed up in positive terms.

By midday there was nothing to indicate his arm and leg were damaged. He was able to walk round and get on with a few chores comfortably. Morton checked to see if he was okay, but he told him he'd had a twinge or two, otherwise nothing.

"Don't go overdoing it," Morton said. "Rest as much as you can."

For the next few days, the pattern remained the same. Violent pain—now in both legs and the right arm—followed by a slow subsidence. Twice Hatherley went to get the car out of the garage, but as soon as he attempted to start it, the pain hit him so hard he dared not risk driving.

He spoke to Morton again, who promised him more tests, although Hatherley could hear the slight exasperation in the doctor's voice. *He does think I'm imagining all this.*

*

That night Hatherley woke after a drugged sleep. The air outside was very still. He got up, blessedly free of pain, and went to the window. He stared out at his lawn and the trees beyond. Some of the tall shrubs shivered as if ruffled by a breeze and he wondered if a deer was moving through them. It was too dark to see clearly. Something emerged, or rather, flowed, on to the edge of the lawn, a deep shadow. Hatherley tried to study it, but its shape remained blurred.

He fetched a torch, but when he returned to the window, the shadow shape was gone. Later, dozing, he thought he heard a rapping downstairs on the front door. It didn't persist and he slipped back into sleep.

* * * *

The following morning, after a particularly uncomfortable transition from the bedroom to the downstairs living area, Hatherley lost his temper, swearing crudely and picking up a small vase and flinging it across the room. As it shattered against a tall mirror, the whole thing shook as though it would dissolve in a rain of shards. As his image in the mirror blurred, he had the bizarre feeling it was Melissa looking out at him.

The thought stabbed at him like the fresh probing of pain, though this time it hit him in the chest. Melissa. Damn her, she'd have enjoyed this. In their rows, especially near the end, they'd both have happily—what? What was he thinking? Struck each other? Caused each other pain, for sure.

He calmed his anger, trying to be objective. Okay, I did neglect her. I took her for granted. I spent too long up in the city, working. I did or didn't do all the things she accused me of. I wasn't an utter bastard, but I was a poor husband. Her accusations were reasonable. But I didn't screw other women. It wasn't me that had an affair. She turned to Donald and I was the injured party.

He straightened the mirror and picked up the broken pieces of the vase. Broken. Like pieces of bone.

Pain erupted in his chest, his rib cage. He sagged back, crying out. Arms and legs both flared with new waves. He slid to the floor, gasping, sucking in a huge lungful of air.

Stop, stop, for Christ's sake! Lying on the carpet, face pressed to it, he looked across at a tier of bookshelves, the neatly arranged volumes rising up. There'd been a small table there. Not any more. He remembered what had happened to it. The whole sordid event came flowing back to him. It was never going to go away.

He twisted his head and glared at the mirror, though he couldn't see himself in it from this angle.

"Is that it? Is that what this is about?" he shouted. The house was still, inanimate, the air frozen, indifferent.

His body answered him with more pain. *Oh yes, yes this is what this is about.*

He dragged his cell phone out of his pocket and prodded the keys clumsily, vision slightly blurred. He could imagine Melissa watching him now, cool and collected. She'd always mastered whatever anger she felt, especially when he was losing his rag. It had just made him worse.

"It's Derek. I need to see you," he blurted when he heard the voice on the phone. "I need help." He closed his eyes and let the abrupt arrival of sleep take him. For a while the pain ebbed away.

The doorbell brought him round. He shook himself. It must be Giles Morton. He'd no doubt be exasperated, but at least he'd come.

Hatherley got up. The pain, typically, had gone. He got up and opened the door. The man standing there wasn't the doctor, but Hatherley recognised him.

"Inspector Collins?" he said.

The man nodded, his face impassive. He was tall, a little too gaunt, his drawn features pale, though his eyes were oddly sharp. Observant, Hatherley imagined. He remembered him, the steady, thorough appraisal of facts. What the hell was he doing here?

"You asked me to come, sir. Said you needed help. I recognised your voice—on the phone."

Hatherley's puzzlement must have shown on his face. "I—I'm sorry, inspector. I rang the doctor—"

"Are you unwell, sir?" Those eyes studied him, Hatherley thought, as if they could see the pain in his bones.

"It's nothing."

"May I come in?"

Hatherley paused briefly, then pulled the door wider. "Of course! Come in. I was about to make some coffee."

"That's very kind, sir. Thank you. Milk without sugar." The detective sat at the kitchen table, casually looking around him. "You say you meant to call the doctor. Do you need him?"

"It can wait," said Hatherley, making the drinks.

"There's a slight irony to our meeting today," said Collins. "You probably aren't aware of it, but it's a year to the day since your wife disappeared."

Hatherley set the drinks down, masking his reaction. "Since she ran off with Donald Welton?"

"Well, we never really established that, sir." Collins smiled patiently.

Hatherley couldn't face those eyes. *A year to the day!*

"Mr Welton maintains his insistence that he never saw your wife at that time. He's never denied she was going to leave you and go to him, but I think we've all accepted she just disappeared. We'll probably never know the truth. I review things from time to time—that's my job, sir. So when you rang me, even though you probably hadn't meant to, well, it seemed appropriate to give you a visit. Is there anything fresh you can tell me?"

"Not at all."

"I half hoped you might have heard something. From your wife."

Hatherley was about to repeat his words, but the pain took him unprepared, throughout his body. Every bone protested so fiercely he cried out.

Collins was quick to respond, getting up, his calm features blurring into a look of concern as he came to Hatherley, helping him sit more comfortably. "I think you do need to see the doctor, sir. What's the number?"

"No, no," said Hatherley, eyes filling with tears of pain. "It's no use. I know what this is about. It's Melissa."

Collins got Hatherley to the living room and managed to manhandle him gently on to the settee, spreading him out among its cushions. Hatherley was clearly in agony.

"Your wife, sir? She's responsible for this?"

Hatherley nodded. "It must be her."

"In what way?" said Collins, evidently puzzled.

Hatherley gritted his teeth against another wave of pain. *Maybe,* he thought, *just maybe, there is a way of ending this.* He cursed under his breath. "All right, inspector. I'll tell you what really happened that night. My wife was going to leave me. Donald Welton was coming in the morning to fetch her. But she hadn't gone off elsewhere, disappeared. Not as we all imagined. And I wasn't in Bristol, at that time. That was later."

"Do you mind if I jot this down?" said Collins, taking out a small notepad and pen. He sat in an armchair opposite Hatherley.

"Go ahead. So—we argued. Melissa had obviously been building up to it. She'd made her mind up to go. She wanted to give me a final piece of her mind. No last attempt at reconciliation, we were beyond that. I'd had a few glasses of wine. I was angry. As much at myself as her. Part of me just wanted to say, go, get on with the rest of your life. Another part wanted her to stay. I don't know. I think I was jealous of Donald. I didn't dislike him. It wasn't his fault. What happened wasn't planned. Not initially."

"You fought?"

"Well, for once Melissa lost it. She must've wanted to let the poison flow. She shouted and I shouted louder. So much so she stepped back, probably thinking I was going to hit her. I didn't inspector. I didn't strike her. She slipped. The carpet rucked at the edge on the tiles. Melissa went down. I can see it now. Her head turned and cracked on the edge of a small table under those bookshelves. The blow must have snapped her neck. Killed her outright. I bent down to her but it was obvious immediately she was dead." Hatherley closed his eyes as though re-enacting the whole scene.

"You didn't think to call an ambulance, or the police?"

"Yes, but I hesitated. Selfish, you see. I started to think what Melissa's death would mean. Donald would immediately suspect murder. How could I be sure of proving otherwise? Even if your people had believed me, there'd be the stigma. My friends, my ex-colleagues—what would they think? Life would never be the same for me."

Collins was writing quickly. He nodded.

"I finished the wine, no longer completely sober. Then I did think up a plan. If I got rid of Melissa's body, put it where it would never be found, the world might just believe she had gone off. As far as anyone knew, I was away. Any suspicion of foul play would fall on Donald Welton.

"So I put her in the boot of my car, carefully wrapped in bin bags. I came back inside and cleaned everything up. Fortunately there was no blood. I put the table in the boot with her. And her suitcases, which were already conveniently packed. I added toiletries—anything I thought she would have taken with her the next morning.

"I knew exactly where to take her. About ten miles from here, on the edge of Dartmoor. There are some woods and an old copper mine. It's fenced off, out of sight to the world. I waited until after midnight and drove there. Didn't see a soul. No traffic, which is normal for this area. The farmers were done for the day, most of them asleep, I expect. Up at the crack of dawn, but not at one in the morning.

"It was far easier than I'd imagined. I just got her out of the boot and rolled her over the lip of the shaft. I heard her falling. Long way down. I chucked her things into the mine and that was that. Drove back, still without seeing anyone. Not a single car. I got back and showered, going over every detail in my mind. I spent a bit of time doing a final tidy up and then drove up to Bristol. I've a small flat there.

"The next morning I spoke to some neighbours. No one had heard me arrive. I said it was just after tea time, my usual time. They know I like to spend the night in the flat before visiting the city. Later in the day I met friends and spent a couple of days there. No one had any reason to think I was behaving other than normally.

"Tell me, inspector, did you think it was foul play at the time?"

Collins's face betrayed no emotion. He seemed amazingly blasé given Hatherley's confession. "I found it hard to believe your wife had simply disappeared. Given that she didn't contact anyone, even after a week or so. These things do happen. But people usually get in touch with relatives or close friends eventually. You wife's complete silence was a little odd."

"What happens now?"

"I'll have to contact my colleagues, sir. We'll need to check out that mine shaft. Recover your wife's body. Are you well enough to move?"

Hatherley flexed his arms and then lifted his legs carefully, but there was no adverse reaction. The pain had deserted him. "Yes. It comes and goes." *But if I've got this right*, he told himself, *the pain won't be back if I take you to the mine. It's what you want.*

Collins put his notepad and pen away and stood up, watching Hatherley rise, gingerly. Collins took a cell phone from another pocket and walked to the far end of the room, gently tapping the keys.

Hatherley stretched. No reaction. He heard Collins speak to other policemen. He was a cool customer, Hatherley gave him that. *Maybe he thinks I'm nuts. Maybe he still thinks Melissa did run off. That would be a laugh.*

Eventually Collins came back. "I suggest you try and get a good night's sleep, sir. I'll have two of my colleagues come and keep an eye on things."

"I'm not going to make a break for it, if that's what you think."

It was a tired attempt at humour and Collins smiled indulgently. "No, I'm sure you won't, sir. In the morning we'll visit that mine, if you don't mind. And I'm grateful to you for telling me about this."

"I've been a damn fool," Hatherley said with a scowl. "It's time to put things straight." *And end this pain, this bloody—what, witchcraft?*

* * * *

They drove out to the mine the following morning, Hatherley sitting in the back of the police car between two uniformed police. For once he'd had a decent night's sleep and really did wonder if the pain in his bones had been withdrawn. He recognised the drive along the edge of the Moor, across its open ground, its landmark copse, and the dark wound in the land where the fencing was still standing, though weak, almost pulled apart by years of fierce moorland weather.

Several police cars and two trucks followed Collins's car in a short convoy. The trucks disgorged several men in special gear, who immediately set up what they needed to be able to abseil down into the shaft. It was almost vertical and Hatherley knew these things often went hundreds of feet down. A number of the shafts nearer his cottage had been searched at the time of Melissa's disappearance, but there were too many for them all to have been entered.

Hatherley sat back, relaxing in spite of the situation. It was such a blessed relief not to have suffered from any of the bone-grinding pain this morning. *It's in my mind*, he told himself. *Must be. I'm controlling this. Guilt. How else can it be explained?*

Collins stood just beyond the car, watching the shaft, patient as a dog awaiting an instruction. An hour drifted by. Two.

Hatherley realised he'd been dozing. Collins opened the door, calling him out.

"You've found her?" said Hatherley, clambering out and stretching. Not so much as a twinge in his bones. Suddenly the thought of that year-old body, wrapped in black bin bags, disturbed him. He hoped to Christ they didn't want him to identify it.

"The men are back up," said Collins. "Apparently they haven't found anything. Neither a body, nor any of the items you claimed you threw into the shaft with it."

Hatherley stared at the gaping darkness beyond the fencing. He looked around him. The men were already stripping off their protective clothing, winding up operations. "This is the right place. I'm quite certain. That copse there is unmistakable. There are other mines, a few miles away. I chose this one deliberately."

"It was night," said Collins. "Could you have used another shaft?"

"No. This is it. I'm sure. There must be something—"

Collins was shaking his head. "The men are pretty thorough, sir. If there'd been a rock fall, possibly burying a body, they'd have found evidence of it. The shaft is undisturbed. Nothing has collapsed for a long time. Just a shallow pool at the bottom. Shallow and empty. They trawled it. And there are no shafts running off it."

Hatherley didn't know whether to laugh or cry. *Empty!* Yet this was the shaft. No doubt about it. Of course, there'd be no evidence of his having come here, a year ago. Any tyre tracks would have been weathered away.

"We'll go back to your cottage, sir," said Collins. His bland expression showed no sign of disappointment, though Hatherley imagined he must be annoyed.

On the drive home, Hatherley braced himself, thinking the pain in his bones would inevitably return. But it didn't.

"What happens now?" he asked Collins.

"I'll prepare a written statement for you to sign. We can't do any more at the moment. I must ask you not to leave the area, sir."

"No, that's fine. I'll be here. I might need some shopping, from locally."

Collins nodded. "If I could be here tomorrow, sir, we'll finalise things. Could I suggest you contact your solicitor?"

"Of course."

"I'll need to talk to your doctor."

"Sure."

And that was it. Collins and his colleagues left. Hatherley watched the car disappear and slumped down on his sofa. The mine shaft had been empty! Could the body and the suitcases—the small table—all have simply weathered down after a year? But surely the bin bags at least would have been there. That stuff was indestructible. And the table. It had been tough wood. Worm?

Another thought occurred to him—could someone have got into the mine and found the body? Unlikely. The only way in was by direct descent. No one in their right mind went into those shafts. Besides, they'd have reported it.

He poured himself a large scotch and tossed it back. Then another. After that the rest of the day was a blur. He thought about ringing his solicitor, but put it off. He'd sound slightly mad confessing to him that he had, after all, disposed of his wife. He would have phoned Giles, but he felt fine. Just tired.

Later he made himself a ready meal and ate it mechanically, hardly tasting it. He watched television, though the images and sounds from the machine barely registered. He felt drained of energy.

He had an early night and was soon asleep. Hours later he woke, shrouded in darkness. Tentatively he flexed his fingers, wrists, arms. No response. Still OK. He flicked on the bedside light. 3.06 am.

He went to the bathroom and relieved himself. In the bedroom, he went to the window, peering out at the gloom. The lawn and trees beyond were little more than a patchwork of dark shadows, lifeless and silent.

Something on the lawn drew his attention. Something rectangular, with an open lid. A box? How had a box got there? No, not a box. A case. He squinted. There were smears of lighter colour on the darkness of the lawn, things strewn about. He reached for the torch he'd left on the chest of drawers. When he turned back to the window and aimed the torch beam down, there was nothing to see.

He swore and went back towards the bed. Below him, in the living room, he heard a knocking. Front door. He rushed back to the window and tried to see outside. For a moment something moved in deep shadow, low down on the ground, spreading like a black stain, its movements spider-like, awkward. Again he used the torch, but the light revealed nothing.

Making as little noise as possible, he put on his slippers and went downstairs. He inched towards the front door, determined to surprise whoever was lurking about outside. As he reached for the first bolt, the knocking came again, short, sharp raps. Weirdly they came from the *bottom* of the door, almost at ground level. An insistent tapping—it must be a person. Lying down? That made no sense.

He felt something very cold blow softly in, as if the door was actually open. Which it wasn't, of course. He'd bolted and locked it, and it was draught-proof, good quality workmanship. For a few moments he stared at it, still determined to surprise his visitor. Something warned him off. That cold, unseasonal air. He drew back, right into the room, waiting. The knock didn't come again.

After a time he grimaced at his ridiculous nervous reaction and turned to go back to bed. In the vague light, he saw the tall bookcase and below it, the little table. *The table on which Melissa had broken her neck in the fall.* He made a move towards it, meaning to pick it up and hurl it across the room, but he couldn't bring himself to touch it. In the morning, perhaps.

Upstairs, he took a final look at the garden, but it was no more than a crumpled sheet of darkness, offering no clue as to who had knocked. The trees were shifting in a light night wind.

In bed, he flicked off the lamp, stretching out. Sleep began to lap at him, a soft tide.

On the edge of unconsciousness, the pain began—in his hands and feet, his arms, legs and chest. Bone after bone protested at the sudden, searing agony. He couldn't move a limb, pinned to the bed like a butterfly to a board. He lifted his head, but all he could see was the end of the bed and a thick wall of clotted darkness beyond it that fell away into impenetrable depths. Something rose up from them, a writhing mass of hair crowning a blur of torso and limbs.

The cold draught of earlier returned and washed over him as if he'd been sluiced down with icy water. He ground his teeth, shuddering. Gradually the shape beyond the bed dragged itself up on to the sheets, extending elongated arms. The pain in his bones intensified to the point where he almost blanked out. It spread mercilessly. He was locked, immobile, wanting to scream, but his jaw creaked as it snapped, twisting to one side, his tongue snarled up within it.

It closed on him, that black, mangled shape, those arms sliding under his back and holding him, ever tighter. Something vaguely resembling a face lifted, inches from his own. And he heard the dull snapping of his bones. One by one they were crushed as the grip of the thing squeezed relentlessly, agony heaped upon agony, excruciatingly through every bone in his body.

QUACHIL UTTAUS

Frederick J. Mayer

"Duan de Casa"

I think
Therefore I am
I thought
Wherefore I have been
No one told me
it's a sinful crime
Now I am out of sync
homeless within housed Time…
Upon the dreams' rust
amid the corrupt blues
and darker hues
comes the House Master
Imp Wanderer
The Treader
of the Dust
a collector of celestial dues…
Time Changeling in wind calling
in tombs, in tomes, of changing
of the gods musty shadowing
Ancient Ones
old remains Quachil Uttaus
and I am the remains, the dust.

WE WERE X-MEN
Abdul-Qaadir Taariq Bakari-Muhammad

When I first arrived on your world, I had seen enough of your bad science fiction movies to know that they served at least one truth if nothing else. Human beings in their elegant stupor drift through time, constantly recycling their ignorance and fear. That's another way of saying that had I revealed who I was and what I meant to the future of humanity, I might have wound up in a mental institution or, even worse, dead on some darkened highway. I supposed it would be ruled a freak accident caused by a bum who was under the influence of alcohol. An old friend of mine thought the same thing. People knew him as Melvin Locke. He was a late-night talk show host I found to be unique amongst my travels. I was introduced to Melvin by way of another friend at a local college library here in southeastern Virginia. If I remember correctly, it was in the computer lab on the second floor of Norfolk State University. I began feeling dizzy and nauseated. That only happened when obscure messages from the future would rush into my mind. Usually, I would grab a cup of coffee; that somehow made my headaches go away. This particular morning, I had no such luck. What I did have was the good fortune of meeting the assistant director of the computer lab. Our first encounter was a bit odd in its language. His words to me were:

"Peace God. Are you alright?"

I assured him that I would be fine.

"Just a little headache, but it's interesting that you called me that."

"Why, my brotha? Do you not see yourself as the original man? The maker, owner, cream of the planet Earth, God of the universe?

I was about to answer that question in a different way, but instead I wanted to learn more from this person. So, I kept that conversation at bay until the time was right to discuss it.

Yes, yes, I understand where you are coming from, but can you tell me where the closest restroom is located?"

"Yeah, bruh, as soon as you walk out of the lab, it's like down the hall to your right. Can't miss it."

"Thank you, sir. You are too kind."

"No doubt, but don't be so formal. Om Mekka Tauheed."

"Oh, great, like the hajj to Mecca in Saudi Arabia?"

"You're funny, G."

As I headed out towards the restroom, I saw him place his right fist over his heart and say peace. I noticed that someone had left a *USA Today* newspaper on a nearby table. I grabbed it and looked at the date to see if it was old or new. It turned out that it was new. The date read September 11, 1996.

* * * *

I left the library later in the evening, feeling puzzled and disturbed. The country seemed to be totally unaware of what was about to happened. By the end of the day, I had contemplated how I was going to warn these people and whether they were going to believe me or not. Then I thought about the other conversation I had with Tauheed right before I left the library. It was brief, like the first one. That was a bit intentional. I didn't have time to discuss 5 Percent Nation of Islam theology. Good for him that it had given him focus in life. I had a mission to complete and was very interested in the talk show he recommended. It was called *The Locke Down*, hosted by Melvin Locke. At the time, it was the only show of its kind. I had thanked Tauheed for that information and, with the *USA Today* rolled up under my jacket, I headed home.

* * * *

By the time I had driven back home to Suffolk, Virginia, it was pitch dark but still young in the night. Earlier in the year, I had purchased an RV and parked it near the residence of Mr. James L. Armstrong. He and his wife, Doloris, were retired educators that believed my story about being a former U.S. Marine who had served in Desert Storm. I told them that while being deployed overseas, I had developed a love for photography and vowed to pursue it as a career once I returned home. I even showed them pictures I got off Instagram that I had supposedly taken while I was in Iraq. They were very gullible. I paid $10.00 to download and print those at a now defunct Kinko's that merged with FedEx. They never questioned the sincerity of my academic goal of becoming a photojournalist. In fact, they had even given me recommendations to two local universities. I received phone calls from Norfolk State and Old Dominion on a daily basis. Each asking me to tour their campus. The '90s must have been the quiet before the storm, or that's the kindness trust money can buy when you dish out $500.00 dollars a month to live on someone else's property. Even if it is under false pretenses.

* * * *

To pass time, I fiddled around with my ham radio and a gaming system now known as the Sony PlayStation or, as some die hard gamers refer to it, the PlayStation 1. I had modified both to help me decode messages embedded in my headaches. There was still about 5 hours before Mr. Locke was to begin his broadcast. I had decided to take a nap until 12:15 a.m. I placed the newspaper over my face in hopes that, with my modifications, it would provide me with some answers by the time I woke up. One thing for sure, living near a country road disturbed only by a rare truck passing by allowed me to have a substantial amount of rest periods.

* * * *

I awoke around 12:45am to images of people covered in soot with fire burning their backs. The rest of the images were fuzzy, but I knew that whatever was going on, it was just a distraction. If I could get through to this Melvin Locke person I could explain what I had dreamt or rather saw. I walked outside of my RV to see every beautiful dead star that the eye could behold. The temperature had dropped as promised to a brisk 15 degrees. Down from the 50's from yesterday. This Melvin Locke came on as promised playing what he called bumper music. Most of it from a Canadian folk artist known as Jordan Featherfoot. His show was being broadcasted from Dogon Radio 1555 AM in the city of Old Kamby, Virginia. On that night, it was open lines. This was the night people could call in and talk about whatever. I was in luck, but hesitated on calling. An hour had passed and after all the foolishness that I had heard, I realized my dream would probably sound just as crazy.

* * * *

I had to rethink what I was going to tell him. First I was going to introduce myself. Then if that didn't hook him I was going to mentioned an important letter I had in my possession titled Return to Sender. I had hope that the letter I possessed would suffice. Yet, if it didn't I was just going to have to tell him and his audience the truth of who I am and what my purpose was for being here. With the amount of calls he was receiving I didn't think I would get through. Needless to say, I did get through and week after week we had become distant friends. I had also become a regular on his show. He and the Locke Down audience had given me the name X-Man. I kind of felt honored. Tauheed called me Brotha Supreme X. He often in a joking manner referred to me as the brotha from another planet that actually talks. After 911 I never heard from him again. It wasn't until 15 years later that the mere thought of him had rushed its way back into my life.

* * * *

I had received an anonymous phone call from a woman asking me to meet her at a local Starbucks in Portsmouth, Virginia. I don't know how she got my number, but she went on to tell me how she was this big fan of mine and was an avid listener to the Locke Down show since he began broadcasting in 2004. That threw me for a loop. I laughed and for once in my time on Earth called someone else crazy. After calling her a fraud I explained to her that Melvin Locke has been on the air since the early 90's. Then she told me that based on my timeline that was correct. So, then I thought she was some kook that's been listening to too many of Mr. Locke's time travelers and was just trying to pull my leg. I had a good sense of humor better than anyone, but this lady was persistent and it was pissing me off. I was getting ready to hang up on her until she spoke about my headaches. No one knew about my headaches except for Tauheed. And I hadn't spoken to him in years. I don't know what the hell happened to him. He just up and vanished. After she mentioned my headaches I had a ton of questions for her. Yet, she had thrown me for another loop. She wanted to meet me at 9:00am and warned me not to stay up listening to Melvin. Now I was convinced she was off her rocker. Mr. Locke has been off the air since his retirement in early 2003. Ian Noory is now the host of the show and it's been renamed the Kingdom of Kamby. He doesn't do a bad job, but it's just not the same since Melvin left. I reluctantly agreed to the meeting. That call had intrigued me. I thought what could it hurt? It was going to be at a place that was heavily visited. So, there was no need for me to worry. I told this woman that it was a deal. Tomorrow at 9am sharp.

* * * *

I had left work early that day because I wasn't feeling well. I took some Ibuprofen to help get rid of my migraine. My headache had disappeared, but not my restlessness. It was 2am in the morning and I clicked on my Google Chrome app to bring up my web browser. The funniest thing I could have sworn just yesterday I was using I-Google to access the interweb. I mean it was the best and some would say the only one to use. That Steve Gates and his Applesoft company sure know how to build a computer. Anyhow, I went to my Yahoo homepage and typed in Melvin Locke. I found the official link to his website. I clicked it and the next thing you know I was somehow listening to a live and current broadcast of his show. This was somehow the real thing, and I had no answers as to how or why. I was afraid to call in. In fact, I was afraid to even pick up my cell phone. Now I was wide awoke listening until he signed off. I was in such a shock I have no idea what that program was about. And to reinforce how late it was I could hear Barry Mitchell perform the World News Polka like he often did to sign off ABC's Late Night News. I heard him clearly from the television I had left on in the living room. I needed something to relax me and put me to sleep. There was no way in the world I was going to miss that meeting at 9am. So, I thought about having sex with Whitney Houston my favorite r&b artist. She was so sexy, full figured, and could sang her heart out. I am so glad she divorced that drug using bum Bobby Brown. If she hadn't she would have died of an overdose just like he did years ago. I laid down and pictured us on a tropical island at one of those clothing optional resorts, and the whole time I was rubbing her bare ass she was singing to me my favorite song You Give Good Love.

* * * *

The next day I walked into Starbucks with a giant monkey on my back. Man, was I tired. I guess me and Whitney must have made a baby on that island. The good thing about is I was at the right place to pick me up. Normally I would have ordered a shot of espresso to go with my coffee, but on that day, I asked the cute cashier behind the counter to make it four. She sure had a nice ass or was I still thinking about Whitney Houston? Thirty minutes had passed and I was getting impatient. I should have known that someone had probably hacked my computer and lured my dumb ass there as a joke. The crazy X-Man had fallen for another otherworldly scam. I reached for my leather jacket and skull cap so I could get the hell out of there. Right before I got up the cute cashier slipped me a piece of paper. I looked at it and it read Peace God give me just 5 more minutes. I am manager not an octopus. As I sat down with my mouth opened for all the world to see, all I could slowly whisper to myself is what-in-the-fuck-is-going-on?

* * * *

When she came back to the table I was still in shock. My headaches began to rumble so hard they replaced my shock with a searing pain that made me massage both of my temples.

"Lord, man, you and those headaches. Here, take this—it's better than that bullshit Ibuprofen you eat like M&M's. I wished out of all the agents they had spared you this tracking device. You look ruff brotha. How long has it been for you? Twenty years by my calculations."

* * * *

"Who in the hell are you?" I said as I took the pills, confident that they weren't poisonous.

"If I told you, you would probably jump up and arouse the attention of those police officers over there enjoying their free coffee."

"Yeah well try me."

"Okay then, darling, buckle your seat belt because what I have to tell you will make the hair on your chest disappear, and you won't feel a thing. Not only that, I think you will still get up and draw attention to yourself. Shall we continue?"

"Look, lady, I know you hacked either my computer or my fucking cellphone just so you could fuck with me about my conversations with Melvin. You wouldn't be the first skeptic that approached me. So, just get on with it, Why are we here? You can start by humoring me as to why you called me God and agent."

"I've been a manager at this Starbucks since 2004 under the name of Seline Knight. Prior to that, I was a 5 Percenter with the name Mekka Tauheed. You know, like the hajj to Mecca in Saudi Arabia. I played the black masculine computer geek in touch with his perceived cultural heritage. It's what the 5 Percent Nation of Islam called 'right knowledge of self and kind.' You could say it was a disguise within a disguise. I acted the perfect self-righteous, misogynistic-but-caring black male nationalist that one could ever hope to play. Like you, I was given a distraction until my real purpose here in this world threw itself on me like a cold splash of water to the face on a hot summer day. That's about the time you came along with 911 in the wake, or in your case, your sleep. My distraction was the memory loss of my superior sexual identity. Who knows, man, maybe we are interdimensional versions of Marlin and Dory. The two adult characters in the movies *Finding Nemo* and *Finding Dory*. You needed help finding out the loss of your true identity, and I needed help remembering I was like no other woman that has ever existed, transgendered or otherwise. Now let's see that sexy President of Netflix, Laverne Cox, make an original series out of that. Brotha, I see that look on your face. You don't seem convinced."

"I'm not…in the least."

"Honey I figured as much. From now on you will have the floor. You need to remove those construction workers that's got shit all up and down your memory lane. Here's a suggestion why don't you start from the first conversation with your friend Mr. Locke."

"I think I'll do that. For some reason, it feels as though it happened yesterday."

"With the power, you hold it just might have. Oh, shit wait a minute. I almost forgot. Short term memory lost-wink."

"What's that?"

"It's a miniature remodified ham radio in addition to some tech I stole from my boyfriend in another version of this world. It will keep you and I together no matter what dimension we slid into. Now tell me about Melvin."

"Lady, you are some kind of crazy. Anyway, I always called or was allowed to get through during his open lines. I told him and his listeners that I was preparing the world they lived in for a new beginning. Yet, all I really did was relegate myself to a late night prime time slot on his show. Still, I continued to informed them about their destiny. I even had the symbols on my body that were moving around and interlocking together like steampunk gadgets. The only problem was the were only visible to me. It was as if a something had been turned on in me."

"Some kind of agent perhaps?" said Seline.

"Yes, an agent but other things as well. I was also sent here to build a relay station once I was sure that this was the right Earth. Some of his audience found that difficult to believe, but I did exactly that fusing my ham radio with my Sony PlayStation. One caller said it sounded too much like E.T. The Extraterrestrial. I responded by telling them out of all the worlds I have visited, which were numerous, I never once saw this movie to understand their skepticism. I was being truthful and they were cracking jokes. Melvin suggested that I was some kind of dimensional time-hopper with no proof that I had been anywhere. I so wanted to tell them about my headaches that were connected to pivotal events that I watched violently unfold. The USA Today paper I found was one I discussed after the fact. I stated in a broadcast back in 2002 that I had actually envisioned the Twin Towers being turned to rubble. I never said anything because I was afraid that it would throw me into yet another alternate Earth. He seemed to buy that line of reasoning. He said that it coincided with the space-time continuum."

* * * *

"Oh, lord child. The space-time continuum? I supposed you never seen the Back to the Past trilogy either? You know the one were the lead actor was trying to stop the evil Dr. Biff from infecting his great, great, great grandfather with Parkinson's disease."

"No can't say that I have."

"Wow none of the Earth's you've been to seem like they were any fun. JS."

"JS?"

"You know JS—just saying. Oh, never mind, I don't want to know. Just go on with your story. Jeezus Christ."

* * * *

"Melvin soon told me that he was contemplating retirement within three to four years. When he told me that I had to act fast. Six years had passed and I saw no change in the world based on my appearances on his show. Then around Halloween of that same year I had an idea. I went on his show to talk about something his world was familiar with, such as mythology. My headaches had decreased dramatically, and I could think more clearly. It was time for me to introduce my true self to *The Locke Down*. I told him that I wasn't going to use any technical language that his human mind couldn't comprehend. So, I kept my language basic even though I was dying to speak Kobol to throw him a hint. It was one of humanities oldest classical languages."

"Kobol, you say?" said Seline as she looked with disbelief.

"Yes, Kobol. I also stated to him that I was from a race of people that humans would consider to be gods. For years, they used magic to create multiple worlds, timelines, and dimensions. Nothing was impossible for them to wish into existence. They had deemed themselves perfect, but one of them did not. This particular god was known as the First Mason. This god started a ranking system in order for each other god to prove their worth as Almighty. To do this, they had to explain their magical powers by using science and the formulas the First Mason's invented. If a god could do this through scientific explanation, the First Mason would have deemed them worthy of their title and power that came with it. This was a clearly a challenge, and Melvin agreed with me that it was. I could tell that Melvin was immersing himself in my story. I went on to say that each god had accepted the challenged one by one as if doing it for charitable organizations. Melvin found that humorous. Once all the gods had accepted the challenge, the First Mason upped it by making them agree to make this a law. They had to agree that until they had mastered science, no magic would ever be used again. For ages, they had to deal with this law because they could not figure out the First Mason's scientific formulas."

* * * *

"I can bet I know what happened next. They gave up trying."

"You are so correct. They had unanimously decided to abolish the law and restore their powers. Like I told Melvin there was just one problem. The First Mason had hidden their powers within the formulas. They had been tricked into consolidating their powers for the First Mason to possess. They were of course foolish, but not completely powerless. As a fail-safe mechanism, they wish their spirits in the form of Yonic or Yoni symbols into the vastness of the cosmos to avoid total extinction. Countless numbers of these symbols in the form X seeded so many worlds at once the numbers were astronomical. The First Mason feeling cheated of victory created what is known as phallic symbols to destroy X symbols out of jealousy and fear. It resulted in just mutating the symbol and not destroying it. For all that it was worth I had failed miserably."

"You failed miserably? Are you saying that you are the First Mason?"

"Like I told Melvin, not only that, but I am that who created him and anyone who has ever lived. I am the God who goes by many names. I had regained my consciousness, but not my powers. I could not command thunder and rain. I did not speak to him about his aunt Lorraine that died of brain cancer when he was 17 years old. That information spooked him out. He had never spoken to anyone about his aunt Lorraine. I know because he prayed to me when she died to tell her he said I will see you in heaven one day and that he loved her very much. He hated me, though.

He blamed me for taking her so soon. He was in shock. No one knew that. I could tell that he was now starting to take me a lot more seriously. I could hear it in his voice. He was so distraught that he went to another caller who was still doubting my claims. She stopped questioning me once I told her that her real hatred wasn't really aimed at me, but at Rabbi Stevenson who had convinced her to have an abortion, only to find out that he and his boyfriend had decided to adopt two beautiful newborns that needed a stable home. I asked what made her the angriest? Was it the abortion or having unprotected sex with a man of the cloth that hid his sexual identity? She gave me a big fuck you and hung up the phone. I didn't get to tell her she was H.I.V. negative and had no worries on that end, but she would also never have any children of her own. Unless she adopts."

"You are such a bastard."

"No, I am God that technically speaking created these bastard humans. many of them. This is not how I intended things. I sent my symbols out to destroy the X not for it to attach itself to it. And you know that don't you young lady? I know who and what you are now."

"Oh, really? Do enlighten me, First Mason, or do you prefer God?"

"I prefer to win this game of chess that's been played for far too long. But to answer your question, you are one of their agents sent to sound the alarm of my whereabouts to the other gods."

"That is correct."

"Now that's funny do you know these people have written stories about you. They think you are seven different angels with a big bugle to activate some gigantic alarm system. Had I known that these creatures were the result of my early drafts, I never would have revised my formulas. How long do the "powers that be" come for me?"

"Sweetie, your destiny depends on all that you told Mr. Locke. So, tell me the rest."

"Very well, I will. After I had revealed that I was his creator, but could not outperform Charlton Heston's parting of the Red Sea. Many of his listeners considered me an educated fraud. A good story, another caller claimed, but still fraudulent to the core. I think they like me better when I was X-Man."

"Okay ,but you are still not telling me why they really called you X-

Man. Now spit it out!"

"I will, patience please. We wouldn't want to arouse the attention of those officers over there enjoying their free cups of coffee, would we?"

"Point taken; go on."

"A year before Mr. Locke retired, I came across a letter I was trying to decode since Y2K. Another foolish distraction invented by the human propaganda machine to spread deception all over the world. That let me know that he was here and two steps ahead of me."

"He? You mean the other agent?"

"Yes, but don't interrupt; I am almost dome. As I was saying, I shared this letter with Melvin and his audience on another open line that for the most part was dedicated to me. He never openly considered me a guest, but once I read that letter to him, I knew that would change forever. I explained that the latter I had in my possession was from my last visit to an alternate Earth. It contained information about an agent sent to find me. This agent never found me and decided to take matters in his own hand by going rogue. I have that letter with me that I read to Melvin and his listeners about that agent. You know who I am talking about, don't you?"

"I do, and like you someone will find and capture Iblis Shaytan and return him where it belongs."

"And where is that, exactly. It's like I told Melvin one night, there is no such thing as heaven or hell. Every single human being that has ever lived is still here on this Earth. Most of them have spent an eternity yelling in their graves to let them out, hoping someone will hear them. Some small children and animals can hear them, but they tend not to say too much. The rest just watch history unfold as they await their family and loved ones to join them. Do you know some of them thought they could use the space shuttle to leave the Earth? And if that didn't work, they tried rockets. What a waste they are. Again, had I known. Anyways, the letter read:

June 1, 2014

Dear: Cherise,

I hope this letter finds you well. I trust you and your family have had a weekend of fun at Disney World. Now you probably thinking how do I know you went to Disney World for the weekend? Three words "your Facebook profile." It was linked to people in some shape, form, or fashion that knows us both. Rest assure I wasn't spying on you. I just needed to get in contact with you. So, please don't rip this letter up. Wow now that I think about it Tasha must be 13 and Lil Steven what 9? It's funny how time flies. Anyway, it was 15 years ago, on this exact date that we were supposed to celebrate my new job in the government's theoretical physics program in California. I had given up putting in applications at

USA Jobs website, but they finally came through. The next thing I knew I had an interview in D.C. They were really interested in my ideas on time travel and spatial mechanics. I only asked them to allow me time to get myself together so I could pack and try and renegotiate the lease on my apartment. They were like kool would 90 days be sufficient? Sheiit with the money they were talking I wanted to leave for Cali right after that interview.

I always think about it. Within ninety days my life the one that included you was going to change for the better. I knew my concept on reversing time would impress the right people. You and some of our friends use to laugh at me about pursuing foolish ideas. What was it Nate use to call me? Oh, I remember brotha from a different hood. They always looked at me funny when I would explain why I came up with the idea. I told all of you how much I missed my grandmother the woman that raised me. I wanted to go back in time to let her know that I was going to make it in life and be somebody. I didn't want to be another nigga either dead in the street or rotting away in some prison cell. I know your mom use to tell you to find a real man. Someone that wanted real things in life for his family. Man, did her attitude do a 360 when she heard Uncle Sam had offered me a job. She was like can I do this for you son? Can I do that? I never wanted her to be my personal maid. I just wanted a mother-in-law to trust that I was indeed in love with her daughter and wanted what was best for the both of us.

Yet, that's not exactly what happened now is it? You wouldn't listen then, but maybe you will now? Inspiration can come at any time. As a matter fact, it did one night at work. You never know when or in what manner it will come. You just have to grab it and go forward with that energy. Now for the most part that's what I did. Just as soon as I got off from work on the ferry. I started to write down the mathematical formulas that were running crazy in my head. Now technically I didn't wait. I called for a bathroom break to jot those ideas down on a piece of paper. You know how bad I had trouble remembering things. I do remember that time at the restaurant at the Golden Corral. You asked me to get up and go get you some rolls because the waitress was taking too long. So, when I came back without them, but the phone number from that same waitress sticking out my back pocket you were pissed. I apologized all the way home, but you were not trying to hear it. We made love that night and I promised to never disrespect you like that again and I meant it.

Several days had passed by since that moment. We had planned to get married. You remember, don't you? We both knew as well as your mother that we were broke. I never liked the idea of you working as a housekeeper cleaning all those damn rooms for a few measly dollars. That's why if you can recall is the reason I went back to school, to get my masters in mechanical engineering back in 97. It's also the same reason that I asked my job for more hours at work. School and more hours at work the j-o-b was going to be tough and I was up for the challenge. Then you turned around and asked your job to do the same thing. I was pissed off. Yet, that's the kind of woman you were. You will do whatever it takes to make things work for the better. They simply don't make people like you nowadays. More time went by and we were barely seeing one another. I accepted that because we were both working towards a goal.

Then one night at work during the late spring I met Taveena. Like so many others she used the ferry to get to her job. She was a nurse that worked at a nearby hospital. I was smoking me a cigarette near the staircase and I noticed her when she drove pass me to park. Right from the jump something told me to not even bother with her. I finish my smoke and went back down to the engine room. The ship would be pulling out soon. I used to hear my aunts say all the time a dick ain't got a conscious. And there I was proving them right. I just had a few more weeks to go before it was time to move on with my life and all I could think of was sexing that sista down from her head to her toes. She was fine as hell and I had to get to know her. Please don't stop reading. You really need to hear the rest of this letter.

As it turned out Taveena had recently started working the night shift to put herself through nursing school; which she attended during the day. Right off the back we had something in common or so I thought. It took the ferry 45 minutes to cross the James River form one side to the next. She would often get out of her car to enjoy the warm nighttime breeze. Her conversations were normally geared around the future and doing well in life. I liked that about her she had goals just like me. Now more than anything she talked about all the sci-fi books she liked to read. There I was staring at her ass in that tight nursing uniform she wore and she was talking about spaceships and some new Star Wars movie that was coming out soon. I didn't care about none of that shit. As strange as this might sound to some people not all geeks are into science fiction. I just really liked math and science. I could care less about a damn

Artoo Threepio or Jabba the Solo. Who really gives a fuck? All I know is that I was feeling her and I wanted some pussy. Sorry to put it like that, but you know I am going to keep it 100.

The next time I saw her I decided to pretend I was all into that Captain Kirk shit. She was eating it up too or so I thought. After several nights of trying to holla at her ass, she made a move that I didn't see coming. Taveena knew all along that I was feeling her. She told me that if I wanted to get with her I needed to do something for her. So, naturally I asked what was it she wanted me to do. She looked at me with those pretty brown eyes and I looked back at her hoping she could read what was on my mind. It seemed like the boat had stopped moving. It was then she reached back from the driver's side of her car to the backseat and handed me a book. The book was titled "Return to Sender" written by her. All 500 and some pages. I was surprised that she was an author. That meant she had some intelligence too. In a way that was good and bad. The bad thing is I was going to have to put time in her. Time that I didn't have. It was the end of April and time was pushing.

I told her that I was impressed with her accomplishment. She told me a lot of the book was based on things that happened in her alternate life. I was like yeah that sounds interesting I can't wait to read it. What I was really saying was what in the fuck is this bitch talking about. She went on and on about how everybody that has read it already really enjoyed it and said she was wicked with the pen. She wasn't really bragging just confident and proud of her work. I still wasn't going to read the shit, especially after she said it was a sci-fi romance. Five hundred and some pages of mush shit. Give me a damn break. It just wasn't happening. I took it and just as soon as she drove off in her Honda Accord I put the shit in my locker downstairs. I didn't see her until the next following weekend.

That Friday night she drove up with some dude in the car. I was like damn I knew she had a man. She was too fine not to. Yet, I didn't see a ring on her either. I was so caught up in everything else I never thought to look or ask. I was like fuck oh well. She hurt me to my heart when she introduced me to her husband Patrick Beamon a fucking bellhop. He was a tall real light skinned thin dude. The all cheerful and nice to meet you kind of shit. I said to myself I know this nigga weak. Then to top it off he had on a black t-shirt with little Marvin Martians going around his collar holding hands. Not to mention his jeans were raggedy with strange calligraphy that read Helter Myskelter. What did she see in this guy to marry him? Taveena asked me to show her were the ladies room was on the boat. Just as I thought he would he stayed behind to socialize with the other passengers.

We walked to the other side of the ship were the women's restroom was located. She was about to asked me about that damn book. I kind of figured she would so I lied and told her I read it after she had asked. Then she grabbed me by the hand and took me into the restroom. Just as soon as we were in there she locked the door. It was one of those small restrooms that could only fit two people at a time. She asked me again if I read her book before we went on any further. I couldn't believe it at the time what was about to go down. It all happened so fast. Without thinking I said yes. I didn't want to miss that door of opportunity. The next thing you know we were having sex.

So, there we were, going at it. We were so into it that we had lost track of time. Then we heard her husband outside of the door calling for her. She told me to stay put and she would be in touch with me. With the quickness, she left from out of the restroom. It was three days later until I heard from her again. The next time I saw her she was on her way to work. She had acted like nothing had happened. All she wanted to know was when I was leaving to go to Cali? I told her in a few days.

All of a sudden, she started crying. I asked her what was wrong. She told me that she was sorry and that she would never see me again. I was okay with that it was all good. I knew that it was a onetime thing so I didn't sweat it. There was something about the way she looked at me that made me feel a certain kind of way. At the time, it was hard to explain, but of course I know now that it was a look of pity. As I watched her drive off I couldn't help but think she was a weird, but good piece of ass. The same weekend things turned for the worse.

I had just got home from work. It was the same morning you dropped of those brochures of Los Angeles. I must have just missed you. I was getting ready to call you, but I started bleeding from my eyes and nose. It scared the shit out of me. I had no idea of what was going on. All I know is that I was afraid. It didn't help that when I went into the bathroom that made things worse. My eyes had stop bleeding. They were now pale and my pupils turned yellow. I ran out of the bathroom and drove myself to the hospital. By the time, I got there I had blood coming out of my ears. Then there was this strange feeling in my head like something was moving around inside. The next thing I know I woke up in the ICU with you holding my hand. I hate to remind you of all of this, but please continue reading. I am almost done.

When the doctors told me that my life would never be the same. I thought they were playing some cruel kind of joke. Things got real when they showed me the video of my legs falling off as they tried to put me onto a stretcher. All they could tell me was that whatever I had it began in the urethra I use to have. They had to cut my entire penis off. That messed me up psychologically. They sent me a shrink and a sexologist to talk to about an alternative sexual lifestyle. I never knew but one way to have sex. I thought alternative lifestyle meant you were gay. It was during those sessions when those doctors wanted to know detailed information about our sex lives. We both hated answering all of those personal questions. Doctor or not it made me uncomfortable telling all those people our business.

I knew then that I had to confess about me cheating on you. If I could have remembered who she was I would have told you and doctors. Then I saw that look on your face like you had already known. What I didn't know was that I had been in the hospital for four weeks. They claimed that I was in and out mumbling words that they couldn't decipher. They even told me that my lapse in memory would continue to get worse. I thought I had heard it all until they told me I was in the care of the CDC (Center for Disease Control). Was it that serious? It must have been because they had you to sign a disclosure agreement not to mention this to anyone. This is why the names in this letter as they say have been changed to protect the innocent. So, if you are reading this you are probably saying tell me something I don't know. I will do exactly that.

After they finished poking and drilling every bit of information out of you they told you that you couldn't see me anymore. The only way that we could remain in contact was through social media or snail mail. That thing about your Facebook profile was told to me by them. It was all a setup. For the past 15 years, they have been keeping tabs on you. Considering what we've been through that's not surprising. Trust me these people are relentless. You don't' know this, but they send me from one hospital to the next. Currently I am somewhere in California. They never tell me what city just the state. Yeah, I finally got to Cali just not the way I wanted. Even if I knew where in Cali I couldn't reveal it and if I did you still wouldn't know. They screen all my letters and watch me like a hawk. Most of the time it is a nurse or some soldier. It depends on the facility. This one is a great one. Excuse me if that sounded too enthusiastic. It's just that over the years I have had my share of hospitals. And not all of them have been hospitable.

It means the world when you have a nurse that is sincere. If it wasn't for this one nurse, I never would have typed this letter. I will call her nurse Patricia. Her name immediately bought to focus some dark images. They came and then they went. I told my doctors that and all they did was added more dosage in my medication. Nurse Patricia seemed to be always by my side when I would wake up from a heavy dosage. Sometimes it was a day and sometimes it was several days. Now each and every time I woke up she was always reading something. I never bothered to ask her what she was reading. I supposed in a past life I hated to read.

Yet, for no reason other than curiosity I asked her why she reads so much? She told me that she loved it. She went on to say that some books just seem to take you to others places. It allowed her an avenue to escape the harsh realities of life. I flipped when she asked me would I like something to read. I said sure why not? I asked to humor her what did she recommend. She handed me a book titled "Return to Sender." I couldn't believe it. She told me that the author was a friend of her cousin. That interested me a lot. This time I asked what happened to the author since she said was. She said she didn't know about the author's whereabouts, but her cousin died in New Orleans during Hurricane Katrina.

My next question was had she herself read it? She said not yet because science fiction was not on the top of her list. She took it because her cousin said it was good. I told her I would read it and let her know what I thought about it. The author's skills were impeccable. To say it was a page turner would be an understatement. No on the contrary this book hit home in more ways than one. It just completely pulled me into the characters and the story line. Cherise the story line was about us down to the letter. Listen to what I am saying. The resemblance was mind boggling. It took me two days to read it. After I completed it all I could do was scream at the top of my lungs. I was a madman. I kept calling your real name.

Do you really want to know why? Well here it is. The book was about a biracial brotha from a parallel universe. He is from a world that looks exactly like ours except they call it Sender not Earth. In his world, black and white people have declared war on all the other races. An underground movement was started to counter attack the invading armies. The war went on for 50 years leaving devastation all over the planet. His kind was losing so they came up with a plan. The plan was to find a world that was free from racial tensions. Why he chose our world in that regard I don't have a clue. They sent him here to our world to raise an army of biracial soldiers to eliminate their enemies. He recruited some through a form of mind control. There were known as the Millennials. He also impregnated most of his victims.

He then went on to kill thousands of people here on our world if their D.N.A. was not compatible with his own. The ones who were went missing never to be found again. He enjoyed working with the females in this world. This alien was often sadistic in his dealings with women. After, he had accomplished his goals he decided to find him a wife and leave children here in our world as spies. He eventually got a job as a bellhop and met a nurse, who became his wife. He tormented her daily and threatened to kill all her family members in a Charles Manson like way. He even forced her to leave clues of her predicament to those who he knew would not pick up on her situation. At least not in time. As a couple, they had sex with tons of people. Sometimes as a couple and sometimes individually. Many thought they were swingers, but the reality was something altogether different. She disappeared the latter part of 1999.

Shortly after that he met a housekeeper; who had recently lost her boyfriend due to some strange accident. It was later revealed that her boyfriend had fell terminally ill. They got married and had two kids a girl and a boy. Their name were Tasha and Steven. Cherise if you get this letter run. Your husband is the alien in the book and he has been playing us all along. I know this might sound crazy, but nor I or the government are taken this lightly. They are looking for all of you at this exact moment. One last thing and I hope it isn't true. According to the epilogue all they will find is a note in your home saying "Returned to Sender."

"Once I finished the letter, Mr. Locke wanted to know was this agent successful. I told him in his world he might have very will been a god. I had no information on him other than this letter that was written by someone who's probably dead. In fact, that entire world may be defunct. Nevertheless, this agent provided a blueprint that this world would be conquered in a similar fashion. Mr. Locke found my story to be fascinating. He is such a unique individual. When I started his family line they had just learned the importance of fire. Some of them scared of their own shadow. Now there he was questioning my sincerity-albeit then in a nonchalant manner. He went to one last commercial break that took longer than usual. As I expected when he came back I could feel him from a far. I knew that I had completely hooked him line and sinker as they say. He wasn't going to admit it. He did want to know what was this agent's next move? I told Melvin that his next move had already been made. This agent had become more tactical with his concept of chess. Naturally Melvin wanted me to explain that. I told him that he could see his work all around us. It's all about the DNA and gaining favor with the winning side. Iblis was never evil, just miss understood. Hell, I killed more people than he did. Floods, earthquakes, wars, famine, disease, and so many other things, which people blame him for. He figured that if he could be born and raised amongst you and do his part in the natural progression of human evolution, that might get him a ticket back home. Again, he has done this based on what he perceives as nature correcting itself. The final cog in human development was the sexual revolution during the 60's and 70's. It paved the way for a new era, which like you humans always do-misnomer things. Third wave feminism and its focus on queer theory is the incubator for human advancement. This agent saw that too. He realized that murder was not the way of the future. People needed to be spoon fed. So, with the help of a few others he took on the name Stan Lee and used your mythology to brilliantly show what you all are destined to come. Melvin should have been in denial by now, but he wasn't. I had him remember?"

"I do indeed, continue."

"He asked me if I was talking about the guy who started Marvel comics. I said bingo. I asked him why do you think that there are so many comic book movies out in the theaters nowadays? It was his plan all along. Especially, his beloved X-Men. Queer rights and comic book movies are the revolution that is being televised. It's the male gender that has always been the mutant gene of what was already perfect. I know because I created the mutation to be first and foremost even if it had to kill to do so. Now this agent you call the devil in some circles has figured out a way to capitalized on my mistakes. I always considered the other gods to be lesser than me. Anything they did was weak and inferior. I am a jealous god and I wanted everything and anything to bow down to my grace. I have failed at such a small task. I thought that if I could corrupt the human chromosome that eventually I would be knighted in this game of chess, but know I see that this will never be. I told Mr. Locke was that a type of heaven would be established on this world like no male will ever see. All men that are selected to stay will eventually be biologically converted to a woman. And in so many ways it's happening already. I even told gave dear Mr. Melvin the date that men will be no more. June 6 in the year three thousand and."

"I have heard enough." Seline motioned the officers to come in her direction, while at the same time telling her employees that everything was okay and to continue working. "These ladies will escort you to a holding facility until the proper authorities arrive to take you back home and I can promise this it's not going to take thousands of years either. Like you said the world is about to receive more people like us. A cosmic supernatural renaissance long overdue. You might not believe this, but I wished we could have done this a lot earlier. I was so sick and tired wearing that costume with that shit constantly dangling between my legs. I fuckin hated it with a passion. Yet, the powers that be said they needed a confession and now they have it. Everything is in due time I suppose. When I see my beautiful nude feminine body in the mirror, I know for a fact that nature has chosen the correct gender to represent her everywhere. This body may not live to see the date you gave Mr. Locke, but a picture speaks a thousand words. Mine, like so many others, will say we were X-Men.

✗

EMPRESS OF THE DARK DOMAIN
Allan Rozinski

*She can seduce all creatures of the night
—the wolf, the crow, the owl, the snake—
bend starlight and moonbeams to her will,
Empress of the Dark Domain.*

*With a gentle sigh of breeze,
flowery meadows and stands of trees
dance and sway and murmur songs
of adoration in her wake.*

*She sails in at twilight of the waning day,
is fond of play in fallow fields,
all nature to her would surely yield
should she ask, though she rarely may.*

*Sprites and fairies lend their hand,
rendering aid with magical dust and sand
sprinkled into eyes to effect the spell of slumber,
each delivered unto her bewitched land.*

*At the warning light of dawn,
she gathers her robes of shadow and form,
the revels of the night now all but done,
she fades into the dark vault opposite the sun.*

SOME BATTLES CANNOT BE WON

Paul Lubaczewski

He felt the presence in an instant. He was here!

Dammit! He'd have to go, and he had to go now!

His phone was out in an instant as he headed for the lobby. He punched in the shortcut and waited for Carol to pick up. He was talking as soon as the line clicked, "Carol, the man who pays you a fortune for not asking questions!"

"What's up boss?" she said briskly.

"I need my things picked up at the Pan-Pacific and a ticket leaving Shahjala ASAP, don't care where except out of here by some distance, and not coach," he said stepping towards the waiting line of cabs.

"One of those trips?" Carol said with practiced smartness.

"Yep, yep, chop chop on this, I gotta go now. No time for customs, no time for anything, no time for anymore Bangladesh," he said getting into the vehicle. He could hear Carol's fingers tapping on a keyboard in the background already.

"I've got you first class to Luxembourg, no customs, this is costing you a king's ransom," Carol said automatically.

"Which I have in travel expenses for just such an emergency. I'll call you again from the plane," he said clicking the phone shut. Well, there was today's meeting shot to hell. Thankfully, he hadn't had too many important things in his bags, so whoever went and collected them wouldn't be getting anything important for their rifling through his things looking for valuables to pocket.

He watched the streets of Dhaka go by from inside the cab. He wasn't upset to be leaving, the place was a mess. Billboards everywhere, dust and pollution coating every available surface. The cab he was in had probably been washed just this morning, it was for the high-end trade after all, the driver had even spoken English, but still it was taking on a brown sheen. White had probably not been the best choice for many of the billboards and the banners that hung between the northbound and south bound lanes, they all looked tan to his eyes.

Dust brown, dust, everywhere you looked. Like another town he'd been in once, one he'd called home.

* * * *

Johnathan Bishop hated coming into town for anything, but a farm is never as self-sustaining as you want it to be. You learn to forge, you learn to brew, you learn to grind corn into flour, you try and learn everything, but no matter how hard you try it's not enough. Sometimes you've got to take some of the coins and script you keep in a tin can hidden in the privy, and you have to ride into town for supplies.

Hardlesty was as good as any town he supposed, but in all the building that had happened over the years, it was dusty. He'd read somewhere that you had to plant something in the ground to hold the ground together when you built, or the soil dries out. He'd done quite a bit of reading before coming here, before he moved his family here. Jonathan didn't want to fail at this. He didn't want to go back east his tail between his legs and see all the things that reminded him of the war.

The war had gone everywhere, and it had been brutal to everyone it touched, most things out east reminded him of the killing now. He had had a little bit of property to come back to, and he had had a Captain's pay stacking up, not to mention the money he'd saved before the war. Jonathan had options, and he chose the one that let him leave. There was a whole land out there that needed farmers and ranchers, and that had barely seen the war at all, he aimed to live on part of it.

Even so, he avoided town, there were no bad memories here, nothing had every been burned to the ground here. No women raped, or children slaughtered, at least not any more than any other town. The streets of this town had never run red with the blood of youth wasted on the hard ground. Jonathan had just discovered, he didn't much care for people anymore, he knew what they were capable of.

The war might be over, and there might be peace in the land, but that didn't mean everyone forgave or forgot. The nation's strife had left its mark on all, like the children of a couple who bicker and brawl all into the night filling unlit bedrooms with the smashing of glass heard through walls. In wanting to be away from his own hurt, he could rarely stand to witness it in the eyes of others while they spoke. They might not even think themselves carrying the hurt with them, but he could see it in their eyes.

Johnathan was wishing for a drink of water as he was pulling the wagon into Hardlesty. The dust of the road here and the dust of the town now coated him and his conveyance with a layer of brown grit. It made no difference that his neckerchief had been red when he left the house this morning, it was reddish brown now, the color of dried blood. He thought he could feel the dust grind into his teeth with every swallow.

The wagon rolled to a creaking halt as he pulled up on the horse's reins. Carefully unhitching them from the vehicle he tethered them to the post in front of the General Store. Before he went looking for any beverages, there was still the list to give to Henry the owner of the place. Hopefully, Henry's boys could have it loaded before he even got back from sampling the rat piss they called beer here. He noted the other wagon similarly tied, but loaded now in front, and wondered who else had come into town getting supplies. He couldn't help but wonder if they were in the whore house if they left the wagon like that, getting another supply they didn't get the way they liked it back at home.

His boot creaked on the bare wood that made the store's porch. They were dusty too, but you could see the gleam under the dust that indicated it had been polished first thing this morning, a remnant of a military life. Henry was behind the counter, asleep in his chair when Johnathan walked into the store. Jonathan politely cleared his throat. Henry's bone-thin body jerked at the noise, his eyes flying open showing confusion for a second as if he had no idea where he had woken. The man recovered quickly though and was on his long legs in a moment, but as he stared at Jonathan, his eyes were still wide in shock at this intrusion into his dreamworld by reality.

"How you doing today Henry?" Jonathan said smiling matter of factually as he strode through the dimly lit store to deliver his list.

"Oh, my word Jonathan, you couldn't have picked a worse time to come to town, and no mistake," the man stuttered wiping sweat off his brow, as he propped himself up behind the counter.

"How do you figure? One day's as good as the next to take my money," he drawled.

"Not this one, Bill Addison is in town gettin' supplies too, he's over at the saloon, drinking it up and telling everyone who'll sit still to listen what done happened. That's his wagon out front," the storekeeper stammered out.

"Aww hell Henry, those were my cattle. Bill just likes to stir up trouble and you know that." Johnathan shrugged unconcernedly.

"Did you have to shoot the kid, though?"

"I just put one in the seat of his pants, big strapping young man like that will heal up in no time. I told him to let them go, I told him to get the hell off of my land. So, what does the fool do if not go for his rifle! He's lucky I only put a slug in his ass and not his head, it would be an honest mistake between the two," Jonathan grinned.

Henry tittered at that nervously but added, "He's still sayin' he's sore mad at you. And drinking like an injun'. I'll get the boys to fill you up as fast as I can, but I'd stay out of sight if I was you. That man is spoiling for a fight, and he wants it with you."

"Maybe I'll go see what Andrew's about then. But before I go give me a bottle of soda water, will you? I got miles of dust in my mouth," he said sliding a coin across the counter.

"You actually drink that stuff straight from the bottle?"

"Well, I was going to get beer, but if that fool is tearing up the saloon, well I need something to get the dust out of my mouth," he smiled taking the bottle.

Bill Addison, the bane of his otherwise placid life. The man was a canker sore of a human. Jonathan knew deep in his heart that the whole reason for trying to steal those steers from his land was pure mischief on the man's part. Some people can't get far enough away from the past, it seems they spend their entire life trying to flee it. Others, well they wallow in it, they wear their perceived victimization as if it was some badge of honor, even if they were in the wrong to start. That was Bill Addison all over.

Major William H. Addison, Confederate Soldier of the 9th Tennessee Infantry, veteran of Shiloh, man who was still fighting the lost cause. He was also known as Bill Addison hateful drunk who abused his wife, his children, his neighbors and anyone else who couldn't get away from him fast enough. Jonathan had no idea what Bill had been like before the war, it didn't matter to him, that was not who he was dealing with now.

Once Addison had found out Jonathan had been a Captain in Sherman's army, the man made it his life's mission to torment him. Their properties touched at one spot, and it took all of Jonathan's turning the other cheek to keep that simple fact from becoming a range war. He'd caught the man's damned fool nephew trying to herd some of Jonathan's cattle on to Addison land, probably at his Uncle's bidding. He had told the young man to leave off and get off his land, the boy had gone for a rifle slung in his saddle a few feet from where he was trying to gentle the cows, it had taken a mighty fine shot to only shoot him in his hindquarters.

He was positive Henry was right, Addison must be furious. The right or wrong didn't enter into it at all. His plans thwarted, and his nephew punctured where he kept his brains, must have driven him to a fit. Which he was now venting on anyone foolish enough to be within ten feet of him at the saloon. Jonathan had other places he could go. Andrew was the town undertaker, but he usually kept a bit of beer around the place to go with the best whiskey, and he had a sardonic wit that matched Jonathan's own these days. Andrew would be a safe place to sit and talk and drink while that idiot Addison either drank himself unconscious or finally staggered over to Henry's to climb aboard his own wagon to take it home.

When his feet hit the main street a gust of wind went down it to greet his presence it seemed. He felt the dust it brought coating him all over again. Jonathan turned towards the direction of the town's only gravedigger's house which also doubled as the town mortuary. It had the second nicest front room in all of town, after the whore house, of course, opposite sides of the same coin really. Creating life and disposing of what's left after it.

It was in Jonathan's best interest to cross the street. His way would take him past the saloon, and if he walked right by the door with Addison in there, the soused rebel would be sure to spot him. It wasn't that he was afraid of the man, but nobody needed trouble, Jonathan had a wife and a son to think about now. Not to mention Addison had numerous children to care for from that wan-faced long-suffering wife, with her eyes that spoke of drunken rages and terror.

Every footstep that took him within line of sight of the place seemed like thunder in his ears. Jonathan felt sweat starting to roll rivulets through the dust that coated his face. He had to resist the urge to run, he hadn't done a damned thing wrong, and a less patient man would have shot the boy dead for going for the gun on top of rustling. Hell, a lesser man would have shot him over the cows.

The mortuary was directly in his sight now, and he could almost taste Andrew's beer already. Yet fleeting moment later and he could already see that beer flying away from him when the swinging doors to the saloon slammed open behind him. Jonathan half turned to look, already sure of what to expect. Addison standing on the porch of the saloon swaying slightly, drunk as a lord, and angrier than a burning hornet's nest.

"You got a lot of guts comin' here Yankee!" the man bellowed into the street.

"Addison, I just come for supplies, same as you," Jonathan said turning to face his tormentor. "Now, why don't you get yourself back in the saloon, and I'll go about my way. Henry's already got your wagon waiting for you. Neither one of us need talk to each other more than we already have."

"I don't WANT to talk to you Yankee. I demand satisfaction for what you did to Jebadiah!" the man bellowed drunkenly as he stepped off the porch and into the dusty road.

"Now Bill, the boy had two of my steers and was trying to lead em off. Be reasonable, I could have shot him dead right there and then! I didn't do him any harm that sleeping on his stomach for a few months won't cure," Jonathan shrugged. He heard a few unhelpful guffaws come from inside the saloon. He was trying to calm this fool down enough for him to go back in, and making Addison feeling he was being made a mockery of wouldn't help any.

"Just like you damned Yankee bastards," Addison snarled weaving onto the street, "one of us is hurt, and you just stand there saying 'Well I had no choice' like that makes it any damned better!"

"Bill if you could tell me what choice I had, man is robbing me and makes a move for his rifle, he should count himself lucky I didn't shoot him dead," Jonathan barked back getting angry himself. He could feel this spiraling out of hand quickly, and he could feel the unseen audience staring at them both from every window facing the street. They were getting a show now, nobody would intervene, the drunk had the floor until he fell over onto it.

His nemesis came to a stop in the middle of the road, standing between two ruts. Jonathan was surprised he didn't actually trip over them to get there, "I'm gonna give you a choice right now, you want a choice so damned bad." Addison spat a stream of tobacco juice that sent up a cloud as it struck the ground, "Either you draw for it, or I shoot you dead where you stand!"

This was exactly what Jonathan had been trying to avoid, he had no doubt the fool would try to make good on his threat. As drunk as he was, he doubted Addison could hit the broad side of a barn, but he could get lucky. No, the best way to deal with this was to try and shoot him in his gun arm, and hope he lived, the distance wasn't too great, Jonathan was sure he could make the shot. The whole town had seen the idiot call him out, everyone could see Addison had the weapon to make good on his promise, or at least attempt to. Didn't seem that Jonathan had a choice in this at all.

He reached down, and loosened his holster, hearing the gun crack free from the leather, and said, "If that's the way you want it."

"That's the satisfaction I demand Yankee! Johnson! Get out here and call it," Addison bellowed.

Another man, Jonathan had made his acquaintance but didn't know him well, fell out of the bar at Addison's caterwauling demands. His eyes were wide as he looked at both of the men, he stammered out, "John, y'all don't have to do this, you know nobody'd think less of you if you didn't right?"

"He ain't got no CHOICE," Addison spat the word out with disgust, "and he damned well knows it."

"What he said," Jonathan said quietly, just loud enough to be heard by all up and down the silent road.

Johnson walked a few steps into the road, "If I cain't talkin y'all out of it, I'll call it loud for you on three! Fire till yer empty, hopefully, neither of you get killed, y'all got young uns!"

He stared at Addison now, there was nothing else to do but look at the man he was hoping to not kill here. The face covered in dirt same as him, stubble and deep lines where a set of sorrows and his drinking had dug into him deeper than the sun and the wind ever could. He could tell by the stains, the man had eaten here in town, fresh sauce on his shirt told the tale of that. He'd met the man's wife, Jonathan knew there hadn't been anything on his shirt when Bill left the house. Jonathan couldn't help but wonder, with a town full of witnesses if he wouldn't be better off killing the son of a bitch right here and right now, for her sake if nothing else.

No, he came here to get away from all the killing.

Jonathan turned to Johnson and nodded to indicate he was ready. Addison seeing that just bellowed, "Aww god dammit Johnson, get on with it already! I want to shoot him, not paint his damned picture!"

Even the wind died down now from it's out of season blowing of a moment ago, as Johnson cleared his throat, "Ummm, well OK then, umm on three then. ONE..."

Johnathan's hand flexed.

"TWO!"

His hand drifted towards his thigh holster, his eyes intent on Addison. "THREE!"

Their shots went off simultaneously, BAM! BAM! Even drunk the man had had a fast hand. But Jonathan could see as if in slow motion something was wrong, Addison was falling off balance to his right! It would put his chest in line with the shot!

He didn't see what happened to the man. There was too much smoke, and worse, he was too overcome with shock by a sudden pain in his shoulder! The drunk had stumbled his way into not missing him either! Flames went through his chest along the path the bullet had burned! A gasp escaped his lips, and Jonathan sank to his knees clutching at the wound, his hand feeling the warm wet of his life spilling over it!

As the smoke cleared, he could see Addison lying there. The fool must have thought he'd be clever and dive away as he shot. Either that or he had just drunkenly stumbled as he drew out his own weapon, either answer could be the truth. One thing was clear just looking at him from there, Addison would never get to tell anybody which the correct answer was.

Jonathan watched through eyes blurry with his own tears and sweat, almost uncertain of what he was viewing. There was a man who had not been in the street before, striding purposefully towards Addison's fallen body. He looked to be a white man, but he was dressed like a Mexican Caballero or Vaquero. It was hard to tell what his face looked like, it seemed blurry, something Jonathan was willing to write off to the tears in his eyes. It was odd, though, his outfit was as clear as day, beautiful almost, in its deep black the dust seemed unable to touch, all of the tassels that went with it, a deep crimson that matched the man's crimson shirt.

It seemed to him, he could almost see the man's skull through his translucent skin as the man reached a hand down towards Addison's inert body.

The air shimmered around Bill's corpse as the hand neared it. Jonathan's eyes widened now, as, before his eyes, he saw the form of Addison rising up from his corpse and taking the man in black's hand! He could definitely see a skull in place of the face of the new man as it grinned at the shade of Bill that it pulled up to its feet! It didn't have much choice in grinning.

Jonathan had no doubts as to what he was looking at now, it was the Grim Reaper come to claim Addison's soul! Judging by the wound he had in him, come to claim him next! He dragged himself painfully back upright, as the shade of Addison came away from his mortal remains. Jonathan had only a moment! The thing hadn't spotted him yet! While there was life there was hope! As fast as his failing legs could take him he took off down the street towards where his wagon waited. If he could get away, he might yet still live! But one thing he was sure of, he knew it in his pumping heart quickly losing any blood to pump, there was only one way that waiting here could end!

His first thought was to grab his own horses until he saw Addison's wagon standing loaded and with his horses back in their traces. He could never have said why, but some hidden voice said that he'd need to run a good long way. A fast horse was nice, but if all you had was that and the clothes on your back, you wouldn't be getting far! But a wagon load of supplies could put many a mile between where you were, and where you could feel safe again!

He dragged himself onto the seat and clicked the horses to move! Over his shoulder, he heard a voice call out, as final as the sealing of a tomb, "YOU RUN ALL YOU WANT BOY! I'LL CATCH UP WITH YOU SOMEDAY! I CATCH UP TO EVERYONE EVENTUALLY!"

As he drove the horses to a gallop, he felt sure as sure could be that he was the only one that had heard that, except for maybe shade that had been Bill Addison.

* * * *

As he fled, he could feel the demon behind him just staying where it was. With a moment to think calmly, he began to believe the thing was giving him a head start! He could feel the distance lengthen as he rode like it viewed this as some kind of game. It reminded him of back at the farm when their old tom caught a mouse. The evil cruel old bastard would let the poor terrified creature run loose from under his paws. Its terror bleating away in a series of squeaks, the false hope of freedom and life so tantalizingly close to its panicked little black eyes, only to have that hoped snuffed out as the cat leapt upon its back. So close to escape, only to have the hot breath of the cat's mouth around its neck, to feel the cruel sharp fangs digging in and drawing blood yet again. If you didn't kill the poor thing yourself out of pity, the cat would do that for hours. No matter what Jonathan was now, he was going to run as far and as fast as he could! He could practically feel the claw hovering over him, and the hot breath of the cat as he whipped the horses to go faster!

He ruled out going home, for one thing, it was the first place the man-… no, he had to be honest with himself if he was going to survive, the reaper would look for him. Secondly, he didn't know, could the reaper kill a man himself? Or was he just the one to come to collect those who died? He couldn't risk Martha and Johnnie like that. And for what? He suspected his life lasted as long as he kept running, so to tell them he had to leave? Or drag them from the farm to run with him? He had his own problem, it was unique to him, and a man shouldn't do that to the woman he loved or a son that deserved a chance at a normal life of his own. Home was out of the question.

It wasn't until the sun was starting to set that he finally pulled on the reigns to stop. He hoped this was enough distance to buy him a night's sleep if it wasn't, he'd have to walk, the horses needed to rest. But, he suspected he was fine for the now, he could still feel the presence of death, but it was a long way off now, like a minor irritation to the psyche that one cannot explain. It wasn't a hot and fiery feeling of terror and flight anymore like it had been back in town at least.

Funny thing was he wasn't really tired now, or thirsty, or even hungry. Jonathan would have thought that he would be considering all that had happened. Mentally he felt a bit fatigued, but his body just felt, nothing at all. Not even pain from the wound he received. Moving carefully, he rooted through what would have been Addison's supplies until he found what he needed to do something about that, whiskey, a needle, and thread.

He didn't know what his situation was in terms of life, but he did know he couldn't be leaving a bullet hole open on his chest. Carefully he pulled back the rag he had wedged into the wound on his way out of town. He was expecting the worst of it, for it to start bleeding again until he could sew it shut, he had to steel himself to even look at it. Jonathan had been shot in the war, he knew what it felt like to be wounded, but you couldn't make him look forward to the view of it.

As the rag came away, he started at it in shock! The thing wasn't bleeding at all! What was, he had been sure, a mortal wound showed not a drop now! It had been enough to bring the Reaper to call, and now it didn't even ooze!

Whatever the reason, he still knew it had to be closed. Grabbing a bottle of whiskey from the supplies, he poured it over the wound. To his further surprise, it didn't hurt nearly as bad as he'd expected. Neither did the lengthy and careful process of digging out the slug with his knife. He could feel it, it stung a bit, but it should have been pure agony!

Jonathan sat there after the wound was finally closed, ruminating as he stared at the fire. Something about him had changed when he had run from the Reaper. What kind of changes, and to what extent, he knew not, but by running he had bought himself time to consider it all.

More time than he realized to consider what the reaper meant with this game.

But he'd find out.

* * * *

Years passed, and he kept moving. He'd stay somewhere long enough to make some money, and then move on. A few times he overstayed his welcome, and he would begin to feel that presence, that niggling over his shoulder that told him that the cat had found him again and was looking for another swat. He didn't age, nor did the wound ever really heal. He could eat for taste, but anything that came in, left with only the digestion of rot to it, he was never really hungry.

What he had been the day Addison shot him dead, but not dead, was all that he would ever be. There was to be no growth, no sacred manna of life anymore. He found out how much he'd been unmanned, how little humanity was left in him after that day the hardest way. The only time he had fallen in love in all of the time he had run. She had been a prostitute in New Orleans, named Bessie. He was lonely, not just for the companionship of a woman, but also something less temporary than her trade implied. Frankly, he didn't care about her trade, a woman had to make a living with what she had in 1915, and that was what she had to work with.

When Jonathan felt the tug on him and went to run, she ran with him. She kept running right along beside him for ten years. She might have kept running with him until the day she died if he had let her. He just wasn't that selfish of a bastard. He could see her days of having children were being used up by her time being with him.

While he could commit the act, Johnathan had no life in him, nor, it turned out could he create life from him.

A woman with no children, or grandchildren to care for her in her dotage had a death sentence upon her in that world. He could not promise he would always be there, with the cat always on his tail looking for just the right time to pounce again. He'd cried about it, he set money aside for her for a while, what he figured a good dowry for her would be. Jonathan went to tell her he had to leave, but she had already known. She had his bags packed for him and waiting when he had gotten home from work that day.

"You ain't like other men Jonathan Bishop. You ain't aged a day since the day I laid down with you for the first time. But I've seen enough of you to know, you got problems other men don't have to go with it. I guess you think it's time for me to grow up and settle down, and I know enough about you to know, you cain't never settle down," she said tears brimming in her eyes, but her jaw resolute.

He went over to her and held her for a long time, before she spoke again, "Did you love having company, or did you love me, Johnathan?"

His voice was like gravel, thick with held back tears when he responded, "I loved you, Bessie."

"Well then, we'll always have that, and I suppose that's all that really matters, in the end, isn't it?"

"Yes."

* * * *

When she died at the ripe old age of 79, he made a point to go to her grave to leave flowers. Just like he had done with Martha and Johnnie.

* * * *

Jonathan would never learn why death had decided to make him his toy. He had thought on it often and had always come back to only pique on the part of the Reaper. The thing Johnathan had discovered about himself over the years was, he was good with money. Hiding it, moving it, and investing it. By 1925 Johnathan had solid investments, his instincts were good enough that before the crash of 29 he moved his money around, and barely lost any, the same thing in 2008. As the money grew, he hired people, who hired people. It all grew into an enormous web, all the lines crossing and crisscrossing, all existing to protect, and hide the spider inside.

He hadn't had to go to Dhaka, but Johnathan still kept moving, and he had figured to combine his safety and business. He had no idea how the Reaper had discovered him here so fast. The Reaper had gotten close enough once before that Johnathan had sworn he heard the monster's spurs jangling before he'd been able to affect his escape. But he had to admit that time, he'd been half testing the tether that bound him to the taker of souls, to see how close he could let him get, and what would happen. If Jonathan was really being honest with himself, it was right after he had left Bessie, and he thought he might want to finally die. The Reaper never put in a personal appearance before Jonathan ran, but he felt him close, as close as he could feel the monster today!

Johnathan snapped out of his reverie when he realized that the car had stopped. As he looked around he saw traffic was now quickly backing up, already there were cars stacking up behind them. It happened in what seemed an instant, one minute they were cruising along at the speed limit, the next, a parking lot as far as the eye can see!

Johnathan rapped on the window to get the driver's attention. "What's happening?" he demanded urgently.

The driver turned to him, his dark features smiling, "This time of day, could be anything, sir! Probably an accident, but could be anything, could even be a traffic light is out!"

"Well, how long do these things usually last?" Johnathan demanded.

"Hard to say, boss, could be fifteen minutes, could be two hours," the driver shrugged.

He didn't HAVE two hours, from the feel of it, Johnathan didn't feel like he had fifteen minutes.

He heard in the distance, the metallic jangle of a spur on concrete.

He didn't have five minutes!

He had to move now! Johnathan threw the door open and lunged out of the cab, the voice of the driver over his shoulder, "MISTER I GOT SOME AIR CONDITIONING IN THE CAB! YOU DON'T WANT TO GO OUT THERE! HEY, YOU OWE ME MONEY FOR THE RIDE!"

Johnathan began to run forward. There might be still some chance, some hope! He heard the other door of the cab slam open and shut, heard the driver yell after him, "I GONNA CALL THE COPS! YOU SEE THEN HUH?" A moment later he could hear the exasperated driver exclaim more quietly, "Crazy damn Americans!"

Johnathan was running now, full hard fleeing. The macadam pounding through the thin soles of his monk straps, jarring him as he went. Doors were opening on cars, drivers with nowhere to go, trying to see what all the commotion was about. Some probably hoped to slow him down or trip him up just out of pure mischief!

Suddenly in the midst of the panic, and the terror of the moment, in the midst of his most dreadful overwhelming desire to flee, it all stopped. Johnathan had been running for over a hundred and fifty years now. He was tired of it. A resignation passed across his very soul, his feet slowly wound down their pounding run, to a jog, to a walk, to a full stop. For the first time since the end of the war, he was sick and tired of running. He'd run across the whole world and across a century and a half, and what had it gotten him? Nothing but having to run more.

He stopped and turned. No part of him was truthfully surprised to find not a line of cars in Bangladesh, but a dusty dirt road in a forgotten Oklahoma town. He had heard the spurs getting closer as he slowed, he knew that the Reaper would be there. Johnathan did not feel perturbed to find that he would be meeting the Reaper here. It was fitting, the only thing more fitting would have been the battlefield of Shiloh. But death had only flirted with him there, he had yet to make his move like he had on so many others that day.

The man appeared in the distance walking towards him. Jonathan could see that his appearance hadn't changed over the years. But except for his clothes, neither had Jonathan. Looking down at himself, he noticed now for the first time since he'd gotten out of the cab, his clothes hadn't changed anymore either. Nothing had changed, right down to the clothes he had put on that morning, oh so many years ago!

Instinctively his hand trailed down to his thigh to where his...

"Yeah, you got your guns boy!" the reaper called out to him. "You gave me a good run, but now I figured we'd settle this like men!"

Johnathan saw a figure move out of the corner of his eye. He turned his head to see the shade of Bill Addison stepping towards the side of the road. "This how it's gonna be, I waited all these years to find out how it ends. I know you know how to draw Yankee, so on three!"

"That just it?!" Jonathan yelled to the figure who was striding into position, "We just gonna draw for it?!"

The eyes both black as night and piercing like blue light simultaneously bore into him for a moment, until the Reaper spoke, "Seems only fair boy! You led me on a merry chase, seem a waste to end it on a whimper like you were some deer who ran from an arrow in its belly. Just trailin' along behind you with a knife in my hand waiting until you fell over! Would seem, how they say, anti-climactic. Naw, better we draw for it this time!"

"Looks like I got no choice then," Johnathan said quietly.

"Looks like you never did," the Reaper seemed to smile, it was still hard to say the Reaper had a choice, the skull still lurked and hovered over his face after all.

"ONE!" Addison shouted.

Jonathan's hand floated above his gun.

"TWO!"

The Reaper's dropped towards his own pistol in its holster.

"THREE!"

The air erupted with the cacophony of the guns! They both got off one shot each! Before either could fire again, visibility vanished in a cloud of smoke from the guns! Johnathan felt a bullet bite into his arm, he could still fire again, but he couldn't see his target to fire! No gunfire was coming towards him either, though. Where the air had been dead calm suddenly an errant gust of wind showed him why! The Reaper was lying flat on his back!

Johnathan's other hand automatically went to clutch at the wounded bicep, before he realized, he was in no pain to it at all. Looking at it in disbelief he saw, that there was no wound to hurt, just torn clothing! In a flash of insight, he yanked at the buttons on his shirt, so he could see the wound from all those years ago, only to see that there was no sewn-up injury there anymore either!

When he looked back up, Jonathan could clearly see the figure just lying there in the dirt. Cautiously he strode towards it. Funny he didn't remember wearing spurs that day he fought Addison, but he could hear them jingle as he walked today. Addison had gone back to whatever hell he'd been let out of for the event, it was just him and the Reaper now.

Only it wasn't. It couldn't be. The figure lying in the dirt was no longer clothed like the Reaper, but like some kind of medieval peasant, no longer the man in black he'd fled from all those years ago! There plain as day leaked a bloody wound on the front of his tunic where he'd been pierced to confirm his identity. Yet still, this blond haired blue-eyed young man couldn't be the devil he'd been fleeing for 150 years now!

The tear stained, dust covered face looked up, the head raised a little from the dirt, so the man could view him. "I guess you won huh? To be fair, I never could get the hang of guns. Don't you ever worry about it none, though, I didn't throw this, you beat me fair and square."

Jonathan leaned in close, he could see the young man was dying quickly. There was like a pulling sensation to the entire world for a moment, like the entire fabric of the world stretched as it dragged something away from the body lying in the dirt! A moment later, there was nothing on the ground and the blond-haired blue-eyed man standing right next to him, healthy and hearty as could be!

"You know why I let you go? You wonder all those years? Because I thought maybe you had it in you to beat me. But before you start thinking you won something, "he said laughing, "I'd look at the new cut of your jib!" And with those final words, the man was gone altogether, leaving only the faint echo of his laughter.

The dirt road went with him, and Jonathan stood there in the street in Dhaka again. Driven to see what the Reaper had meant he looked down at his arms in front of him. Gone was the good homespun Martha had made for him. The suit that he had been wearing earlier had not returned to replace it. In its place was a black coat, black as night, so black you thought you could see stars swirling in it! Johnathan whirled to look at his reflection in one of the car windows.

He saw a man in black, black shirt, black coat, with a swirling face that one minute was a skull, the next his own face! No matter what form it was, the eyes looked both blue like the ice that froze Satan fast in place in hell or black as the endless night. Now he knew the final truth, there was no victory, only flight.

Nobody ever really beats the Reaper.

NYKTHOS
Marlane Quade Cook

The moon climbed high behind a shifting gray veil as two figures trudged through the glade of trees. Without a word, Grandmother stopped. She indicated the ground where her grandson was to dig. The boy loosened the dirt with the spade and dug a small hole. The old woman clutched her shawl with one hand and bent over the frigid soil as she reached into the earth.

"It's a bit cold, Grandmother," he said quietly. "Are you sure it will grow?"

"The Dragonclaw always grows if well tended, child," the woman said. "There's more to be told, but tonight we must hasten to plant it. We do not know how long her labor will be."

The boy nodded as he packed the ground over the plant's clawlike root. The leaves that dripped from the stubs of withered branches were still red. A haze seemed to cling to it: a faint misty glow.

Her hand reached out for his arm as they walked slowly back toward the cottage. "Come talk to me later. I will have work after the others are asleep. There is always much to do after a birth." They could hear a woman's cries from the house. The boy drew a deep breath and nodded.

The well-worn path that led to the cottage door was where they parted ways. He wandered toward his grandfather, who leaned against one of the outbuildings while seated on a short barrel around a fire. Aunts, uncles, and cousins milled awkwardly around a fire that gleamed in a clearing amidst the houses of the little settlement.

"Here," the old man extended a mug to the boy, who gratefully accepted. "The old ways pass on, eh, Killian?" the boy nodded again.

"We weren't expecting this one so soon. May the tree flourish. May the child flourish." he raised his own tankard.

"Grandfather," Killian ventured, "does Grandmother know that this will be a…?"

"A Nykthos? A child of the dragon, the ancients called them… Won't know 'til we see the eyes. But the tree must be planted, each generation. We planted last when your sister was born," he shrugged, "Not a glimmer of red among you. But we weren't ready this time." He shook his head. "I wish she had told us sooner. But that's past and can't be helped. You get the knowledge this time. That's good. Means your grandmother sees a level head on you. It's a sacred trust, being Keeper."

* * * *

They walked through the village under the noon sky. Killian often took the ten-year-old along on errands and odd jobs; a mentor to the boy, who was his pale shadow. They stopped first at a market stall to look for earthenware jars the Grandmother might use to store herbs. A stall-minder glanced at them, made a strange sign with her hand, and the uncle scowled as he moved the boy along.

"What was that?" the lad asked.

Killian shrugged unconvincingly. The boy noticed others make the same gesture when they thought he wasn't looking, though not all took the trouble to hide the sign of warding.

"Come, Conall, the market is not worth our time today," his uncle said with a baleful glare around them.

They turned back to their horse and cart, but as they went they heard an old woman's shout, "Young master Killian! I hope your family has in mind its protection! Remember the Dragonclaw!"

The boy looked up with a question on his face, but Killian ushered him firmly toward the cart.

When they arrived home, Conall's mother and great-grandmother were in the garden. The boy ran up and began talking in a low, urgent voice. "Never you mind, child," his mother said fondly, eyes soft and mournful.

"You can't protect him forever, Colleen," the grandmother said, not unkindly, nor pausing in her work as she spoke. She moved from one clump of plants to the next, sometimes gathering, sometimes pruning, sometimes pulling weeds that grew entangled in the plants.

"He's mine to protect!" the young woman snapped. She gathered the boy close to her as they moved briskly away. Conall looked back, his deep red eyes bewildered.

Killian ran an exasperated hand through his dark hair, "what am I supposed to do in all this?" he mused.

"You are the Keeper," the grandmother said levelly, driving a spade into a stubborn clump of roots. "You mind the Dragonclaw, watch, and wait. He's just a boy. There's time."

* * * *

A matter of days later, Killian went out to tend the tree at daybreak, as was custom. Daybreak and dusk. As he approached, he stopped still with horror.

Their grandmother's little garden was half-trampled, rocks and path torn up in disorder as if a bewildered beast had charged through. Colleen stood in the center of the destruction; an axe in her hand, and the Dragon-tree was in splinters.

"What have you done?" he said in horror, "this place is well nigh sacred, Colleen!"

"I know what you're trying to do!" His sister shrieked, weeping. She drove her fingers into the earth and wrenched a chunk of the splintered root free. "It's this, this thing that will poison him if you decide he's evil! And who are you to decide?" She shook the clump of claw-like plant fibers, the earth staining her hands and dropping heavily to the ground. Mixed with black stains of the earth, Killian could see the red tinge of blood. She had lacerated her hands in her frenzy.

"Colleen—sister—listen!" Killian pleaded.

"He's just a boy! He's your nephew! He's not the Devil's child as they say."

"None of us say that! Listen, please!"

But she would not hear him. She hurled the axe at him and as he dodged, she dissolved into sobs and ran, flinging the twisted and crushed root away from her as she went.

Later, Killian followed the old woman down the path, stepping around or over the devastated plants, apprehension flooding him. The tattered hem of Grandmother's ancient woolen dress swept the stones and gravel with a stately grace as they came to the center of the ravaged garden. He worked to retrieve what was left of the root and handed it to her. She shook her head uneasily. "It is too badly damaged. There's little time," she growled, "we must begin again. This is bad, Killian. I have never heard of such a thing."

In the back of the house was an old trunk, piled high with old wooden boxes, surrounded by the clutter of the season. "Give an old woman a hand," she bade him as she began to uncover the trunk. Eventually they pulled it open, and from its depths she drew another box, ornately carved and ancient. This she reverently opened, and withdrew a small bundle wrapped in a scarlet cloth. "it may be too late," she mused, "and Colleen may well destroy it again. We must hide it this time, and tell no one."

She placed it tenderly in his hands, "plant it tonight, under the moon. And we must hope it flourishes."

One night, several years later, Killian had just returned on his meandering path to tend the Dragonclaw unobserved, when he came upon a circle of the men out behind the house. It reminded him of all those years ago, when Conall was born. A few smoked; a few cradled their sleepy children, who clung contentedly to their fathers' worn jackets.

"We could lock him up," one suggested quietly.

"Ah, even if we had a place to hold him, could you bring yourself to do that?"

"What can we do, wait?"

Killian stood quietly in the darkness for a few moments before approaching the fire and finding a seat on a stump of timber. "It won't be long," he said quietly, "We'll be able to help him soon."

"Have you seen the lad lately?" an uncle muttered, "Wild as they come! Furtive. Angry. And Colleen's as bad. She'll stop you if she can."

"I know."

"And can you get him to take it? will he still trust you?"

Killian shrugged, "I can only try."

Killian rose to go out at dawn, but he found others already stirring. Voices were hushed, movements slow, heads bowed. He sought his grandmother, "what happened?"

She shook her head, "We're too late, lad. Go dig up the Dragonclaw, and we'll hide it away again."

Baffled, he left, but on the way met an uncle walking dejectedly up the path, eyes red with repressed tears. "John, what happened?"

"Ah, Killian, you tried," he said sadly, with a reassuring clap on the shoulder. "They'll be bringing him back soon. That is, what's left of him." The older man's voice caught, and halted.

"What?" A cold horror began to creep over Killian.

"They got him. A crazed mob. Some from the village said he'd been killing livestock. We're lucky they didn't come for us all."

"Merciful God, no! Killian's voice choked the words, and emerged in a whisper. "I was almost ready—a matter of days… Oh, God, Colleen! This will kill her! Where is she?"

John shook his head and there were tears in his eyes, "she went after him. No one knew." He paused and shook his head. "if only she'd come home for help. But she didn't. She must have seen it all. Then she threw herself in the river. I'm so sorry, boy. We've only now found out."

Killian fell to his knees. His uncle's stolid grip on his shoulder was a world away.

Everything was quiet and still. the dew soaked through to his skin. He was dimly aware of other voices, other hands urging him to stand, encouraging, empathizing. The keening, mourning call of women. So far away. Only one voice cut through.

"…Terrible loss." it was sweet and lilting, foreign-sounding. He blinked. The face in front of him was olive-skinned, dark-eyed, concerned. Her long black hair fell back from a bright scarf. A colorful shawl was around her shoulders.

"You're not from here," he heard himself say as he fumbled for words.

She gave a smile so lovely his heart twisted. "No," she said, then was abruptly solemn. "My family is traveling. Passing through. but we know of such trouble. Your kinsman was special, and I am so sorry he could not be saved. Doubtless you tried your best."

Killian nodded mechanically.

"My mother is helping the women of your family. You don't know me," she ventured, "but it seems you could use a friend, and I thought... you might like someone to go with you. To dig up the herb?

He stared wordlessly, and this time her smile was shy, "As I said," she told him gently, 'we know of such things."

* * * *

Diama stared at the far wall where bunches of herbs hung drying out of the sunlight. Nearer to her seat on the old couch was a window filtering in sunlight between a pattern of branches. The shadows played on the floor and the table of books in front of her, reminding her that a world waited outside. Her mind was drifting far away.

"He married her eventually. She was a Gypsy girl, they say."

"What?" Diama started out of her reverie, "sorry, Auntie, what was that?"

"Only our family's history, child," Aunt Bea snapped," And it's important, since..."

"I know, I know." She flopped back on the couch, silent for a second before another thought caught her. "Was the woman Killian married really a Gypsy?"

"*Romani,* I should say," Bea corrected herself with a rueful grimace, "If there's any truth to that part of the story. Not social to outsiders, as a rule, so it's strange—unlikely—that their family sought out Killian's. But, who knows what might draw someone in. Sympathy? Curiosity? Herblore? Something less tangible? Regardless, Killian married some young woman, wherever she came from. He eventuallly passed the lore of the Dragonclaw on to their daughter, who passed it to her son, and..." Bea shrugged.

"Wait—her son wasn't—Grandpa?"

"My father. Yes." Bea hid a startled smile at the girls' quickness.

"Hmm," Diama pondered. "So why didn't he pass it on to you?" Bea shrugged and went back to wiping down her jars. "Are we nearly done?" Diama asked anxiously, "I promised Ebenn we'd race our bikes."

"Very well, then," Bea retorted, "but I expect to see you soon, my girl."

Diama gave a smile that was half a wince, and rose to go. At the same moment they heard a gentle knock at the door. "Coming," she called cheerfully, darting back in a whirl of black hair for a book she had forgotten. A young boy poked his head around the corner. His skin was pale and the eyes that scanned his aunt's sacrosanct workshop were a deep, bright red.

"In or out," Bea grumbled, "just close that door. We don't want the little ones wandering in here."

The boy grinned brightly, 'Yes, Auntie," he replied, but flung the door wide as Diama rushed out and they collided, sending each other sprawling.

"Are you hurt, Dia? He asked in alarm as he picked himself up. Diama struggled to rise to her feet.

"Don't coddle the girl," snapped Bea, softening the words with a wink, "she's twice as tough as you are."

Ebenn chuckled, then frowned as Diama took a few limping steps. Bea frowned as well, and started toward her. "I'm fine," she said with a smile, groping for the banister to steady herself.

"Sorry," Ebenn began.

"Nah, it's nothing. Let's go. Bye, Auntie."

They closed the door, and the girl sagged against the wall.

"You're hurt!" Ebenn said accusingly, "Why didn't you tell her?

Diama shook her head defiantly, jaw set. Then she smiled. "You can help, though," she said, and held out a hand. He put it around his shoulders and helped her hobble down the stairs. Her leg creaked and popped as she moved.

Diama was still limping the next day when Bea took her to the herb garden bordering the woods. Gravel paths meandered through the sage, lavender, catnip, and many others whose names she was learning. In the very center was a low rock wall built

in a circle around a small, gnarled tree. Its bark was greenish-gray, and its sparse scarlet leaves clustered on the branch ends like droplets.

Bea talked while they weeded, pruned, and watered. She would tell Diama about the plants and their uses, then drift into folklore. The girl only half listened.

"Auntie, I think I need to rest," the girl ventured after nearly an hour, steadying herself against a small fruit tree.

"Nonsense, girl. When I was your age I worked outside all day long. Your generation spends far too much time indoors..."

"I don't want to go in...just to sit down..."

A gentle scuff of the gravel was the only sound Diama made as she fell.

****

"A fainting fit," she heard Bea's voice grumbling as she came around, blinking. She was in bed. Her head throbbed. With relief she saw who held a glass of water to her lips.

"Mama," she said hoarsely, I—"

"Shh," her mother urged kindly. "Rest, sweetheart."

Even with the pounding in her head, Diama noticed her mother was still wearing her work clothes. The expensive business suit seemed unsuited to a sickroom. And Diama wondered why she was sick.

"The girl's feeble, Mariah," Bea was grumbling. "What have you been feeding her? She needs good food and more exercise."

"I know my child," Diama's mother said, with an edge in her voice, "and I know how to care for her. Her nutrition is impeccable. She gets plenty of exercise. The doctor agrees with me, though they are starting to recommend medication." Mariah smiled reassuringly at Diama, though sadness and worry vied in her expression, along with a subtle expression that suggested Bea should tread carefully.

Bea made a scoffing noise, "Medication? For what? Tell me what it's for and I can make a tea to replace it."

Mariah sighed and set down the glass, "Not everything can be cured with herbs, Bea. They say it's something rare."

Bea scoffed again, 'Like a Nykthos isn't something rare? You start letting doctors look at our children and—"

"MY child, Beatrice," Mariah's dark eyes flashed as she stood and turned on Bea. "I think you'd better leave. She needs to rest."

Diama was soon taken back to the doctor. The evening afterward, two small figures snuck outside the dining room window to eavesdrop on the adults. It was the family's habit to gather and discuss important events. The two preteens wanted to learn what they might not be told, and since it was early summer the window was half-open.

Diama's mother and father were sitting close together, Bea was on the far side of the table, a few aunts and uncles were scattered in between. They didn't all live in the big house, though they visited almost every day, and tonight an entire generation of the living family plus Beatrice, their elder, was present.

They caught the last of what Mariah was saying as they cautiously crept under the greenery to eavesdrop.

"…Rare genetic illness."

The family went silent.

"We've never heard of it before. It's not usually fatal, but it's why she gets hurt so easily and ill so much. It explains her passing out because of—other complications. It has to do with the way her body is put together, and…it won't get better."

"Is there anything they can do?" Uncle Elias asked in a solemn voice.

Mariah was silent for a minute. Diama stretched to see if she shook her head or nodded, but Ebenn tugged on her sleeve as a reminder to stay out of sight. The adults went on for a while in low tones about what Diama was to do or not do. She rolled her eyes theatrically in the shadows and made hurrying-up motions with her hand.

"The good part is," said Thomas, Diama's father, "she could live a long, full life."

"Unless the disorder cripples her." Mariah interjected in a taut whisper.

"Will she be fit to serve as Keeper?" Bea's voice was abrupt.

There was an awkward hush.

"*That's* your concern?" Thomas was incredulous.

"Superstition and folklore are the least of our worries," Mariah's voice was harsh, nearly shaking. "You want to know if she can tend that damned plant 'just in case' Ebenn goes crazy? That's what this is about?"

"You know what the Nykthos is," Bea replied.

"Do I? Do any of us, really? Mother's doctor said he's an Albino. It's a lack of pigment, not a curse!"

Bea sighed, "it is beyond science, beyond doctors," she said quietly. "He may look like an Albino, but we know it's something else. In our family, every generation or two, there has always been a Nykthos. And nearly every Nykthos has gone mad or become murderous. And there is *always* the Dragonclaw, and *always* its Keeper, in case they are needed."

The children drew in a horrified breath and stared at each other through the gathering shadows.

"This is our blessing and our curse, our heritage," Bea continued, "Ebenn is a good boy, but so was Connall, and so was Zethiel. Devla was the sweetest girl I ever met, until she tried to kill me. Each was Nykthos. Killian and his grandmother, Pavda, and Father—Germain—all kept our family safe. All did their duty."

"Well, if you expect Diama to physically keep Ebenn under control—!" her father rumbled.

Outside, the girl turned her wide eyes to Ebenn with a grin, "can you believe this?" she whispered. Her cousin frowned.

"Calm yourself, Thomas," Bea said archly, "it's not quite that. If needed, any with strength could restrain: older cousins, uncles. But only the Keeper who has planted and tended the tree can harvest the claw, brew it, and administer it to the Nykthos. It is the way."

"Of all the superstitious mystical shit…" Thomas burst out.

"I assure you, it is very real. There was a time that all in our family accepted this. It was an inevitable role we all filled. Those who married into the family," there was a weighted pause, as if Bea was giving her in-laws a withering glance, "were given to understand that they were bound to the same duty."

"Regardless, we may have years before he shows any signs. But this is why our family has always stayed so tightly knit: we care for our own."

"Like you care for my daughter?" Mariah's voice lashed out, "Ignoring what is happening to her when it is in front of you every day? Avoiding the point with—all this?" The scuff of a chair roughly pushed back was followed by quick, angry footsteps. The children under the window guessed Mariah was leaving the room. The slam of the door confirmed it.

"All this modern convenience," Bea groused, as if to herself, "conformity, ease and pampering, scientific breakthroughs. We forget things that are real. We forget ourselves."

Some low murmurs at the table expressed varying opinions, and as usual with the family, enthusiastic discourse followed. Diama pulled on Ebenn's sleeve and signaled him to go. When they were out of earshot in the darkening backyard, they stood silently for a moment.

"What was that all about?" Ebenn whispered as if out of breath.

Diama threw out her hands, "I have no idea! I can't decide which one of us they think is weirder!"

Ebenn shook his head, eyes downcast. "Not weird. Evil. They think I'm evil."

"No!" she insisted, "that's not quite what they said—they said—well, that you might go crazy. But I don't believe it for a minute. You're the kindest person I know, Benn. You're my best friend..." She gave him a smile and a friendly squeeze on the arm.

"They said... They said something about you. being a Keeper? Like a keeper of me?"

"No, I think that's just—this stupid plant of Aunt Bea's. In the herb garden."

"She won't let me go in there. I guess it makes sense, if it's something to poison me with later."

"Benn! I'm sure it's not like that—you know, she's obsessed with herbs! She even thought they could cure Grandma of cancer."

"Maybe they could have. Chemo didn't work."

Diama paused sadly. "The point is, that's how Bea thinks. Herbs for everything."

"Like she believes in monsters? Am I a monster? Maybe that's why my mom went crazy."

"That was different. Your mom was...well, depressed, or something. But it had nothing to do with you, and it definitely doesn't mean you're evil!"

"Let's just forget it, Dia. It doesn't matter what I am, it's what they *think* I am." He paused and stared into the dark silhouettes of the trees beyond. "I want to be alone for a while." He quickly vanished into the darkness.

Diama was left alone in the gathering night. Her mind raced with troubled thoughts as she gazed after her cousin, then up at the cobalt sky above. Soon it would be expanding velverty blackness, with only the tiniest glimmers to lighten the immensity of the universe. It seemed an enormity that might crush them if not for the relenting light of those small, distant stars.

* * * *

She and Ebenn drifted apart in the years that followed. She saw him less and less, often at a distance from the garden. When she waved he would look away as if he hadn't
seen her.

When he joined the family at meals, for movies, or for joint school studies with Diama, he was mostly silent.

Mariah and Bea could often be heard speaking in raised voices. Thomas was quiet, but often present. He came to check on Diama's schoolwork, offered to take her and Ebenn to the library or movies, often joined her when she watched sitcoms in the living room.

Diama continued her gardening with Bea, but the hours were shorter. The tension was palpable, and the girl mostly obeyed her medical restrictions because it annoyed her aunt.

One day, When Diama was fourteen, Mariah approached her immediately after returning home from work, "Diama," her mother said. "I have a surprise for you."

Diama smiled quizzically in spite of an unease creeping over her.

* * * *

That evening, the cousins sat across from each other on opposite sides of the sleek U-shaped couch, pretending to read. Diama fiddled with her fingers, tracing the slight raised nub of the pale gray fabric.

"I guess my parents are taking me somewhere," she ventured quietly.

Ebenn nodded, but didn't look at her, "they want to take you away from here." He didn't say "from me," but the words hung unspoken in the air.

"It can't last forever," she said, "And I don't *have* to go to this school, even if it is designed for 'special needs' students." Bitterness and defiance struggled for control of her voice.

"No, you should," He smiled sadly, but when he looked up the red eyes were grim. She had never seen an expression like this on his face. "If it helps you. Besides, you should have your own life away from here." Again, she felt the unspoken words, "from me."

"What about you? What will you do?"

"I won't go to college, that's for sure. Maybe I'll have your dad show me how to work on cars. Maybe I can wear sunglasses." He gave a mirthless smirk. and was silent for a moment, "I'll never have a normal life, Dia," he continued, "but maybe you can."

"Normal's boring, Benn," she said with a faint, sad smile. But she wondered if maybe he was right. Maybe it would help him if she could show enough courage to try. Yet, part of her prompted with a small, insistent voice, what if she could help him more by staying?

* * * *

"How's everything there?" Diama sat next to the phone in the common room, where she called home at least once a week. Personal phones were not allowed in the dorms.

"Fine," her mother answered. "nothing ever changes here." she gave a light laugh, but Diama detected unease in her tone.

"What's wrong?" she asked, "Is it Ebenn?"

Her mother hesitated. "Mom!" she insisted.

"He's—a little withdrawn, honey," she said softly. "But he's okay."

"Maybe he should help Dad more. They used to work on cars together, maybe Benn should take it up as a trade. He'd like that. It would give him something to focus on."

"That's an excellent idea. I'll mention it, sweetheart."

"And you, Mom? How are you?" a strange feeling was nagging at her.

"I'm fine, Sweetie. Don't you worry about me. How's school? How's physical therapy?"

"P.T.'s good," Diama answered, "hard, but good. I think it helps me feel stronger. They say to expect setbacks and flare-ups. School, well— it's okay. Nothing much has changed in all this time except the courses. There's always someone calling me "DIE-ah-ma" instead of "DEE-aw-ma." she exhaled a laugh.

"It's wonderful you're making progress! And you're getting to the doctor okay? You're careful when you go out?"

"Mom, I manage. I've been here three years!"

"I know, honey, you're seventeen and you know what you're doing, but I worry about you."

* * * *

I'm home!" Diama called through the door into the kitchen. the house was surprisingly quiet. It was late evening, and usually the place was filled with cheerful noise. Something wasn't right.

"Hello? Mom?" she called, "Dad?"

"Dia?"

The voice was quiet. She turned and saw her cousin standing in the shadow of the hallway.

"Benn!" her smile quickly faded, "what's wrong?"

"Dia, I—"

"What? What's going on? Where is everyone?"

"Benn!" she strode forward and took him by the shoulders, pulling him into the light. She was shocked at how haggard he looked. He shrank back.

"They're all at the hospital. Even Bea. No one expected you."

"I wanted it to be a surprise. I used my own money for a bus ticket. What's going on?"

"It's your mom."

"What?" Diama froze.

"She collapsed. I'm so sorry. I'll call them for you. Here." He guided her to a chair at a nearby desk and went for the house phone. A minute later she heard his voice, "And nobody thought to call the school? Let her know?" She had never before heard Ebenn angry. Upset, sad, scared, but never angry.

"Someone needs to come get her. I don't have a driver's license, re-member?" The bitter edge to his voice was also new. She felt dazed, but her heart was pounding. Ebenn brought her a glass of water and hovered awkwardly nearby.

"Is there anything else you need? I don't know much about your—ill-ness. I don't know how to help."

"Water's great, thanks. I should get salt and protein soon. it was a long trip…" She felt herself staring at the beige wall. This was supposed to be an adventure ending in a reunion, not…

A few minutes later Ebenn reappeared with a plate of leftover food from the fridge, hastily re-heated, and a salt shaker.

"Thanks, Benn," she said with quiet appreciation, reaching out for his hand as he set the plate on the desk and crouched next to her. He wasn't returning her grip, merely waiting for her to let go. His expression was un-readable. She remembered with a sudden jolt of sadness the day his mother died. He was so young. So lost. She anticipated her own sadness. And part of her felt she had no right. She had left them. She glanced at the plate. Aunt Agnes' Moussaka. Normally her mouth would water at the thought of it. Now she had to force herself to eat.

* * * *

Diama was with her mother in the hospital for a short time before an emergency surgery. It was the last time she saw her alive.

When they returned to the big house they felt a keen sense of stillness and emptiness. One of their own was gone. A sense of loss would linger in the old family home, perhaps forever. To Diama it was a deep and cruel blow. Her mother, her gentle nurturer, fierce champion and defender, her hero, was gone. She silently hugged her father, then left to her old room. He was trying so hard to be strong. She knew he wouldn't begin to grieve until he was alone.

No one knew where Ebenn was.

Later, Bea knocked tentatively on Diama's door.

"Come in," she wiped her tear-stained face and pulled herself into a seated position.

"I don't pretend," Bea said, sitting next to her on the bed, "to know how you feel. I don't understand your illness, and you think I have nothing to offer you. I understand loss enough to know this is the worst of all possible times for you, and I am sorry for it, but it *will* get worse if we don't do something. Ebenn needs us."

Diama looked up with red-rimmed eyes. She squinted, trying to read Bea's expression in the semi-darkness.

"We will talk more after the funeral. I am sorry, girl. She was my niece. I have buried parents and sisters. I have seen my generation wither and fade like an untended vine. Now death touches the generation I helped raise. Those who could have been my children, if things had gone differently."

Diama saw a strange softening in the woman's time-worn face. "There is a cycle to things," Bea said softly, "but it can be painful."

She rose and turned to leave. In the light from the half-opened door she saw a folded walker and a pair of knee braces leaning against the wall, where Diama had hastily stashed them.

"What are these for?" Bea asked in surprise.

"They're for me," Diama answered, "when and if I need them." She instantly went on the defensive.

Bea nodded, dropped her eyes, and slowly left the room.

The day after the funeral, two police officers came to the house. They had questions, but no one had seen Ebenn. Diama heard the comments and whispers, low discussions of what her cousin may have done, followed by the hushed tones of family members shocked at the suggestions. Ebenn was such a good boy, a kind boy, a little different yes, but never…

She rose from the gray couch where she sat with her father, squeezed his shoulder reassuringly, and strode from the room.

Last summer Ebenn had moved all his things to a room in the basement. He kept it dark, and listened to loud music on earbuds so no one would complain. He came out for meals, not always with the family. At night he disappeared. He was there now, curled in a fetal position on his bed. Diama stood at the foot of it and glanced around the room before she spoke. Shelves of books, magazines scattered everywhere. A desk with a laptop and some loose paper with writing or drawing on it. There were also some auto parts laying on the floor, and an old TV.

"What are you doing here, Dia?" His mumble was almost a groan.

She sat lightly on the edge of the bed. He seemed to flinch from her.

"What are you into, Benn? What's going on?"

"I—I don't know what it is," he whispered hoarsely. Then, after a moment, "it settles over me and I hear this voice, from deep down inside. deep and fierce, like—a monster. And I don't see anything except a red mist. I can't think until it's gone. It's coming more and more, Dia. I can't stop it. And the dreams, I dream—"

Her eyes were wide and her heart beginning to race. Oh, God, Bea had been right...

"Horrible things. I see what Conall did. What Zethiel did, and Devla, screaming, clawing, covered in blood...and more. I see villages from the middle ages. I see ancient places, stones and...prehistoric huts, I see—too much. I'm losing it, Dia. Better go back to school, where it's safe."

"I don't think so, Benn." She said calmly, "I don't think I'm going back."

"You should. You have to."

"And leave Dad? Leave you?"

"Dia!" he sat up, a desperate look on his face, then huddled back, shaking, "I don't want to hurt you."

"You won't. You wouldn't."

"How can you know? You know what Bea said. Look!" He rose abruptly and stalked over to a laundry basket in the dark corner of the room. Diama realized how tall he'd gotten. So much time had passed.

"Look!" he tossed her a shirt. It was stiff with a dark, crusted stain. He threw another on the floor at her feet, then emptied the basket. A pile of bloody animal bones fell out on the heap.

"My God, Benn," she whispered, and after a moment ventured, "you don't know what happened?"

"No," he began to weep, head in his hands. "I'm going crazy, like all of them, like Mom, like Devla...all of them!" Ebenn burst into sobs and curled his arms over his head, sinking to the floor. Diama crouched gingerly beside him and put her arm around his thin, shaking shoulders.

"You're not crazy, Benn," she said, her mind suddenly ice-clear, eyes lost in the room's dim light and the shadow of her hair. "You're Nykthos. And we're family. We'll figure this out."

"Diama." He grated out her name in a way that startled her. "You do what you have to do. Don't worry about me."

She nodded and tried to hold back the tears, holding and rocking her cousin as if he were still a small boy.

* * * *

Diama leaned heavily on her father's arm as they walked with Bea to a small hut on the edge of the woods. It was like a walled, vine-covered pavilion, surrounded by shrubs of fragrant herbs. The path wound to the front where a windchime fell softly against itself in the subtle breeze. Inside, it was simplistic and peaceful. A woven rug was in the center of the room, a sculpted bowl placed to the left. Candlelight danced along the walls. A small fire burned inside a rock well off to one side, near the wall. A small iron pot hung from a tripod over the embers, spicing the air with the sweet, unfamiliar scent of the Dragonclaw herb mingling with the incense smoke rising from a censer that stood on a low table against the opposite wall. A candle next to it caught the features in a gilded Icon and brought them to life. Bea was so so Old Country, Diama's fleeting thoughts interjected. Yet the serene face of the Saint gazed at her from the dark tones of the painted wood, and something in her responded with a deep sense of calm and comfort.

"It's so ceremonial," Diama whispered.

"As it should be." her aunt replied, filling the stone bowl from the hanging cauldron. She set the bowl on the rug, gesturing to Diama where she should sit

Diama lowered herself to the rug with the black stone bowl before her. Her joints popped and she wondered at her chances of getting up again. She closed her eyes and breathed deeply, slowly. There was a soft scuffle of footsteps as the others left. The door was ajar, letting sharp threads of evening air pierce the warm fragrant space. In the smoky haze of incense and herbs, her mind grew dreamy, and eventually slipped away, hearing a soft, wise murmur drift down the ages.

Words half-remembered, passed down in dreams. So this was why they didn't write their lore. They bequeathed their dreams. There was Grandfather, and his grandmother, and the milling shades of so many more. As Diama staggered through the mist of the dream, there was the sense of a message from ancient times. It was as if generations of her ancestors were with her at this very moment, cautioning and instructing her. She opened her eyes as the door was slowly pulled open and a damp mist rolled through from outside. From the darkness Ebenn crept, red eyes luminous in the dream-haze. He was hunched over, half crawling, fingers clutching the air like claws. Fingers stained dark. Chest heaving as he gasped under the weight of the red-dimmed vision he had described to her.

"Nykthos," she whispered, barely recognizing her cousin in the monster. She was surprisingly unafraid, though the realization of what he had become threatened to break what was left of her heart. Only the peace of her ancestors' wisdom kept her from weeping at the night of the aunguished, maddened form lurching toward her, terrible though it was. She remained seated on the floor, in a loose cross-legged position she already regretted in her hips; her hands cradled the heavy black bowl. Dragon shapes wound around the vessel. She felt their sculpted forms on her fingers, a soothing connection to the tangible. A steam wafted from its depths. The Nykthos approached, half-loping like a wary animal. His red eyes gleamed maliciously, but somewhere beneath the flame of bloodthirst she felt he knew her.

A further pang of melancholy shot through her as she realized that perhaps this was why they had been friends since childhood, had always loved and accepted each other. Because when it came to this moment, he would trust her, and she would do anything to save him. And for once, it no longer mattered that her body was weak. It didn't matter how she had to struggle at school, or to travel, or in everyday life, or whether others understood. This moment, everything was clear. She was unfaltering: still and inscrutable as the night beyond the thin walls, as the darkness of the carved stone. She was the only one who could save him.

"Ebenn," she coaxed, "here." and she held out the bowl. He approached cautiously, casting her furtive glances. But as she remained serene, he slowly grew calm, and took the bowl just as the strength in her fatiguing arms began to fail. He tasted tentatively at first, then gulped until the bowl was nearly drained. Then he gave her a long look. Tears welled in her eyes as she felt there was an accusing aspect to his stare. But then his eyes cleared of the madness for a moment, and there was her old friend. He gave her a slow nod, and a corner of his mouth twitched in a fleeting smile. Then he sank to the floor and curled in on himself. His eyes closed.

Diama's grief burst within her. Legs painfully weak from long sitting, she didn't try to stand, but slid herself along the floor until she was next to him. She put an arm around his shoulder and laid her head on his still body.

Some time later, she heard a faint, shuffling step at the threshold.

"It is done," said Bea, and Diama nodded through tears, not seeing her aunt's approval or caring if it was given.

Ebenn eventually stirred, and Diama held her breath in suspense. He looked up at her with the eyes of innocence and smiled as he once had. She wept even more now, for she saw what the herb had done. It had taken away the bloodlust, the fury, and the madness, but it had also taken away his maturity, his intellect. He was a child again in his mind, and would remain so.

"It is a last resort," Bea said softly.

* * * *

As Diama finished the story, she looked down at the girl by her side. The child gazed up with wide eyes at the gray-haired cousin of her grandmother.

"And now," said Diama, "please help me to my chair. I've been up too long." The girl loaned an arm and the strength of her ten years as she guided the frail form of the tall woman across the herb room to the wheelchair that waited in a corner. Nearby, a pale, red-eyed man was building a small model of clay, humming with the distracted innocence of a child.

MY SHIP OF DREAMS

K.A. Opperman

The silken sails are filled with wind,
And with the moon's blue beams,
And ere the silver mist has thinned,
I board my ship of dreams.

I sail across the seas unknown,
On slumber's aimless streams,
With stars and silence all alone,
Aboard my ship of dreams.

The sirens of enchanted isles,
With flesh that wetly gleams,
Allure me with resistless wiles,
And tempt my ship of dreams.

But I remain horizon-bound,
Indifferent to their schemes.
Fair lands with golden sunrise crowned
Await my ship of dreams.

I keep my lone and stalwart course,
Past shattered quinquiremes.
And yet I feel a dim remorse
Aboard my ship of dreams—

For I will nevermore return
To realms of men, it seems.
My one companion
Aboard my ship of

A WISE AND PATIENT MOTHER
Laura Blackwell

Even before the other wise-women told me, I knew this son would be a hero. He was a huge baby, bigger than any of my others. To distract myself from the pain of birthing, I bit down on a tree-limb and dug my fingers into the sweet earth to clench fistfuls of dirt and stone.

The youngest wise-woman tried to catch him, for bathing children in clean water was her work, but he was strong; he turned over and crawled alongside me. He was still smeared with blood and earth when he found my teats and began to suckle.

"I believe this one will do what Grendel could not," she said. I believed it, too, but I wanted to hear more; though the youngest wise-woman was clever and quick, and supple as a sapling, she was ever as green as that sapling's wood. She was a creature of potential, not experience.

The oldest wise-woman saw all things through her three white eyes. "He is the last champion for a thousand years," she said, voice rasping like stone against stone. "He is our best hope against the kindling-folk."

The kindling-folk's bodies were thin as the sticks they used to start the fires they loved. They used fire to soften their food so their dull teeth could eat it, fire to clear our forests for their fields. They tore the stones from our earth, cut the living trees from our forests, sullied our water with their filth. How could creatures with such useless teeth have such insatiable appetites?

"I will raise him to be the greatest hero the world has ever known," I swore. "He will drive the kindling-folk from our land, and the earth will flourish in the care of bee and bird, worm and wolf. And us, who came before all."

I did not name him. My children find their own names.

I fed him milk from my teats and blood from bears. As he grew cleverer, the oldest wise-woman taught him to find his way above the earth and within it. As he grew bigger, the youngest wise-woman gave him tree-limbs to thrash about, then tree-trunks, then trees entire. As he grew stronger, I taught him to seize a boulder with one hand and throw it over a mountain.

When we were not teaching him, I watched to see what he could do, and I waited.

After he'd grown enough to cross a river in one step, he visited the kindling-folk's towns. He brought back meat for us, whole and hairy, its lungs like the wings of birds. The oldest wise-woman said that this was because the kindling-folk could breathe nothing but air. This made a kind of sense; fire makes its meals of wood, but it is air that feeds its appetite.

One day he brought back more than gifts. "I am called Ydrede," he said, "for when I bash in the roofs of their buildings, they run and cry in fear."

"Do not let the kindling-folk name you," I begged him then, the only time I have ever begged. "No good can come of it. Have you heard the names they call your wise-women? They call the oldest 'hag,' the youngest 'witch,' and me they call 'troll-wife.' They call us children of Cain, though he was a monster of their folk and not ours."

But he called himself Ydrede from them on.

One day, the kindling-folk sent forth a champion of their own, a man less twig-like than the rest. The oldest wise-woman saw fire in his soul; it burned with his longing to prove himself by conquering fear, by conquering my son Ydrede.

No man of the kindling-folk was strong as Ydrede, so they stole from my stone children to craft a weapon to use against him. They stripped the shining blood from the veins of rock, and they used their fire to harden it. The bright thorn they fashioned was harder than stone and sharper than grief.

Ydrede stood in the clearing, tossing a tree from hand to hand, waiting for his challenger. I waited behind him; although the champions were to fight alone, a mother must always watch.

At last the kindling-man bumbled out of the woods, wearing a skin of fire-hardened stonesblood, bright and brittle as an insect. The sight of Ydrede, tall and strong and broad, drove him back a step. It would have taken half a dozen of him to reach Ydrede's height. Then he signaled to his own folk, and they removed the bright carapace from him. He was just meat then, tiny and exposed, with the shining thorn in his hand.

One blow would crush him. Ydrede roared and swung the tree.

The kindling-man danced backward, and the swing went wide. Lucky for him. I laughed.

Ydrede paced, letting his feet fall more heavily, creating gusts that stirred the dry leaves and drove the watchers back in fear. He shifted the tree to his other hand as he lunged, and he brought the club crashing down at the kindling-man.

But when the tree crashed against the ground, the kindling-man was not there. He was running full-tilt toward Ydrede, thorn sheathed and head down. When Ydrede lifted the tree and saw neither meat nor blood in its splintered branches, he did not see the tiny man heave his bright thorn across the place where one boulder-wide foot joined to one mighty leg.

Ydrede roared again, this time in pain, and he fell to one knee.

"Rise!" I screamed. "He is a dry twig, and you are a mountain!"

The kindling-man darted out, fast as fire without his stonesblood skin, and he drove the thorn into Ydrede's wrist. Ydrede growled like an avalanche and dropped the tree, his hand hanging loose.

I saw the dark blood gush from hand and foot, and I cried out. But Ydrede was hale and doughty; he flung the kindling-man from him, and the thin limbs spun in the air until the kindling-man landed on the ground, skidding in the leaves and tumbling over himself.

If it had not been for the leaves, the fall might have been enough to finish him.

Ydrede could not stand, could grasp a weapon in only one hand, so he made himself a log and rolled toward the kindling-man to crush him. The thorn was stuck in his wrist, and he grunted as the weight of his own unstoppable body drove it further in. The kindling-man lay hunched, unmoving. I sucked in my breath and waited for Ydrede to roll past that place, leaving bloody ruin behind.

When Ydrede neared him, the kindling-man rolled in a different direction. Instead of crushing the thin limbs under his hilly shoulders, Ydrede half-rose with the kindling-man clinging to the tangles of his hair. He reached up to bat him away with one hand.

It was the wrong hand. The kindling-man seized the thorn, wrested it free, and drove it into Ydrede's eye.

When Ydrede fell this time, he did not rise again.

I screamed until the earth shook and a river burst its banks. It tumbled Ydrede's body to pieces, and I was glad; it denied the kindling-folk their trophy. His head would adorn no-one's hall.

I had lost my grandson Grendel and his mother, my watery daughter, to one champion of the kindling-folk. To another, I had lost Ydrede. My wise-women and I were losing the rivers, the forests, the stones, the very earth to these invaders.

I retreated underground, and I slept for a long time.

The kindling-folk spread across the land, consuming all in their path. They erected taller buildings with sharper corners. They poured new kinds of filth into the water. The land bristled with shining, man-made thorns.

In my sleep, I birthed new children. The green-children who survived were tough, greedy vines; the water-children poisonous and strange. The children of earth and stone were mighty as ever, but they, too, became sly as they grew around the thorns.

I do not know what wisdom is left to guide them. The youngest wise-woman has grown thin and forgetful, the oldest blind in all her eyes. I have slept too long, and my veins are clotted with poison and anger and fear.

I do not know which of my children will be the next hero. Perhaps a forest-child will snake roots into their buildings, collapsing them from inside; perhaps he will snatch up trees and club down all he finds. Perhaps a son of stone will roll from the mountains and crush them all. Perhaps a water-daughter will wash away their towns, then pull each of them under and drown their weak lungs that understand only air. Perhaps a daughter of earth will open her maw and swallow towns whole, returning metal and sand and stone to their home.

All I know is that the thousand years are nearly spent, and we will come for the land that is ours.

I watch, and I wait.

DRAGON FOOD
Franklyn Searight

Timothy Harrick, as early as the age of three, was obsessed with dragons. He knew they were inclined to savagely bite and grow to prodigious dimensions. He had never heard one, but suspected they were equipped with voices able to drown out the trumpeting charge of a raging elephant. He learned a lot about them from dreams he had at night, from stories read in comic books in which their ferocious appetites were mentioned, but especially from Saturday morning television programs designed to entertain the younger set.

The shows had not especially troubled him, but did warn to keep his distance if one approached. Fortunately, they had never come close enough to bite him, but were frightful enough to cause alarm if one had occasion to glance his way.

"Timmy!" shouted his mother from the floor below "Breakfast is on the table. Hurry down if you expect to have a ride to school."

"Awe, Mom, do I have to?" he yelled back.

"Yes, you have to go to school, but you can walk there by yourself if you want to."

"All right, Mom. I'll be right down."

He had packed his school bag the night before, and was already dressed. All that needed to be done was slip the straps over his shoulders, comb his sandy-colored strands one last time, and grab his smart phone from off the dresser. He would not be able to use it in school without teacher's permission, but would feel naked without it, almost the same as he would without his NICs cap which he carefully fitted to his head, standing before the mirror.

"Get a move on," shouted Mother from below. "I'm at the door now and I'm not waiting much longer. Really going."

"Be right there, Mom," he said, knowing her words were uttered to hurry him along, but was equally certain she was not kidding. It would not be the first time she had left without him, leaving him to walk the three blocks to school on his own. If she had done it to teach him a lesson, it had worked, sort of. She was as good as any of his school teachers in motivating him to action and expecting the best from him, he reflected, giving his cap a rakish twist.

He skipped lightly into the kitchen, spooned a sugary pile of cereal into his mouth and chewed rapidly before swallowing and following it with another, gulped down the glass of milk his mother had poured and raced to the front door, his school bag bouncing on his shoulders.

"It's about time, young man. You just made it."

Timmy knew she was not being serious as they walked to the car. She would have waited a while longer, he believed, but not much before she would drive away to work, leaving him on his own. He did not want to be by himself, at least not outside the house, for fear monstrous creations would begin to take center stage in his mind. As long as someone was with him, he believed, he was safe; the bulldozer-sized critters would leave him alone and wait until he was by himself.

He opened the passenger door and slid into the seat beside her as she inserted the key into the ignition.

"Mom," he began to ask, settling back on the seat, "did you have dragons chase you all over town when you were a little girl?"

She took her eyes off the wheel momentarily, backing out of the drive, and glancing at him. "Of course not, Timmy. We've had this same conversation before, often enough, and I haven't changed my answer. The slimy serpents are legendary creatures who never existed except in songs and fables——make believe stories.

"Stop believing they are real!"

Timmy knew she was wrong, but also knew better than to challenger her. He would have stopped asking her the question long ago if he could have, but could not. It was something embedded in his psyche which could not be rooted out no matter how hard he might try.

"How about other creatures?" he wondered aloud. "Gryphons, Satires, wood nymphs and similar cryptids?"

"Of course not. Where did you hear of those? They're legendary creatures, too, all of them. None of them ever existed."

"So nothing ever scared you when you were a little girl?"

"Nothing," she told her son. "Oh, there must have been some things—-little things like boys pulling my hair when teacher wasn't looking."

"Why, Mommy?"

"Because they were boys and because I usually wore my hair in braids. It was such a tempting target they couldn't resist."

"Sure am glad my hair isn't braided," he thought, reaching up to touch his curly locks.

"I'd never pull your hair, Mom," he assured her.

"I know you wouldn't, dear. You were brought up to respect and be kind to others. Not every boy acts that way often enough," she said, coming to a stop at the first intersection. "Some little children are made to feel poorly about themselves and take out their resentment and frustrations on others who are as defenseless as they are."

"Oh," said Timmy, not quite understanding, but assumed it was extremely important and something he should keep in mind while interacting with his friends.

Timmy skipped out of school later, happy his educational bout for the day was ended, and headed for home. He walked as far as he could with two of his buddies, engaging in light-hearted, frivolous banter, pushing and tripping each other for fun. He had no fear of walking this stretch with his chums as long as he was not alone, certain he would not be bothered by anything objectionable prowling the streets, especially mythical beasts.

Timothy was nine years old, ready to go into the fifth grade, when a calamity visited the town of Saltville where he lived. The Slasher, as the sinister perpetrator was aptly named, perpetrated the first of seven grotesqueries. With an uncontrollable appetite it had bitten off the head of its victim, decapitating it at the neck, severing the artery and squirting blood in all directions. An all-out manhunt was conducted by the local authorities to no avail. The populace was cautioned to stay inside their homes, especially at night, directions the people followed for nearly a month.

"Wonder who's responsible," speculated Tim's father around the supper table one evening, considering the latest atrocity.

Maybe it's a shape-shifter," ruminated the young lad, thinking of the new word he had recently learned.

"Maybe," agreed his dad, absently.

The attacks continued, the sensationalism raged on and on before finally dying down. People returned to their customary activities unafraid, shoving the incident deep into their consciousness. And then another atrocity was committed, this time late at night in a public toilet facility. For the next few weeks the newspapers were consumed by accounts of the latest outrage. The police department, straining under the ridicule of taxpayers for its inability to capture the assailant, were given notice it would be their collective heads that would roll if something were not done… and soon.

Timothy was well aware of what was happening to frighten the people of Saltville so terribly, but not for a moment did he believe it was a demented, crazy person responsible for the massacres. With the certainty of naive youth, he knew a dragon was responsible. Only such a creature could be so brutal and uncaring for mankind to do what had been done. And had the papers not mentioned the imprint of tooth marks on the neck large enough to be caused by a dragon, or was it only something he imagined reading?

He spent hours after school at the local library searching through volumes he had already scrutinized in the past, along with new ones making their recent appearance on the shelves, hunting for mention of what dragons tended to consume. There did not seem to be an overall consensus as to their dietetic preferences, nor did he find any mention of human beings listed among their likings. He suspected they were omnivores, able to eat both plants and animals, but was not certain. Even the Internet did nothing to further his quest, so he concluded as long as people were not specifically mentioned, it was safe to keep them *on* his list of dragon foods and continued to identify the fire breathing creatures as possible culprits.

Nearly once a week, for the next month, a decapitated person was discovered at a lonely site, and then suddenly, as quickly as they had begun, the atrocities ended. In time the speculations of responsibility stopped and moved to the back pages, hopefully gone forever.

Saltville became a quiet town again and continued that way for the next ten years until Timothy reached the magical age of eighteen years, and he would soon graduate from high school. Already, he had researched several colleges he might consider attending, and soon began registration proceedings at State College. What especially interested him was the science department and the course offerings in biology and animal husbandry. Rumors were also circulating of plans to add a class devoted to cryptology which he had known since his early years referred to animals whose existence was unsubstantiated. He toyed with the notion of becoming a cryptozoologist and beginning a career proving the existence of dragons.

As Timothy matured, growing taller and stronger and more confident in himself, he insisted everyone now call him Tim——Terrible Tim, he thought, flexing his muscles before the mirror.

Juvenile thoughts of treacherous creatures receded in his mind as he marched toward adulthood doing those things involved with being a teenager. Life became more exciting, more intricate, as his earlier modes of behavior seemed to crawl into a vault where they were more easily controlled, safely absent from his consciousness where they no longer troubled him.

Alas. the time came they emerged again, born anew and as troublesome as before.

He was eighteen before he began dating the fairer sex, the first few times combining groups of friends his own age, usually classmates. Dating was an experience he no longer feared, being quite comfortable in the company of others, but he looked upon the day, or night, as it might be, with a slight degree of trepidation to take the next step of being alone with the female companion of his choosing.

Graduation day was rapidly approaching, bringing with it prom night, a gala event he eagerly anticipated, followed by assorted parties which he planned to attend. He intended to invite his favorite and newest girlfriend, Corrine, a somewhat shy but extremely attractive youngster whom he had been courting frequently by now. When he did ask, she reacted with a controlled enthusiasm, hemming and hawing for a few seconds before accepting. Timmy, err Tim, mentioned they would be accompanied by mutual friends for at least the first part of the evening. Then they would scatter, some going to favored restaurants or bars if they happened to possess fraudulent proof, or more house parties which would last until the coming of dawn and others to motels for additional frivolity.

"Sounds exciting," Corrine enthused. "Mom told me she had been looking at special prom dresses and shoes——things like that——and we'd be having a special shopping spree just for women."

"Neat! Don't know if my folks have anything special planned, but Dad did mention he'd foot the bill for a tux and not to worry if expenses leapt into the stratosphere. It's a grand-time event for graduates and he'd do what was necessary to see everything went smoothly." When they parted that evening, he gave her a peck on the cheek, their first starry-eyed exchange thus far, and after she went inside he walked home feeling as though he were skipping on a cloud. The following weekends were spent by the pair acquiring their respective formal attire, telling each other on the phone of how their respective plans were getting along.

The big evening arrived and Tim knocked on Corrine's door holding a plastic see-through box containing the loveliest corsage he could locate. He was decked out in a natty tux, his hair slicked down, and wore a red carnation in his lapel. Corrine answered the door herself and greeted her suitor, who believed for a moment he was seeing a dream come true. Her gown was an outfit of heavenly pink, matching beautifully with the accessories, and her hair was treated recently at the beauty parlor with curls cascading downward in gentle waves. She gently touched the offered container and smiled sweetly at him as she accepted the corsage with a coy thank you. She invited him in to meet her parents, and Tim bashfully followed her with a slight tremble.

"My, don't you look handsome, Tim. Come in and meet my folks. You've met my mom, but not my father yet. Pops wants to look you over and give his approval. But don't worry, he's a neat guy and wouldn't dream of saying anything offensive."

Tim entered the vestibule and followed Corrine into the living room. The father invited him to join him on the couch where they chatted for a few minutes, getting to know each other, while the mother assisted Corrine in pinning the flowers he had brought onto her dress.

"Have you heard the latest news?" asked her father.

"I'm not sure. What is it, sir," he replied, uncomfortably.

"Well, the Slasher's been at it again," he continued. "Another body, decapitated like the others, savaged and partially eaten was found in the back aisle of Desmond's Grocery Store."

"Oh, no," said Tim. "Not another one."

"Yup. 'Nother one. Whatever animal is doing this, it's the smartest and quickest I've ever heard about, doing its gruesome work without being caught or even seen. Mind you, I'm not talking about blood and gore on the battlefield——which is understandable. Fact is, I did a bit of soldiering myself years ago in 'Nam."

Tim's immediate thought was of a dragon being on the prowl, but it was an infantile idea everyone would scoff at, and he knew it. Instead, he said, "Think it's a terrorist, sir?"

"Course, I do. Who else would wantonly destroy a life for no reason? Can't understand what satisfaction they get in killing innocent people."

Standing up, he continued, "Now, you two be careful," he cautioned. "Stay out of dark alleys or any place not well lit. I expect you to return our little girl to us in the same condition she is right now. Say one o'clock."

"You can count on me, sir. She's very important in my life, also."

The father nodded, satisfied, saying: "Have a great evening, you two, and don't do anything I wouldn't do," he added with a grin.

"Yes, sir."

Tim escorted Corrine to his father's car, borrowed for the evening and recently washed, its interior cleaned, polished and scented. He opened the door for her to slide onto the passenger seat.

The following hours were a fantasy Timothy could imagine only in his wildest dreams as they danced together cheek to cheek, Tim somewhat awkwardly but not overly self-conscious, conversed, joked and laughed with their friends as they enjoyed the best time possible.

The crowd swilled goblets of punch, rumored by whispering voices it had been spiked with a bottle of rum when the chaperones were not look-ing. Tim drank more than he usually would have, but only because it was a warm evening and dancing caused him to overly perspire, while Corrine did not imbibe nearly as much, more restrained and unwilling to act as freely as the other young ladies.

The evening was getting on when Tim excused himself to visit the little boy's room, as a number of his friends had already done, some more than once.

He left the company of Corrine and made his way to the men's room returning nearly fifteen minutes later because of the long line to use the facility. He had not missed much of the excitement, but found Corrine had left during his absence with the same objective in mind. Many of his friends were on the dance floor strutting their favorite moves.

"She'll be back soon," said one of Corrine's friends. "Went to the la-dies' room with Barbara to powder her nose."

"Fine," thought Timothy, wondering why she had to powder her nose. It had looked fine to him. He sat back to watch his friends on the dance floor, moving cheek to cheek with their dates in slow steps, closely monitored by concerned parents walking about to see nothing untoward occurred.

Corrine was back in a few minutes, her gown slightly ripped at the shoulder and bottom hemming, and ruined by small specks of red splattered along the side. Tim attempted to question her about her appearance but she was intent upon dancing and tugged at his arm until he followed her onto the dance floor. All she would say, averting her eyes, was she had left the building to get some air when something chased her down the street. No, she had no idea who or what it was, only that it had frightened her considerably.

The gaiety continued until Principal Murray walked to the microphone and announced the last dance of the evening was about to begin.

It was the grandest, most exciting dance of all, believed Tim, pressing Corrine closer to himself and tentatively brushing her lips with his own. He was about to whisper something when Principal Murray stepped to the mic again, his voice agitated and face blanched, his hands slightly trembling as he glanced at a note.

"Just a reminder," he began. "I want all of you to be on your guard when you leave here tonight and be extra cautious as you go about your plans. Walk in groups as often as you can and keep inside when you're in your home."

"What's with him?" asked someone in the crowd.

"Sounds like there's trouble," said another.

"What could it be?" wondered a third.

"Maybe the Slasher is on the loose again," suggested a timid teenager coming from a distant table.

"Naw," insisted a deep tenor voice next to her. "If the danger were so great he would have told us more of what's going on."

"I'm not so sure of that," Tim said to Corrine, leaning over. "He might have decided to not make a big thing of it, whatever it was, and not get everyone overly excited."

The midnight hour came much too quickly and everyone seemed quite reluctant to go on to other planned functions. They stayed at their seats in no hurry to stand up and leave with their other classmates. Excited whisperings and wild speculations floated about the tables as the groups attempted to assess the danger, if any.

"Maybe someone has been assaulted," considered Tim's best friend.

"Perhaps another body has been found," said a nearby youngster.

"Badly mutilated."

"Whatever happened," said Corrine, "I'm taking it seriously. I'm willing to skip the breakfast hour, Tim, if you are. I'll feel safer at home."

Timothy agreed with her, a bit disappointed as their tickets for the coming event had already been purchased.

"Bunch of pansies," said Randy, sitting across from them. "We're going on to the meal and eat our fill—-and your share, also. Right, Betty? We're not going to let wild rumors scare us away."

"If you say so," said his date, compliantly, "but…"

"Suit yourself," said Tim. "I told Corrine's parents I'd have her home by one and I intend to keep my word—-Slasher, or not."

"Maybe we should join the others," Corrine disagreed, haltingly, "seeing as you already paid for the tickets."

Tim replied in the negative, a growing agitation defeating his appetite. They said goodbye to their friends and as they strolled away, he felt the beginnings of a trepidation. For the first time this evening Corrine and he would be alone, and as the moments passed his anxiety grew greater, alleviated only by the lovely vision walking beside him. Her very presence seemed to thwart the encroaching unknown.

In the car, she sat on the edge nearest him, leaning her shoulder towards him, so closely they almost touched. She must have sprayed more perfume on, he decided, enough to make it exotically intoxicating. He could think of nothing special to say, nor could she, so he bent over and adjusted the radio until sprightly music filled the void of their silence.

"It was great fun," she exclaimed after a while. "I had a wonderful time."

"Me too. I'm glad you enjoyed the evening…our evening,"

"I did. Especially all the time we spent dancing together."

"Me too," he said again, lapsing into silence once more.

"Are you hungry?" he said, finding his voice and stammering. "If you are, maybe we can find an all-night fast-food place and get a bite to eat."

"No thanks. The meal they served was quite enough. I'm stuffed."

"Really? You ate almost nothing at all—-thought you'd dwindle away."

What was he taking about? She had eaten her meal and then finished his.

"Wasn't as hungry as I expected to be," she said.

"I was thinking of maybe a coke…or coffee…or perhaps some ice-cream."

"Sounds nice," she agreed, reconsidering. "Something light. It's still early, though," she amended, as the car turned onto her block. "I have some sherbet in the fridge. Why not come in for a while?"

"No thanks," he returned. "If your parents are anything like mine, they'll be up waiting for you. I don't want that, and you must need your sleep to stay as pretty as you are."

Tim was surprised at his reluctance to accept her invitation as it would delay for a while the anxiety he would experience during his drive back to his house. He wanted to kiss her goodnight, extending the good feelings they shared, but it could happen now or later. All he knew was the moment he was alone, there would be nothing to calm his nerves.

"Think I should probably leave," he decided.

Reaching her house, he edged the car over to the curb then ran around to open her door. She stepped out daintily, careful not to trample on and crease her already spoiled apparel. On the way to her porch they recalled the wonderful time they had which they would remember forever.

Standing at the entryway with his hand on Corrine's shoulder, he pulled her toward him. She closed her eyes and lifted her lips to his level, slightly smiling.

The youngster leaned forward just as her nose elongated into a snout. Pointy projections sprouted from where ears had been, and prodigious scales covered her frontage. Her mouth opened wide... then wider and even wider. He had no time to move before the shapeshifter edged closer, its horrific resolve to bite off his head.

Tim attempted to get away, surprised a dragon's mouth contained so many and such enormous teeth.

The NIB; AND A BRIEF STUDY IN COSMIC IRRELEVANCE
Christian Riley

> Beyond lonely Pluto, dark and shadowless, lies the glittering realm of interstellar space, the silent ocean that rolls on and on, past stars and galaxies alike, to the ends of the universe. What do men know of this vast infinity, this shoreless ocean? Is it hostile or friendly—or merely indifferent?
>
> —James Strong

We look now at the great expanse just beyond a region of the galaxy ostensibly referred to as the Oort Cloud, and approximately 1.73 parsecs from the gravitational focal point of the nearest planetary system. It is here, in this stretch of space, that a single nematocystic interstellar biosphere, located on the outer rim of an extensive web-like bloom, separates its tethers from a great many identical others. As this detachment occurs, vibrational waves are displaced across the entire bloom (an expanse with an indeterminable radius, but one of which is not presently less than 0.0015 parsecs in length). The sounds of this detachment are composed of various "clicks" and "whistles," and augmented by a series of deep, watery notes. This acoustical conglomeration is categorically neutral in statement, however, void of any and all emotion.

Of course, the isolated biosphere is deaf to this music. It is now an independent resource, surrounded solely by the hard vacuum beyond its transparent body. Using both radial and coronal muscles, the sphere aligns a cluster of subcutaneous chambers in such a way as to manifest a fixed course—a course designed to intersect the gravitational focal point, as previously noted. The sphere then facilitates an internal fermentation process, suggestive to that of respiration.

The fermentation product is carbon dioxide, and it is released into the aligned chambers. As the expansion of these chambers reaches maximum internal pressure, the surrounding cutaneous membrane—the *mesoglea*, of sorts—undergoes a local trans-differentiation; wherein a finite patch of cutaneous cells temporarily gains permeable characteristics. This transformation opens the cluster of extended chambers to the vacuum of space, into which carbon dioxide is slowly released, resulting in a sudden yet steady acceleration of the biosphere.

* * * *

Homo rhodesiensis stands in the sand above an eastern shoreline, observing the distant crash of waves. The morning is painted orange under gray, with the rising sun having yet to break the flat horizon. Belonging to a tribe, he is a young male who has momentarily stepped away from the others, for the purpose of wonder, or in search of distinction, or perhaps a combination of both. He squats, defecates in the sand, and it is here, from this line of sight, that he sees a dull mass lying near the waterline. With the rise of color in the east, the mass illustrates a gleaming, reflective quality, which effectively stirs *the male's* interest. He stands, and then walks, approaching the curiosity.

It is nothing he has seen before: a translucent, bulbous crown, with long, curling adjuncts descending from a central core. The object is strangely plant-like in its appearance. Is it food? Perhaps a fruit pulled from the sea? No. It is *Chironex fleckeri*—the box jellyfish—and it lies rigid in the sand, sustaining the immediate opinion that it is nothing more than a harmless form of vegetation.

All the same, the hominid adheres to instinct and chooses a stick to poke at the strange entity. He does this several times, and upon observing no form of intelligent reaction, the hominid deduces that the mass is indeed harmless. Deferring to natural curiosity, he then reaches out with his hand and grasps the elongated appendages.

At once, he associates the pain with a force of nature, such as the breaking waves beside him; the stinging is absolute and uncompromising. The hominid vaults backwards, stumbles, then falls on the sand. He holds his hand before his face, as if to study it, but his eyes are sealed shut. He screams and howls until he loses control of his body as it convulses.

In the minutes that follow, this *Homo rhodesiensis* will gather only fragments of his experiences within the elapsed timeframe. He will feel the grittiness of the sand pushed against his face as his body reacts to the pulsing pain. He will vomit, and then consider that he is choking on a foreign object, as his respiratory system enters into an imprecise pattern. He will observe a partial sunrise, while the burning expands beyond that of his fingers and into his chest. And finally, after he loses total consciousness, he will become like that of the creature beside him: motionless, and rigid; his body has succumbed to heart failure.

* * * *

Hypothesized as a spherical region of space containing trillions of roaming comets and other icy planetesimals, the Oort Cloud can just as well serve as the hypothesis of a star system's preservation mechanism—inasmuch as trillions of comets traveling at high speeds along respective orbits can presumably serve as a sound, destructive force to all approaching celestial dangers.

However, trillions of comets are also plausibly immaterial when compared to the vast amount of empty space contained within the Oort Cloud. The nematocystic interstellar biosphere has an average diameter of a mere 63,645 kilometers. (Its pliable surface, serving as a passive barrier, is never consistent.) Yet the biosphere has a mass of 3.7753×10^{24} kg. Combined, these characteristics will become distinguishable as the entity passes through the cosmographical boundary of the selected star system, and subsequently enters the Oort Cloud.

It is a passage that will take thousands of years. Yet in this time, despite the vast enormous space within, and the cosmically insignificant size of the biosphere, it is certain that the entity will collide with more than one fast-moving object.

At the very minimum, ice dust will gather along the prominent surface of the sphere; the creature will absorb these particles through the process of osmosis; the particles will separate into water molecules, and individual metals and/or aggregates; and the subsequent products will be filtered out, with a select amount of water molecules being contained and stored for future use. The remaining metals and/or aggregates will eject back into space through an elongated, free-floating *manubrium*.

At the very greatest, a planetesimal of remarkable proportions, traveling at a high speed, and along an antagonistic path to the biosphere, will present itself. The ensuing collision will form a cavity within the biosphere's elastic, cutaneous membrane; the depressed measurements of this cavity will be in direct proportion to the planetesimal's combined size, velocity, and mass. The depression will eventually collapse, fold around the planetesimal, envelope it completely, and the biosphere will then begin a digestive process; wherein, over indefinite years, the rock will be digested, filtered for segregation, and then assimilated within the biosphere, or rejected back into space.

* * * *

In a hillside cave overlooking what in time will be referred to as the Rhine River, *Homo neanderthalensis* stands with his back against the dying light in the sky. He holds in his hand by its hind legs the skinned carcass of a small mammal. To his immediate front, three other hominids sit around a fire, each of them busy with a task: one male is sharpening a stick with a chip of onyx; another male is using a small rock to crack nuts against a large stone slab (he appears modestly entertained); and a female is at this male's side, separating the cracked nuts from the hulls. The female discards the hard casings to a pile on the ground, and the round nuts she puts into a leather pouch.

Over the next few minutes, in what appears as an orchestrated procedure, the members of the tribe perform a series of maneuvers. The small animal is driven through lengthwise by the sharpened spear, and subsequently suspended inches above the fire. The nut-cracking male leaves his place and paces the near hillside, where he will remain until he eats (he is holding a stone axe, sniffing determinedly at the cold air, and listening to the drawing night with great intent). And the female gathers the pile of shells and deposits them into a niche within the cave, to be used later for mundane purposes.

Arguably, there is a certain exquisiteness illustrated within this interval of time, and within these maneuvers (an exquisiteness that is perhaps subjectively abstract in quality, defined in part by the mechanical complexities of hominid physiology), as this entire episode, this "evening dance of *Homo neanderthalensis*," takes place despite the absence of verbal communication. From afar, we can observe it as a silent, beautiful endeavor, one that arbitrarily follows certain laws of nature. And yet, more distinctly, the motions involved within this dance precede and are paramount to the construction of a more advanced society. Without question, the event represents a single pulse toward universal harmony for this species—or a form of stasis otherwise known as civilization.

* * * *

The interstellar biosphere continues its soundless passage through the frigid realm of space. It has crossed beyond the Oort Cloud's perimeter and, as predicted, has consumed and digested more than one planetesimal. There have been no alterations to its course; the biosphere remains locked on to the original gravitational focal point.

What has changed is the activity level within the biosphere's central nervous system. Sensory input has increased relative to the decrease in the biosphere's distance to its core aim; a minutely higher level of particle radiation density has been detected by the biosphere's *rhopalial lappets*. This detection, however, does not elicit any form of excitement upon the biosphere, nor does it cause any form of distress. It serves only as a natural, confirming statement, as the biosphere pushes forward through the darkness of space.

* * * *

In the year 451 AD, Calendar of Man, a most distinguishable incident occurs between two of the greatest military leaders ever to represent that of the human species. It is the Battle of the Catalaunian Plains, and the king of the Visigoths, Theodoric I, has joined ranks with "The Last of the Romans," a Roman general by the name of Flavius Aetius. Their enemy is primarily the Hunnic Empire, led by the infamous Attila the Hun.

The outcome of this specific battle remains, throughout human history, nonspecifically defined. All military sides sustain massive casualties, and the numerous fields of Gaul become wantonly littered with the slain. As bodies lay in piles of thousands, the consequences of the battle suspend forward, into years, and toward a conclusion that seems as nebulous as the black void of space.

What is decisive is the symbolism illustrated behind the past and subsequent future of the two leading characters surrounding this battle.

Flavius Aetius and Attila the Hun begin their lives as state icons, and grow from a childhood that they both share and treasure. Beyond the friendship of their adolescence, they become didactic colleagues, and ultimately respected foes. Yet through the primordial machinations of human appeal, these two men reach profound destinations that are both as different as they are eerily similar.

Due to a state of jealousy, Aetius' intrinsic value to the Roman Empire becomes destroyed, along with his legacy. "The last of the Romans" is subsequently betrayed and killed by his own Emperor, Valentinian III. Finally, the very corporealness of this war hero is unceremoniously cast into an uncharted bog, banished forever to all future payments of respect.

Comparatively, after nearly conquering the known world, Attila the Hun dies from a nosebleed on his wedding night. His body is taken by his generals, and in sound tradition, secretly buried. His gravesite becomes lost forever.

Ironically, within these two lives, one can observe *Homo sapiens'* most ambitious social achievement (world domination), and his greatest form of social decline (unjust exile). In the centuries that will follow, *Homo sapiens'* progress in social evolution will prove significantly stagnant, remaining mundanely locked, so we shall see, to the impulses of their primal desires, and the limitations of their secular interests.

* * * *

In the eighteen months that divide the deaths of Attila the Hun and Flavius Aetius, exactly forty-three abnormally large jellyfish blooms occur throughout the Earth's oceans. One such bloom takes place in what is known as the Thracian Sea, and incidentally below the hull of a merchant vessel presently transporting Persian slaves. Lightning suddenly strikes the vessel, and it sinks. No one lives to describe the bloodcurdling wails coming from the men abandoned to the sea.

* * * *

It is 1932 and Jan Hendrik Oort, the same astronomer who will eventually hypothesize the existence of the Oort Cloud, measures the motions of the stars within a portion of the observable galaxy known as the Milky Way. Upon studying these measurements, Oort discovers a fundamental inconsistency as it relates to the mass of the galactic plane and the mass of the observable material contained within. This observation becomes the birth of a further hypothesis—the existence of dark matter—which postulates that the proven mass within the known universe accounts for less than twenty percent of all total matter. The perplexity of this conjecture provokes a staggering tide within the scientific community and poses the indelible question: What is responsible for this anomaly?

* * * *

The transparency of the nematocystic interstellar biosphere is due to an overwhelming amount of water contained within its core, combined with an absence of chromatophores throughout its structure. The biosphere is unobservable by all conventional means—means that would apply to nominally intelligent life forms. It moves between the cold distances of space, silently undetectable, and is, at this time, entering the inner solar system of the aforementioned gravitational focal point.

To prepare for arrival to its destination, the biosphere releases its single oral arm, a tentacle-like device that extends in length to nearly twice the average diameter of the biosphere. At the end of the oral arm is a thin, ovular membrane, approximately twenty thousand kilometers in diameter, which drags flaccid through the coldness of space.

* * * *

Near the second millennium, in the Calendar of Man, a notable cosmologist by the name of Stephen Hawking publicly postulates that Man's search for extraterrestrial life may be profoundly imprudent. He states the claim that other civilizations, upon learning of Man's existence, may act aggressively to acquire the resources contained on Earth. The warning implies that should a civilization hold the technology for accomplishing such an act of interstellar aggression, there would be, of course, no hope for humanity.

The statement is more noble than brilliant, self-serving perhaps, and one that ultimately falls short of persuasion. For his listeners—astronomers and cosmologists alike—fail to detract their attention from the quest set upon by their curiosity—a curiosity not unlike that which once spurred the need to identify a gleaming mass upon a distant shoreline. Finally, this failure serves to underscore one more tragic lack of evolvement—in this case, an evolvement relating to cognition, as it pertains to *Homo rhodesiensis* and *Homo sapiens*—despite the passing of hundreds of thousands of years.

* * * *

Cosmically speaking, it is a devastatingly short amount of time after Mr. Hawking's ironic admonition, that the nematocystic interstellar biosphere reaches its core objective. Its presence goes entirely undetected, until the sudden point in which its ovular membrane (located at the base of its suspended tentacle) expands appropriately in diameter, and encloses over the surface of the planet.

At once, the occupants of Earth associate the confusing experience to a cataclysmic event. The rotation of the planet comes to an immediate halt, and the ovular membrane releases onto the planet a concoction of acidic vapor—followed shortly by a flood of liquid enzymes.

In the minutes that follow, despite their cries from a blisteringly painful death, the vast majority of humans maintain a stubborn, yet steady hold, to their comically dull convictions of religion, as they utter their final words to an as-of-yet unknown species.

The consumption takes less than twenty-four hours. In the span of what would have been a local terrestrial's single day, the biosphere's digestive juices effectively deconstruct the biological molecules contained on the planet. The planet's organic compounds, in their entirety, are thus transformed into a watery soup, which is subsequently suctioned up through the biosphere's tentacle, and into its core. When this acquisition of sustenance is complete, the biosphere slowly releases its grip on the planet previously known as Earth. And, most notably, the inhabitants, along with their entire history, become lost to a cosmic gravesite, one that eerily parallels that of an uncharted bog.

Finally, after drifting an insubstantial distance away from its ruined prey, and while retracting its single tentacle, the biosphere once again begins the internal process of fermentation. It presently lacks a distinct focal point of which to align itself to, but the biosphere's *rhopalial lappets* soon detect a minute trace of radiation in a region of the galaxy not more than seven light years away. Although this detection fails to solicit excitement in the creature, it stirs a sense of interest. And it is this interest which ultimately decides for the release of carbon dioxide into the vacuum of space, resulting in a sudden, yet steady acceleration of the biosphere.

HOUSE OF THE GRAND FLY
Charles Haugen

A pale cast of orange light shined on Grandma's liver-spotted shoulder, five deep black holes adorning her milky flesh. She stared into her vanity, powdering blush onto her cheeks. The tips of her toes bounced from the tail of her nightgown as someone hummed Sinatra.

I jumped at the sound of knuckles rapping the front door. Grandma jerked her head toward my room. Her frazzled hair masked her features. The shadows concealed me enough to avoid her glance. She didn't know I'd called him. Told him about the holes. About what I saw inside them whilst she slept. What was underneath her skin, wriggling and twisting. Breathing.

Grandma stood from her chair, clumsily dropping her makeup brushes as she cursed under her breath.

"I'm coming. Hold on a second."

She disappeared from view as her gentle steps chambered down the hallway. A second pair of feet pattered behind hers. The front door opened, muffled words barely seeping through the thin walls of our home.

"Come in. Please don't be shy, Doctor Grau. By all means. Whatever would bring you here at such a late hour?"

"I just wanted to check in on you, Grace. See how you were holding up."

"Oh, I'm fine as ever. Nothing quite like living on the beach, falling asleep to the sounds of the ocean."

"How I envy you, Grace. Really."

Their footsteps thudded on the wood floors, marking their approach to the kitchen. When I heard the scraping of the chairs' legs, the creaks of their settling weights, I left my room and tiptoed to the hallway, avoiding their line of sight.

Doctor Grau sat at the table with Grandma. His knees bounced underneath. He took his hat off and pulled a handkerchief from his jacket. His medicine bag was with him, set by his ankles. Grandma stood up, started brewing tea while she clanked the spoons against the cups' porcelain. She filled the cups halfway with sugar before pouring the steaming brew.

"I hope you don't mind it too sweet, Doctor Grau. I've always had a sweet tooth, as I'm sure you remember."

"Oh yes, of course. I hope you've been brushing twice a day, or those cavities will come back with a vengeance." I couldn't see his face, but I knew he was forcing a smile.

Under the dim overhead light, beads of sweat glistened across the back of Doctor Grau's neck. Grandma chuckled, her shoulders bouncing like a cartoon.

"Oh, darling. I haven't had a cavity in many years. Not since..."

She turned her back to him and Doctor Grau tilted his head in my direction. I jumped, startled at his noticing me. He nodded in my direction before wiping sweat from his brow with the sleeve of his shirt. He looked curiously at the handkerchief from his pocket and smiled at me with a two-finger salute.

His mouth grinned, but his eyes screamed.

He stood and walked over to her slowly. I could hear the loose watch on his wrist shaking.

"Say, Grace. You're not breaking out in hives, are you? Your shoulder?"

Porcelain shattered on the floor. Doctor Grau looked down.

Grandma stood statuesque. Her shoulders didn't even rise for a breath. Something wriggled across her back under the nightgown.

Doctor Grau steadied his feet and cleared his throat.

"I'm sorry. The old arthritis gets to me some days. Can't seem to hold a cup of tea anymore without it shaking all about. Well, I guess I should clean that mess up. I made shepherd's pie. Would you like some?"

She turned to face him, her hands gripping the counter behind her. The blacks in her eyes swelled. Her lips twitched into a false curve.

"Grace. Your shoulder?"

"It's nothing. Really. Just a few skin tags that've been there since I was a young lady. You wouldn't embarrass an old woman in such a way, would you, Doctor?"

"If it's nothing, you won't mind me taking a look."

Grandma held her ground for a few moments, staring at Doctor Grau as if testing his fortification, before sighing and slumping her shoulders. She turned around.

"Well, it couldn't hurt, I guess. Right? You've always known best, after all."

"Of course not," the doctor's ears rose. A smile.

I stood on the balls of my feet, trying to see Grandma's back, but Doctor Grau's shoulders hid it from view as he leaned over her.

He unzipped his medicine bag and took out a pair of calipers. Their gleam was shinier than anything else in the house. His hands found focus as they slowly disappeared in front of him.

Grandma shuddered. A strange cough and a twitch of her neck.

"It's okay, Grace. I'm just looking. Relax."

"Okay, okay. Just be gentle."

After a horrible moment of silence, Doctor Grau dropped the pliers. His broad back censored Grandma. As he took a few steps back, I did, too.

"Have you been out of the country recently, Grace?"

"Well, no, silly. I've been right here. Watching over Peter."

"We need to perform a quick procedure. Immediately. It won't hurt, I promise. But if we don't get those things out of you—"

"No. No way in hell, Grau."

Grandma turned back around, cornering Doctor Grau against the table. Her face screwed up until her features folded like the skin of a raisin.

"You will do no such thing. Who else is going to hum Sinatra for me? Who else is going to show me how to care for my grandson? The damned mute. I loved my daughter to death, but she didn't know what it cost, what it took to raise a child of her own! She didn't understand the sacrifices you have to make. She just left me! After everything I'd done for her. One leap into the ocean and she almost ruined everything!"

Grau's fists clenched. His shoulders tensed.

The more that Grandma shouted at the good doctor, and the more her wrinkles creased, new holes started to open like gaping maws of dusk. First on her neck, then her cheeks, until even her forehead and eyelids were covered in black craters that resembled an inverted blanket of stars. Something white glistened in the center of each opening. A squirming, slimy point.

As the yelling grew more frantic, the doctor prepared to restrain her. All I heard were waves crashing against the shore outside. The gentle breeze and salty smell wafting through the open window. And a shrill buzzing issuing from Grandma's throat, merging with her words. Like a thousand microscopic wings beating in harmony.

* * * *

I stood before the dilapidated wooden door. Condensation fogged the adjacent windows that marked the entrance to our once-home. The ocean sloshed heavily against the rocky shore, a lighthouse in the distance circling its eye every few minutes onto the porch. Beneath my feet, the overgrown grass hung over my boots, the blades sharing a browning at their tips. The lone tree sat with its shade beside the house. Its leaves were all but gone. The old swing Grandma built when I was young tilted lightly with each small gust of wind, the creaking dulled against the ocean's call.

I opened the door and stepped inside. It'd been eight years since I was last inside my childhood home. Eight years since Grandma's passing. Dust blanketed every surface, the weak sunlight casting from the blinds revealing millions of specks waltzing through the air. The ceiling bore several black spots of mold that dripped onto the floor quietly. Mildew drifted to my nostrils, accompanied with the vile stench of decay. Likely a rat or feline who'd had its last meal within the walls.

Stepping across the creaking floor, I set down my suitcase and dusted off the couch before turning on every light in the one-story house. My bedroom hadn't changed. Posters of sci-fi films and little toy statues of various monsters and superheroes lined up on the dresser, their features also masked with dust.

Eight years and the house's memories hadn't been altered. Its nervous system frozen in that awful moment. I picked up two of the figures and mouthed a few lines from their respective origins, the strain against my damaged vocal chords ceasing the attempt almost immediately. I tidied up the bed and, for a moment, thought of spending the night there. This room was my sanctuary during many a storm, both natural and familial.

I walked back to the couch as quickly as the thought had come and left. They said I needed to decide whether or not to salvage the house. After two deaths on the same property within such a short time, and eight years of no tenants or inhabiting owners, the city wanted to demolish the house and replace it with a condo for tourists. A perfect location, they said. Prime real estate. Unfortunately, the will left the house in my name. The final decision was up to me, and me alone.

The bottle of whiskey in my suitcase would make a good companion in my seeking a decision. I told them I needed two nights. Two nights to decide if the bad memories were enough to forsake my childhood home, or if the good memories of my mother would incite my keeping it. I poured a glass and gulped the fire. Despite its stinging of my throat usually being more than I could handle, I swished the liquid until it numbed my gums.

An hour in, staring at the fading overhead lightbulb, my eyelids found anchors upon them.

* * * *

"Restrain her! Do it now!" Doctor Grau heaved Grandma onto the kitchen table as his assistants burst through the door. They grabbed her limbs. Her throat vibrated, the chambering sounds like an engine shifting faster in speed. One of the assistants jabbed a needle into her arm, which had taken to a viscous blue as veiny chords pulsated beneath her papery flesh.

"You can't take them from me. I won't let you," said Grandma through gritted teeth.

Doctor Grau picked up his calipers from the floor and rinsed them under hot water in the sink.

"How much did you give her?" he asked.

The assistant looked to Doctor Grau, his face void of color. "Enough to sedate a three-hundred-pound man."

Doctor Grau aimed the calipers at her shoulder and dug into the hole. A ropey, white mass wrapped around the shiny arms, pulling the tool deeper inside. Doctor Grau grunted, yanking the calipers out of her as a long, thrashing thing spilled out from her shoulder. Its body coiled onto the floor as steam rose from its segments.

"What the hell was that?" said the assistant.

"I think they're botflies. But I've never seen any like this," he pulled at another opening. "Usually, people get them from overseas," another grunt, "but the poor lady hasn't left this house in three decades."

A sweltering, leathery snake spilled from another hole. It wriggled across the wood, towards me.

I couldn't move, no matter how hard I tried. My bones leaked ice, my nerves cement.

Doctor Grau followed its trail with his eyes before gasping in horror.

"Peter! Someone get that thing away from the boy. And get him as far away from here as possible. He doesn't need to see this."

As one of the assistants rushed towards me, I stared at the worm. My mouth gaped, and urine trickled down my pant leg. For the briefest of moments, before the assistant grabbed me and carried me away, I could have sworn I saw my mother's face on the head of the worm. Her eyes mournful, but her smile more loving than it had ever been.

* * * *

I woke up to the same light, its bulb now flickering. Sweat stuck to my shirt and the couch's cushion was damp with my outline. I grabbed the glass and filled it until the dark liquor spilled off the rim. The fire consumed my throat, my tongue swishing it between teeth and taste buds. As the buzz continued, the sounds of the ocean returned. Its beating was heavier than before. Windchimes jingled outside, signaling the approach of a storm.

With no ease, I stood from the couch and walked to the kitchen. Shadowy outlines of swirls were embedded into the floor like the memory of flames. Doctor Grau's calipers were still in the sink. The dark, dried blood mixed with brown and black rust. Outside, night cascaded the dead grass. The lighthouse's eye shined on me briefly. I squinted as a throbbing headache emerged from slumber.

I massaged my temples, reassuring myself that imagination had gotten the best of me that night. I was only ten years old. It could've been the trick of the light or all of the horror comics I read late at night to concentrate on anything but the guttural sounds emanating from Grandma's bedroom. I pressed harder, gripping my forehead until whites burst across my vision, until I heard the pattering of footsteps outside the kitchen window.

I knocked a porcelain cup from the counter, its shattering sending fragments across the floor. I gaped at the window and peered outside. Only night and the waves met me. The tree's dead branches swayed in the wind as the rusted swing's chains twisted with each lean. I glanced all upon the yard, seeing only dying shrubs and rock. Movement at the bottom of the tree's shadow caught my attention. Reflective eyes stared back. The head they belonged to was elevated at least ten feet above the tree's roots. The orbs were horizontal and blinking.

I closed my eyes again.

Two nights, that's it, I thought. Two nights. Can I even last two nights?

I looked up. My dead grandmother stood on the other side of the glass. Her eyes gleamed with moonlight. Deep black pores slithered across her dimples as she smiled. Lips wriggling like snakes, she pointed to the ocean with a rotting finger. Yellowed bone protruded from broken skin. Her eyes filled with tears, the pools of light shimmering in waves. She turned and glided toward the shore as the eye of the lighthouse swept across the yard. Right before it engulfed her, something resembling wings stretched from her back. Glass-like, grooved wings that tore through cloth and flesh. Wings that sputtered and vibrated as if she was about to take flight.

* * * *

Firm hands grasped my torso as green blades of grass zoomed past. Multiple cars were parked ahead. Their sirens and lights flashed, blinding me. The assistant set me beside a squad car and motioned for a police officer to come check on me. The tides smashed onto the rocky shore. Buckets of salty waves splashed against the vehicles.

A few officers took out their guns and cautiously approached the house as Grandma's shrieking screams reached a crescendo. The buzzing from her throat vibrated, thrumming through my skeleton. I'm not sure if they could feel it, but I could in every bone. It was the same when Mom left.

Banging and rattling broke from the house. The police aimed their pistols at the door. One of the assistants crashed through a window as Doctor Grau's voice bellowed from inside. He sounded hurt.

Grandma burst through the door, limping across the yard in jagged strides. Her baggy, naked flesh hung from her arms and legs. Sagging breasts swung below her waistline. One of the officers opened fire, clipping her in the back. Black blood shot from the hole, but she only sprinted faster. Tendrils peeked from the openings across her body, twisting across her skin both above and beneath. When her feet touched the rocks, she leapt.

I heard her screeches as the tide swallowed her, the buzzing dying beneath the waves. Officers and medics leaned over the shore calling her name. Doctor Grau crawled out of the house, his arms covered in scarlet. The EMTs ran a stretcher over to him and ushered him onto it. Spotlights reached over the shore as they cried her name out again and again.

When they took me to the precinct, I was told that Doctor Grau had to be flown to ICU. Amidst all the chattering of my status as an orphan and what was to become of the property, I heard them talk about finding someone else in the house before Grandma dove into the tides. Someone that looked like my mother, had she been at the bottom of the ocean for three years.

* * * *

I awoke in my bed. Night filtered through the curtains. The lighthouse circled, mixing with the moonlight on its pass. I held my breath and reached for the whisky. In several gulps, the buzz returned. Muscles relaxed. With a long sigh, I sat up in the bed. The walls leaked black. A single fan spun overhead in erratic, wobbling arcs. I prayed for it to fall off the hinges, to smash my consciousness into a void absent of this place. A perpetual darkness where I could not only sleep but dream of anything other than that night.

On the dresser across from me stood a framed picture of my mother. Her curly brown hair rested on muscular shoulders, a smile beaming like the sun. In her arms, she held me in a cocoon of blankets. My face was hidden. I smiled, thinking back to when she was alive, when we used to run around the house playing hide-and-seek. She never found me when I'd hide in the guest bedroom. Inside a walk-in closet that went much deeper than it appeared. Covering myself with an assortment of wardrobes, she'd give up after several searches. It wasn't until I snuck up behind her and tapped her shoulder that she'd yelp in fright. Fright which turned into choking laughter.

Something slithered through the doorway and into the hall. I jumped from the bed. Just as I had when I was a child, I tiptoed out the bedroom and glanced in both directions. A leathery tail twisted toward the front door before disappearing beneath the frame. I launched myself after it, stopping as I passed the kitchen. In a fast motion, I looked to the window. Nothing.

A deep exhale. Then I sprinted through the front door.

* * * *

"What do you mean, he can't speak?" asked my Mom through the wall.

"I mean his vocal chords are damaged. Does he cry a lot? This type of damage, he'd have to be screaming at the top of his lungs every day for it to happen," said Doctor Grau.

"What are you insinuating?"

"Nothing. My only concern is for Peter's wellbeing. Everything else is second. I don't suspect you nor Grace of any abuse. I know you, Carol. I've known you since we were kids. Known your mother longer."

Silence.

Then, "What's happening to my boy?"

Mom sniffled, a low weeping between sobs.

"I don't know. I really don't. He can still live a normal life, but you need to find out what is causing this before any more damage is done. It could permanently affect his throat, not to mention any chance he ever has at speaking again."

More silence.

Then, Doctor Grau whispered, "Have you been keeping an eye on her?"

The car rumbled along the gravel as we left the doctor's office. Mom ruffled my hair with shaking fingers. Her eyes glistened in the sunlight as she tried her best not to cry.

"I know you can't talk, sweetie. But please, if there's anything happening that I don't know about, you can always write me letters. You can use one of your notepads from school. You have to talk to me, baby."

I nodded. For the smallest of moments, it almost seemed that her tears were not of sorrow, but rather of hope. The reason for this hope, I never pinpointed. A deep-rooted happiness that I never quite understood.

That night, I lay in my bed, staring at the ceiling. Waiting.

As the grandfather clock in my room ticked to midnight, Grandma stepped through the doorway. The silhouette of her small frame elongated with the hallway light and towered over my bed. Her silent footsteps were masked by the creaking of the door's hinges. She seemed to slide over to me, her gown ruffling within a phantom breeze. She knelt beside me. The blacks in her eyes consumed the whites.

"Peter. Are you ready?"

I shook my head, tightening my eyelids to fight back the tears. I kept trying to twist away. I clenched my eyes even tighter, as something wet slithered into my nostril and down my throat. I gagged and tried jerking away. All the while, Grandma's breath grew heavier. A barely audible buzzing filling my ears.

* * * *

I chased after the black thing, stopping at times to listen for its rustling against the dead grass. It led me past the tree and closer to the granite shoreline. A light splash echoed from the coast. I leaned over the ledge. A series of widening ripples met my gaze.

Several feet beyond the dark undulations, Grandma stood on the water. Her sagging husk was now bloated. A deep blue cascaded her body. She walked across the ocean, her feet not altering the currents. Lifting her arm from her side, she pointed toward a rock formation on the shore, broken bones snapping as her body floated closer to it. Her head tilted back, hanging loosely down her spine. She winked at me with cataract eyes.

Mist pooled around her figure before she was swallowed completely. Out in the distance, I heard my mother's voice calling. The tides carried her words farther than possible. Each syllable fading, then deafening, then fading.

Carefully stepping onto the stones, I guided a path along the rocky edifice. Pebbles thumped into the water with each step as the fog enveloped my approach. The current strengthened, brushing against my ankles and threatening my balance. After several leaping strides, I came to an enclosure shrouded by mist. A natural indention in the gravelly slope.

I quickened my pace, finding a rhythm. As the haze dissipated from my sight, I could now discern a glimmering, inky black liquid spilling from the enclosure. I heard buzzing. Deep vibrations that shook the soles of my shoes.

With careful footing, I jumped into the cavern. The sensation of falling into a bottomless void took hold.

* * * *

Grandma eased me up from the bed and held her oily hand over my eyes as something writhed at the back of my throat.

"Just a little farther now. You know where to go," she said.

We left my bedroom and she led me down the hallway. I knew we passed Mom's room when I heard her snoring. Grandma's feet didn't sound off on the wood floors, only mine. A door creaked open before us, despite her hands never leaving my body. She released me as the door moaned shut behind us. I opened my eyes, finding myself in the darkness of the guestroom. The closet was open, endless blackness inside.

From the walls, "You know where to go, Peter. You know where it leads."

My chin quivered, knees wobbled. I cried into my hands and wiped the tears away with my wrist.

From the floor, "Go on. You know what to do."

I went.

* * * *

Inside. The sensation of rocketing through empty space vanished. I pressed against the wet walls. The humidity cooked my skin. The ground was slick, each step a breath away from a slip. As I treaded deeper into the cave, the darkness became too blinding. The echoing dripping from the walls too deafening. I reached into my pocket and pulled out my phone, shined it onto the wall ahead.

Beside the trapdoor that led back to the guestroom, my mother crouched over a lump of writhing, sinewy mass. Her soaking hair streamed into pools at her feet, the ridges of her spine twisting with each movement like a large chain grinding taut. The skin on her face pressed outwards, its outermost parts webbed with blue veins. Mom prodded the bulging clump. The mound expanded and contracted to her touch. Long toenails clacked on the floor as she adjusted, her naked figure caked in glistening sweat.

To her side, Grandma crouched in a similar way. Though her body was far more grotesque than Mom's. Every part of her seemed to dangle to the floor. Balls of squirming things pushed against her baggy skin as if hoping for a break. She motioned for me to come closer. I held my ground, thinking to myself it wasn't real.

Grandma stood, her legs snapping into place as she started limping toward me. I backed away and shook my head as I had when I was a boy. She shushed me, reaching out with those gaunt hands. Black filth dripped from the elongated fingernails. An oozing puss secreted from her glass-like eyes.

I kept stepping backward, until I hit something solid.

"Peter," said Doctor Grau.

I spun around, reeled back in terror. His figure loomed over me, the shadows of his form as tall as the cavern's roof. As moments stretched by, his outline expanded. It now blocked the grotto's entrance entirely. I mouthed a million insults to him, signed a thousand questions.

"Peter, I know. You need to see them. It's for the best."

As he said this, his eyes glimmered in the blackness. Instead of single glares, they bore thousands. Segments of light reflecting like a house of windows.

"You know, I don't know why you always said I hid your face in that picture," Mom's voice gurgled within gallons of ocean water.

I turned back to her and signed, "*What*?" Flotsam and foam billowed out of her discolored lips.

"Take a closer look, baby."

She held out a photo. Its edges curved and hung as rivulets of water trickled off.

Mom smiled at me, the shape of her face taking on a cylindrical impression. Like the head of a worm.

I snatched the picture from her decaying hands and stared into the details. I shined my phone onto the withered photograph.

The longer I looked, the more I saw. Hidden minutiae within the frames of our first memory together.

A small tail hung limply from the shell of blankets. Pasty, leathery skin peeked from a small opening between her shoulders. A barely discernible, segmented neck. Holes in the skin, like craters upon the moon.

I felt Grau's thousand eyes watching my every move, heard the heaving gasps from Grandma, watched the foamy water bubble over Mom's blue lips.

"It's why we're here, Peter. Why we're all here. Why the ocean has called to us for generations. Everything was leading to this. It's finally time for you to speak," said Grandma.

I signed, "Doctor Grau is dead. You're all dead. None of this is real!"

"We are all hosts, willing and unwilling. Now speak, mute."

My Adam's apple rose, the chords in my neck taut. All the oxygen vacuumed out as blood vessels burst across my vision. Grandma lit a torch and kicked my phone away with a skeletal, lopsided foot. The humming of Sinatra reverberated through my throat. A thousand keys thrummed to the rhythm. Deep inside, within the walls of my esophagus, I felt something shift. Countless bodies awakening. Their tails wiggled against my windpipe.

Grandma danced with Mom, their shells haphazardly moving upon fractured legs and within loose skin. Mom burped up water as she laughed. Grandma's eye slipped out of her skull. Grau watched from the blackness as the silhouettes of gigantic wings lightly flapped behind his multi-paneled eyes. Mom and Grandma leaned over as thin layers of skin fell from their spines, pointed extremities reaching from the openings.

The lump in my throat dislodged as I puked out an enormous, viscous corpus of thrashing meat. It bulged and contorted as the air touched it, its silky exterior leaking like an amniotic sac.

They all chanted, their voices vibrating the entire cave. I looked at the trapdoor, then back to them. Grandma motioned to me with her rotted hands.

"Speak, Peter. Go on."

I cleared my throat and licked the ivory of my teeth as I fought back the expectation of pain. I collapsed onto the floor, losing control of my arms and legs as they seemed to disappear from beneath me. My skin felt wet, sticky. I looked to my Mom, who smiled at me with decaying skin. Her cheeks sagged over the outline of her neck. Though she was rotting, changing even, I could tell she was proud of me. Prouder than she had ever been. That hope I never understood found reason. As her eyes split and multiplied, her smile remained. The corners of her mouth stretched to her forehead, hundreds of teeth pushing through her gums in a wide grin.

When I finally spoke, it was with the chorus of a million wings taking flight. The vibrations of a jet engine. The strength of an earthquake.

We all flew away, spreading our scaly parts as we dove into the ocean. Where the tides had called for us our entire lives. Deep in the sloshing waves, beneath the earth's embrace. In a place where we could all sing, dance, and squirm. Where our eyes could catch danger before it came, and our hairy, segmented legs could flex with unimaginable strength before the jump.

Through the burrows of botflies, back into the blackness where my mother would always smile, and where her mother would find a house as grand as she.

Into the depths, we flew forth.

Into the night, where our wings beat swift.

Into the House of the Grand Fly.

THE SMITH AFFAIR
James Goodridge

Fall 1920

I was enjoying the darkness of my combination office/living room when my phone rang, but in the occult detective business you had to be available. Producing a magenta glow in the palm of my left hand—a gift and sometimes curse from a nameless horror from the stars—I lit an Old Gold cigarette from my cigarette box and answered the phone.

"Cavendish here, your nickel."

"Hello? Mr Cavendish? Oh this is such a frightfully bad connection!" complained a female voice at the other end.

"Whoever you are, I can hear you okay. Who am I speaking to?"

"Pamela, Pamela Coleman Smith."

I had heard of her. After a brief click, the static noise ended on her end.

"There," she said. "I can hear you now. We have a mutual friend in Zoe Churel." Zoe was a conjurer acquaintance of ours.

"What can I do for you, Miss Smith?"

"I'm…I'm having a problem at a flat I recently rented and converted into an art studio in Ocean Hill, Brooklyn." Pamela's accent seemed to go back and forth between Yank and Brit." I'd rather not go into details over this connection. Can we meet in the city? It's around one p.m. now. How good would four p.m. be for you?" she asked.

"Where?"

"The 23rd Street side of Madison Square Park," Pamela suggested.

"That would be perfect, but how will I recognize you?"

"I'll have on a gray overcoat covering a red dress, a red turban also," said Pamela. "I like to wear colorful beads, one of them a rosary. I'll know you, I've seen you two before. Zoe pointed you out at one of her Harlem functions a few years ago, but you and your partner left before I could make my way across the room to introduce myself."

I couldn't remember that night, but knew her artwork from Sue's deck of Tarot cards.

"Okay four this afternoon it will be Miss Smith," I confirmed." See you then. Good bye."

I got up from behind my desk and pulled back my window curtains to confirm the rawness of the day, but I thought it best to take my green tinted glasses with me once I dressed, just in case the pallor of the afternoon sun became too intense for my kind. A phone call to Sue upstairs lets her know we have a meeting about a potential affair.

* * * *

A brisk wind went hand-in-hand with the briskness of New Yorkers on their way home from a day's work. After parking our avocado-hued 1919 Briscoe along the park, I brought a bag of hot roasted peanuts for us to enjoy while stationed on a bench waiting for Miss Smith. Sue's gorgeous in a cinnamon-red dress with matching wool coat and black crusher hat. Myself dark suited with my Homburg hat, I didn't need an overcoat. I enjoyed the cool Autumn air.

"Hello, Pamela?" Sue said, seeing Miss Smith before I did.

"Miss Sue, Mr. Cavendish."

I looked up from my bag of peanuts into brown, mousy eyes. Dark hair peeking from under her red satin turban, Pamela is impressive in looks. A thought began to blossom in my mind that she most likely was "passing" like me, although I was an open secret to my friends up in Harlem. I let the thought die on the vine, I'm not here to judge. Sue, in contrast, let her beautiful statuesque Native American/African heritage be known.

"It's a pleasure, Miss Smith." I smiled.

"I feel I've picked too blustery a place for our meeting," Pamela admitted. The Flatiron building discombobulated 23rd Street's wind direction.

"It's all right. Let's find a place more sedate to talk," I said, handing her the bag of nuts as a goodwill gesture and waving off her objections.

Crossing 23rd Street in a western direction, the three of us agreed on a little working-man's diner right before 7th Avenue that served only cackle fruit and bacon around the clock. Once inside, Pamela—who asked that we call her "Pixie"—ordered tea and a poached egg, while I had sunny side up eggs and black java. Sue ordered a plate of bacon, the strips cooked to various degrees from raw to burnt, much to the short order cook's perplexed look. The lights in the diner exposed the haggardness on Pixie's face as she relayed her problem to us. A haunting.

"I came back to the States and my beloved Brooklyn in particular to hopefully pep up my artistic juices. Providence saw me obtaining an apartment just off Eastern Parkway at Prospect Place. The summer was uneventful. But as the leaves changed, so did my situation. One morning I woke to find my bedroom bookcase empty, all of my books scattered about the floor. Downstairs in my makeshift studio, all of my artwork and supplies where moved to the center of the room piled high like a Christmas tree on Boxing day, almost touching the ceiling. As if some phantom crept in during the night while I slept."

"You sure it wasn't the neighborhood rascals, sister?" I challenged.

"No, and before you ask, "Why?"—the next morning, after putting everything back in its place, I found all of my paintbrushes formed into the shape of a pentacle in my backyard, with a mutilated cat in the center." Pixie's voice became sorrowful. "Children know not of such things, only adults sick of mind—and dark forces."

"Aren't you a member of the Golden Dawn Society?" my Sue asked.

"I left that rabble years ago. I belong to the Catholic faith now. But I have not gained their trust because the church and I are not in accord when it comes to women's rights. Please, I need your help," Pixie pleaded.

I advised her, due to her state of exhaustion and for her safety, that it would be best for her to spend the night at Seneca Sue's apartment. She agreed. We would discuss a fee at a later date.

After the drive uptown to 107th St. off of Riverside Drive, Sue found and adjusted a sleeping gown for Pixie, then Pixie stretched out on Sue's North African harem pillows in her living room to sleep. All in all, my doll and Pixie were two bohemian peas in a pod. It was a bit odd, though, in the morning when Sue relayed to me—away from Pixie's hearing—that at one point Pixie woke up then began searching through Sue's living room bookcase in search of a book. Maybe she needed to read before sleep, we guessed. Due to her eccentric nature, we left that issue closed.

* * * *

"I think we should start with a simple seance," said Sue. It was evening in Ocean Hill. Decreasing auto mobile, trolleys, and the now rare to New York horse carriage traffic made their way outside Pixie's flat along Eastern Parkway. Inside we sat around a common circular wooden table, around us like a silent audience leaned oil paintings in different unfinished phases, proof of Pixie's problems. Oil paint, turpentine, along with frankincense was the consequent scents in Pixie's studio.

"I feel odd now not being the conductor of this ghost symphony," joked Pixie, herself a medium." But I will follow your judgment."

"If this doesn't pan out, we have other methods, including Caracki's," I told her, although Carnacki's use of garlic made me nauseated.

We settled down to a lone white candle at the center of the table, surrounded by darkness. As we clasped hands, I couldn't help but notice how exquisite Sue looked in a black satin hobble dress, the sleeves in lace, slightly kinky black hair cascading down to her shoulders. Sue's rose-tinted glasses held any unintended pale moon light filtering into the house at bay.

For what seemed like an eternity, Sue used a variety of incantations to summon Pixie's gauche intruding spirit. Pixie, in a purple caftan and scarf, was inpatient until she slumped forward in a channeling state then threw her head back.

"Beware de ocher mon! Beware de ocher mon! Beware!" Pixie yelled out in a deep male Caribbean patwah voice.

"Who are you?" I blurted out to the bass-voiced mantra that was fading away.

Sue tries to coax the spirit back, but it's fruitless. "Pull her out," I tell her.

"Oh goodness what happened?" sighed Pixie, back with us and nervously massaging her temples.

"You briefly channeled what we assumed was a spirit with a patwah dialect warning us about the ocher man. Have you heard of him?" asked Sue.

"I'm afraid I've never heard of an "Ocher man." Bloody no!" Pixie was defensive. "Sorry, it's just tommyrot to me."

"Well, sister, unless you're channeling your anxiety through a poltergeist..."

"What's the answer, Pixie?" I said. A poltergeist had been my first theory, too.

"Oh, I just don't know. What I do know is, I've had a hat full tonight. I want to retire now, if you don't mind. I could make up the room next to mine for the two of you to rest."

Pixie was up and drifting to the staircase and climbing it before we could answer.

"No, we'll be fine down here," I said to her indifference as she closed her bedroom door. "Sue, you get some rest on the couch. I'll sit in this chair," I whispered, moving a stuffed indigo chair out the artwork room to face the staircase.

"Madison Prescott Cavendish, what are you doing?"

"Waiting, love, waiting," I said with a wink.

Sue blew out the candle.

* * * *

Sensual blood-thoughts wormed into my mind while sitting in the darkness. Thoughts of Pixie's exposed neck, nice and plump during the seance aroused this living vampire. Looking across the room, I can see Sue having a fit of a rest, tossing and turning on the indigo couch. Evil is making its presence known in this house tonight. My fangs start to extend in my mouth. I block my blood-thirst with self control just as I hear the thud of books on the floor of Pixie's bedroom above. I was waiting for that.

"Come on," I say to Sue grabbing her by the hands, pulling her up off the couch.

"Madison. Oh my Maddy! Your fangs are showing! Don't let Pixie see them!"

"I know, and my baby blues are blood red! Now will you come on?!" Sue hates my eyes when they're red like that.

In stealth, we crept up the staircase to Pixie's bed room.

"Pixie, it's Madison and Seneca Sue. Please open the door."

Behind the door, we can hear Pixie's frenzied flipping of book pages as if she must read or die. Taking a couple of steps back, I launch myself at the door shoulder first, smacking it open.

Sitting cross-legged on her bed in a cold-sweat trance, Pixie is deep into *The King in Yellow*. I wasn't expecting that. The damned book that finds a sucker every minute, with it's diabolical verses and a causeway for Hastur himself to enter this reality.

"Give…the…book…to…me!" I demand to which Pixie replies by socking me in my right eye.

"Hold on, Maddy, I'll get her by the—"

A jaundiced, slime-covered tentacle grabs Sue by her ankles, pull-bouncing her back down the staircase. She disappeared into a billowing xanthic mist thats caked and cracked the walls. The sound of her rose-tinted glasses breaking is *not* good for all of us involved in this affair.

I was trying hard not to make Pixie one of the living dead by biting her to get the tome. A hard yank releases *The King in Yellow* from her hands, and then Pixie drops to the bedroom floor in a heap, fast asleep.

My victory doesn't last long. Two tentacles grab both my ankles, dragging me to an unknown fate.

I am dragged down a side hallway to the backyard to join Sue. Even before I get there, I hear loud growls, snarls, teeth-snapping. Sue has made her transformation into a werewolf berserker, her beautiful seance outfit now in slime-tattered filigree. For every tentacle she bites or claws off, another appears, slithering out from under the tattered yellow robe of Hastur himself, stationed like a silent humanoid chess-piece in the backyard. I bite into the tentacles using my fangs, but the texture is too slimy. Tentacles are vining down on us from the ceiling, and damn it, Pixie's sound a sleep!

I've got one last idea. Still clutching the book, I open it and emit a magenta glow, which I press onto the pages with my left hand. The book bursts into ice-cold flames. Hastur screams an unearthly scream. The tentacles retreat and, like a bad taste in one's mouth, we are spat out of Hastur's yellow realm, back in the house, sliding along the floor near the staircase.

"Great heavens, oh my," yawns Pixie, sitting up between a naked Sue and me. We are both covered in Hastur's mucus, having transformed back to a non-horrifying state.

* * * *

During the course of Pixie's move to Brooklyn from England, a person or persons unknown had placed a copy of *The King in Yellow* among her book collection. It was packed and shipped among other items to the States. Procrastination during the summer delayed the debacle due to her working on her art. In hindsight, and no longer in danger, Pixie recalled having found it among her prized books when she finally finished unpacking.

Flipping through the insane gospel to see what the legendary uproar was about, she abandoned it after becoming unnerved. Yet it seeped into her unconsciousness, and she returned to read it in a Hastur-induced trance at night, slowly bridging together the two worlds. Sue not having a copy of *The King in Yellow* explained Pixie's fruitless search the night before. Even our spirit world, sensing the gravity of the situation, sent "Sorrel Neville"—a hoodoo spirit from the Caribbean—to warn her. It was his voice channeling a warning through her during the seance.

Alas, the event made Pixie change plans and return to England, but the cost of traveling back and the owner of the house demanding money for damages put Pixie in a financial mud hole. It was at that point that Sue and I decided that, in lieu of our fees, we would pose for a portrait. Pixie painted us in a variation of the "Lovers" card found in the Tarot deck.

Pixie didn't know it, but the painting was a splendidly blasphemous union of a vampire and werewolf which to this day hangs in the study of our duplex apartment just off the Hudson River.

THE WAY ORDER IS MAINTAINED

L.F. Falconer

It's well dark, but for some reason I awake. I rise up on one elbow, causing my heirloom bedframe to squeak. The clock indicates 3:03 AM. Half open to let in the cool night air, the bedroom window is illuminated by the streetlamp, the sheer curtains on either side rustling in the light breeze like a pair of shivering ghosts. A hollow, metallic *thunk* comes up from the porch downstairs. There's not enough wind to have blown it over, but I've dropped the watering can on the porch floor often enough to recognize the sound. The neighbor's cat is probably down there again. A creature with no respect for personal boundaries, it often crosses the six-foot fence between my home and its in order to snoop and prowl around.

Pulling myself from bed, causing the ancient bedframe to creak again, I cross my darkened bedroom and peek outside. The yard below is awash with the light of the streetlamp out front, all except for the far-left corner which hides in the deep shade of the duplex next door. A chill slithers up both my arms and I lurch back with a gasp.

Someone is walking through my back yard. No—not someone. Merely the shadow of someone.

Stepping back to the window, I peer down more closely. Nothing is to be seen except a shadow upon the lawn. It stops for several moments, as if in contemplation before resuming its course until it's eventually swallowed by the deep darkness near the fence line in the far corner. Is this some bizarre trick of the light cast by a source outside of my view?

For nearly an hour I stand at the window, but the shadow does not reappear. There's no way I can get back to sleep, and to do so now would be pointless. My daily routine would normally begin soon, so decide to simply get an earlier start and head downstairs to put on a pot of coffee.

As it brews, I step to the back door and peek out. In the meager lamp light that barely touches the porch, I can see it. My father's old watering can. A two-gallon beast of galvanized steel, lying on its side next to the wicker table it normally sits upon.

It had to be that cat. But the shadow I saw was not that of a cat. The shadow had been distinctly human.

After lingering over my coffee to use up the extra minutes in my day, I catch the bus which will take me to the train into the city. I am not the only rider here to do this. There are a number of familiar faces who take this same daily trek alongside of me. We have never spoken. We simply get on the bus and get off the bus at the train station, board our respective trains where we're then joined by more familiar faces who share the same routine as we. We do not acknowledge one another. To do so might force us to see something outside of ourselves, so instead, we get on the train where we're supposed to and get off where we're supposed to and go to our respective destinations to do what we're told to do.

There are unwritten rules in this life and to disregard the common etiquette would disrupt the efficiency of the system, for if, in the journey, a person got caught up in a conversation with another they might then miss their stop. Such things we do not want, so we do not talk. We do not make eye contact. We board where we're supposed to board and promptly disembark at our destinations. It is the way order is maintained.

Inside the train station the tile floor echoes the clickety-clack of hundreds of hard heels which hustle across its surface. My own shoes, soft and thick-soled, pop and squeak on tile. But the bustle inside the train station drowns out the pop and squeak so all that is heard is the clickety-clack and the swoosh of swift-moving bodies as they veer around me, assailing me with their invisible weapons of choice. In self-defense, I wear a painter's mask to protect against the converging swarm of colognes, body sprays, deodorants, fabric softeners, hair sprays, and other assorted unnatural scents that brutally assault my respiratory system. My shield is plain white and filtering. No one notices. They simply stream by. I am not meant to be seen.

The air is fresher on the street than in the station, but I do not remove my mask. No one removes their masks, not even those who are meant to be seen. No one wants another to see their naked self, so they hide behind make-up and jewelry, wild hair or designer clothes, tattoos, hats and sunglasses—whatever it takes to distract the eyes of those who see them. Anything to hide their true selves.

In the elevator of the building where I work, every day I ride up with a woman who is meant to be seen. I see her, her high heels, her pencil skirt, her blazer, her red lipstick and pearl earrings. Her neatly coiffed light brown hair. I see what she wants me to see. She does not see me behind my white, filtering painter's mask. She does not see my green coveralls or my soft, thick-soled shoes. I am not meant to be seen.

I disembark the elevator car on the 3rd floor to make my way to the janitorial offices. She continues to ride the elevator up, toward the offices near the top of the building where there is a clear view of the surrounding city. In her job she is meant to be seen. My work is invisible. Unless it's done improperly or not done at all. Only then does it draw attention. My manager doesn't like us to draw attention, so we remain invisible along with our work. And at the end of the day, I reverse the routine and board the train for home.

* * * *

It's 3:03 AM and I have awakened. Outside on the back porch, I hear a hollow *thunk*. More swiftly this time I rise, causing the bedframe to squeal. I rush to the window. I do not see a cat. But I do see someone's shadow walking across the lawn, stopping for a few moments before it moves on to become lost within the deep darkness in the far corner. I cannot get back to sleep, opting instead to descend the stairs and put on a pot of coffee to begin my day.

It is said that 3 AM is the witching hour. I am not a witch, so why am I waking in these dark and silent hours? What causes my watering can to tumble? Perhaps I should move it to a better spot. Or onto the floor beside the table. A cat couldn't knock it off then.

Yet it is not the sound which awakens me, for I am awake when I hear it. So, what goes on at 3:03 AM to completely break my slumber? Just before the sound?

These thoughts follow me to work, but abandon me once I enter the elevator. The sight of the woman who is meant to be seen has banished all distractions. I see the bruise beneath the make-up, the unshed tears shimmering in her eyes. I see her shame and her fear. I break the rule and look directly at her. She knows I see and she tightens her crimson lips and takes a step further away, keeping her shimmering eyes glued to the floor indicator lights.

I am no longer invisible to her. With one moment of eye contact, I breached the wall of the comfort zone. She is meant to be seen, but not as clearly as I have seen. She is meant to be seen, but not by my kind. Keeping our trespass silent, we part company at the 3rd floor.

* * * *

3:03 AM. I awaken. I wait for the hollow *thunk*. There it is, right on cue. I do not rise. I do not want to see. I go back to sleep.

* * * *

Over the weekend, the bus schedule was altered to improve efficiency. We had very little warning. My bus leaves earlier now than it used to which causes me to arrive earlier at the train station, enabling me to catch an earlier train. Except for the familiar faces which trek with me from the bus, I am now surrounded on the train by the unfamiliar faces of strangers rather than the familiar faces of strangers.

I arrive at the office building earlier. I no longer share the elevator with the red-lipped woman who is meant to be seen. Instead, I ride with two men with carefully sculpted facial hair who wear sleek business suits and carry expensive leather satchels which likely contain some very important documents. These men are meant to be seen, and they see one another for they were conversing when they entered the elevator car, they conversed while the car rose from the ground floor, and they conversed as I stepped out of the car on the 3rd floor. I'm certain they continued to converse after the doors closed behind my departure. I saw the men. They did not see me.

I arrive at the janitorial office early enough to have a cup of coffee before my shift begins. I stare out the 3rd floor window while I sip, watching the crowds that move over the street below. All the people have shadows attached to their soles. The shadows follow or lead the people, yet no one seems to notice. People trod upon other people's shadows. The shadows do not care. The shadows simply move on. Yet not a single shadow moves on its own.

A dark cloud covers the sun, erasing all the shadows. But the people remain.

Do shadows still exist in the dark?

* * * *

If 3:00 AM is the witching hour, why is my witching hour trailed by another "3"?

* * * *

It's 3:03 AM. I await the *thunk,* but it does not come. Instead, the crash of thunder rattles the open window. The curtains fly high on the incoming wind, flapping with wild and desperate abandon. A strobe outside flashes bright, outshining the streetlamp, but only for a brief moment.

I rise from the bed, causing the bedframe to whine, and hurry to the window, reaching it just as the thunder rumbles through the night. On the lawn below, a shadow walks calmly toward the darkness in the corner, disappearing just before the rain starts to fall.

After closing the window, I crawl back into the sanctuary of my bed.

* * * *

I spend my weekend cleaning up after the storm—broken limbs stacked and bagged, patio furniture retrieved and returned to its rightful place upon the porch. Father's watering can now sits on the porch floor, beside the small wicker table. I won't be using it anytime soon for the wind blew the pots of herbs from the porch railing, shattering the clay. I sweep the soil and debris from the porch floor. Afterwards, I sit on the porch, drinking tea. The neighbor's cat leaps up to walk the top fence rail. It sees that I see it. It doesn't like being seen so disappears back to the other side.

I know the cat does not come to my porch at precisely 3:03 AM each night to tip my watering can to the porch floor. A cat may be a vindictive creature, but is hardly regimental.

I glance into my teacup. A housefly floats within it. I pluck it out and set my tea aside. After a time, the fly rises and flutters its wings before lifting itself into flight. I had thought it to be dead, but the tiny nuisance has defied the rules of life. It flits erratically about as if it has lost its purpose until it finally vanishes from sight.

* * * *

The woman who is meant to be seen—the one with the red lips who used to share the elevator with me works on the 14th floor. She struggles not to see me, for I often catch her eyes looking to connect with mine. The two men in business suits with sculpted facial hair who I now share the elevator ride with work on the 19th floor. They still do not see me. But I see them. I see them all, all those who are meant to be seen. I try to make certain they do not see me. It is my job to remain invisible. To remain in the shadows. It is the way order is maintained.

One of my co-workers has become so invisible he no longer sees the world around him, not even the people who are meant to be seen. He wears headphones most of the time, listening to what only he can hear, perhaps music or a book or the song of a caged bird, as oblivious to life as life is to him. I wonder what it would be like. I wonder if I should invest in headphones, if only to listen to silence. Perhaps that is all my co-worker hears—silence. I will never know, because to ask him would cause him to be seen, and we are ones meant to remain invisible. I will respect his nonexistence.

* * * *

3:03 AM. I await the *thunk*, knowing it will not come. The snow is too deep. I had to walk through 5 inches of it when I got off the bus after work. It was still coming down at that time, but stopped before I retired for the night. The watering can is probably half full of snow. It shouldn't fall over. I will have to shovel the sidewalk in the morning.

I rise to gaze out at the freshly fallen snow which sparkles and glitters in the lamplight. A line of dark holes extends across the expanse, from the porch steps all the way to the darkness at the far corner. I arose too late to see the shadow. But I see the footprints it left behind.

I shiver and return to my bed.

In the morning, I set my watering can upright before retrieving the snow shovel. I do not look at the footprints in the snow. I do not want to see.

* * * *

I hang a wreath upon my front door. A 3-foot tall, pre-lit imitation Christmas tree sits on a table in front of the living room window. It wears no ornaments. I mailed a card to my brother. I have never received one in return. I watch *It's a Wonderful Life* on TV and drink hot cocoa with mini marshmallows, a holiday tradition since childhood.

At 3:03 AM, I awaken. There is a *thunk* on the porch downstairs. I rise and gaze out the window at the shadow passing through my yard.

"Merry Christmas," I whisper.

It does not whisper back.

* * * *

The woman with the crimson lips who works on the 14th floor no longer works on the 14th floor. Today, demanding to be seen one last time, she went off the roof, screaming all the way down.

The two men I ride the elevator with still work in the building. They still do not see me. Not even when I empty their trash receptacles beside their desks. It is a good thing, for I am to remain invisible.

I wonder, if a person is invisible, can they still be heard? If no one can hear you, do you still scream?

Because I can remain invisible, my manager gave me a small bonus at Christmas. I spent it on a new pair of soft, thick-soled shoes. The new pair is nearly silent when I walk across tiles. No more pop and squeak.

* * * *

Warmer weather and a good spring rain has caused the grass in my back yard to turn green again. It is lush and thick, except where a rutted pathway has appeared which leads from the back porch steps to the fence line in the far corner. I walk the barren dirt until it dead ends at the wooden fence. I press my nose against the cool cedar, breathing in its pungent scent. Then I turn around and walk back, letting my shadow lead the way.

I glance at the watering can which sits upon the porch floorboards beside the wicker table. Every morning it must be set back upright. I contemplate the purchase of new herb pots to adorn the porch rail. Perhaps I will opt for plastic pots this year instead of terra cotta. I can get plastic that looks like terra cotta. Plastic will not shatter like clay. But plastic is much lighter than terra cotta and more likely to be blown by the wind. I could forgo herbs altogether. I never use them. Then I would have no need of the old watering can and could rid my porch of its clutter. Perhaps I shall add borage to the mix this year.

I make a cup of tea and sit on the porch, staring at the rutted dirt path which now graces my lawn. I go inside and retrieve my stepstool and walk the path once more. At its terminus, I set the stool near the fence and mount the steps. Peering over the fence, I can see the back yards of the neighboring homes. None of them bears a pathway. It ends here.

* * * *

My alarm is set for 2:30. I will be fully awake and waiting on my porch by 3:03 AM. Waiting. And watching. Invisibly.

I heat up a frozen meal in the microwave, eating while watching *Jeopardy* on the TV. I say the few answers I know in silence, inside my head. At eight o'clock I retire and fall easily to sleep, undisturbed by anticipation of my middle of the night plans. After all, I know how to remain unseen. It is the one thing in my life I do well.

What I don't count on is over-sleeping. I'd mistakenly set the alarm for 2:30 PM instead of 2:30 AM. It is now 3:00 AM. The witching hour. But not quite *my* witching hour. I can still do this. I have 3 minutes.

Throwing the covers off, I spring from my bed. The window looms like a glowing rectangle in the dark. And in the dark I remain in my swift and silent haste down the stairs. The floor is cold beneath my feet.

I pause my course in the kitchen. What might I encounter out there? Quietly, I ease open the drawer beside the stove and withdraw the chef's knife kept within. My clammy palm wraps around the handle. By the time I reach the back door, my fleeting bravado has vanished and my hand shakes as I twist the deadbolt to open.

Taking a deep breath, I pull the curtain back a smidge and peek out the window to the porch beyond shaded in various grays beneath the distant streetlamp's glow. Above, the ceiling groans unmistakably with movement from upstairs.

A rush of cold envelops my flesh. Now comes the shuffle of footsteps.

Scrunching up against the door, I turn and watch in silent terror as a shadow descends the staircase. A nameless, faceless shade advances with purpose, the footsteps relentlessly beeping in the dark. Beeping. Beeping. Raising the knife over my head, I bring it down and...

...my fist smashes against the alarm clock, silencing the beeps.

I bolt upright in bed and the bedframe cries out against such a sudden move. I stare at the glowing rectangle on the dark bedroom wall, outlined by a pair of wispy curtains. Glancing at the clock on the bedside table, I see it is 2:30 AM. After several deep breaths to catch my bearings, I almost chuckle before pulling myself from the comfort of my bed, causing the bedframe to screech.

I sneak to the open window, pulling the curtain back to peek out. The lamplit yard below is empty—undisturbed. For several moments, I linger at the window before heading downstairs, content that the yard is vacant.

I cross the kitchen toward the back door. I do not stop to pull a chef's knife from a drawer. I do not own a chef's knife. Even if I did, would I dare use a weapon? Only in a dream would I be so bold and reckless. I cannot rely on courage I do not possess. Instead, I will use the one asset I truly have. Invisibility. It has served me well so far.

Carefully easing myself through the back door, I stand against the wall in the shadows on the porch, and wait.

The six-foot wooden fence between my yard and the neighboring houses is a formidable barrier against intruders, unless one is catlike and nimble. The culminating glow of many streetlamps forbids any starlight above. I do not wear a watch. I do not know how many minutes have passed as I stand in the shadows against the wall in the dark, watching and waiting. Hoping to remain unseen.

In the distance, car tires roll over pavement. There is a light on in the duplex next door. It shines dimly through the window. Faint on the horizon of sound is a barking dog and an even more distant siren's wail.

My yard is silent. Empty. Nothing moves. Not even me. Except my eyes and the pounding of my heart. The time must be growing close by now.

3:03. What does it mean? Beyond the witching hour, what is "3"? The power of three? Three points on a triangle. The Father, the Son, and the Holy Ghost. Mind, Body, and Spirit. Birth, Life, Death. The past, the present, the future. What is "3"? Three primary colors. The third heaven—the realm of angels. By itself, "3" is a magical number—charmed, holding a firm place in myth, art, and history. But 3:03? That's simply a "3" and its shadow, bound together by nothing.

Do I hear footsteps on the sidewalk out front? I hold stock still, trying to keep my breaths under control. Sweat seeps out, moistening my palms as I squeeze my hands into tight fists of anticipation. Am I ready to confront whatever it is that's been plaguing my sleep? At what personal cost does one confront their fear?

I pray not for confrontation. I pray for invisibility. I pray to see, but not to be seen.

The night has grown so heavy. So still. Surely the witching hour has begun. I survey every shadow within my view. Nothing moves. I close my eyes for a moment, listening. There is no sound, but I sense a change. A subtle shift inside. I feel like a fly floating in a cup of tea, at once both dead and alive.

Opening my eyes, I see the light in the duplex next door has gone out, all the windows a deep charcoal gray. From my own bedroom window above, I hear my bedframe screech.

Curiosity lures me away from the shadows near the house wall, drawing me further out onto the porch. Near the table, my foot accidently kicks against the watering can. It tips onto its side with a resounding hollow *thunk*. Fearing I might've alerted whomever might be here with me, I stop short.

Another squeal escapes through the open bedroom window above. I hurry down the porch stairs, stepping out into the open upon the well-trod path across my lawn, suddenly brought to a halt when I gaze up at my bedroom window.

In the darkness, the window is a rectangle of silver upon the gray wall. The sheer curtain inside draws tentatively back, revealing a face—a face pale and ghostly. My face. Locked in surprise and wonder.

The person staring down at me—is me.

Frozen in a moment of time, I watch myself watching myself and I glance down. My feet are darkened shades upon the ground.

I am but a shadow. This I now see. As clearly as I've seen it from my window above, night after night in a life unseen. Trapped inside a shadow, I have awakened myself, presented myself with possibilities. Do I proceed upon the rutted path, or step free?

I gaze up at myself, aware of what I'm telling myself to do. Yet I needn't have wasted my time. I have no desire to stray from the rutted path, no wish to ever be seen, for even a caged bird can sing, if only to itself.

This world is made up of those meant to be seen and those who are not, and I am but a shadow that disappears in the darkness, like all the shadows who came before and all those who will follow. I was not the first and I will not be the last. Nothing ever really changes—unless the rules are broken. And when I broke the rules I had to undo what had been done. To unchange the change, I had to send her off the roof. It was the only way, for she could no longer keep her eyes off me, would not allow me to remain invisible. And I have never been one meant to be seen.

Her screams were loud. Mine are silent.

I am but a shadow, and a shadow I will forever remain. I should care, but shadows do not care. Shadows simply move on.

It is a good thing. After all, it is the way of society. The way of the world.

It is the way order is maintained.

THE ADJACENT POSSIBLE
Michael Janairo

Taborgas Ramirez, the electrical engineer, waited for Dr. Heda's signal. A nod meant it was time to hit the button to launch the spatial-temporal adjacency shifter. That would, God willing, send them—Dr. Heda, Taborgas, and three other post-docs—from Lab A to Lab B, which was one hundred meters away, through sterile white walls, cement block, and steel girders. In Lab B, the team's other post-doc—the experiment's control—would greet them upon arrival.

Dr. Heda gazed from one post-doc to the next with hard downturned lips, giving his unshaven face a mixture of seriousness and confidence that Taborgas found so reassuring that he let himself marvel that he—a hardworking middle-class kid from Manila—was about to make a *Star Trek* fantasy a reality in a nondescript basement beneath a used book store, far from the rest of the Advanced Science and Technology Research Center of Tokyo University.

Dr. Heda smiled, something mischievous in his pressed lips. He nodded. Taborgas pressed the button with his thumb.

They had tested the spatial-temporal adjacency shifter before on rocks, clay, sand, glass, empty drinking glasses, glasses half-full of water (and later beer and whiskey, which all tasted fine afterward), petri dishes with samples of bacteria and algae and yeast, mice, rabbits, fish and their aquarium, and sheep. They tested things individually and then in groups of like things, and then unlike inanimate things and then unlike living things, and then mixtures of the animate and inanimate. All tests had succeeded beyond their expectations. In the tests, the shifts from Lab A to Lab B all occurred in fractions of a second. So now, the human test, aimed to give the researchers inside knowledge of the shifter experience.

Taborgas released his thumb and sensed a light so bright he had to shut his eyes. Power surge? he wondered. It was as if his button-pushing had turned on the world's brightest light. Eyes still shut, he sensed many other things all at once: a breeze; the scent of salt-sea air; heat; a rocking-swaying movement beneath his feet; a hoarse voice shouting in surprise, a quick interjection in a booming Japanese voice that didn't sound at all like Dr. Heda's quiet, measured voice.

Taborgas blinked. Japanese was his fourth language. He felt the floor sway. He nearly fell over. Squinting, he slid opened an eye. The bright light shone on a worn wooden floor. Where was this? His squinting eyes adjusted. A low wooden wall. Beyond that: the dark green sea. Were they on a ship? He blinked. The sea roiled and an enormous form broke the water's surface, seawater cascading down its sleek-green body before it crashed beneath the waves. Then, at that point, his bewildered mind finally translated what the booming Japanese voice had said: "Yellow devils!" This was not Lab B at all.

He looked around. Scruffy men with hard eyes, scraggly beards, and rolled sleeves stood nearby. Some stood with legs wide, planting themselves on the wooden desk of a ship. Others grasped hanging ropes. Most had white skin. Some had tattoos. Their gazes moved from the sea to Dr. Heda, him, and the other post-docs. Taborgas knew these judging looks; they made him feel like nothing more than a dusky phantom materialized out of thin air. None of them looked Japanese.

A new voice, also in Japanese, shouted: "All ready there, Fedallah?"

Fedallah? Taborgas turned. The floor continued to move. His stomach roiled; he was glad he hadn't eaten that morning.

A tall figure in a beard and dark suit nodded knowingly at Dr. Heda. The bearded man's skin was pale white, but was he the one who had spoken Japanese? More surprising, Dr. Heda half-hissed a reply in his native language: "Ready."

Ready? For what? Taborgas looked around: wooden deck, wooden mast, ropes dangling, ropes tying up sails. Another bearded white man shouted in Japanese.

Taborgas, busy translating white people speaking Japanese—"Lower away then; d'ye hear? Lower away, I say," had been the shout—also felt a strange doubling within himself: conscious that he still held the button that had launched them from Lab A to here—whatever adjacency this may be—and that he was still part of an experiment, while also feeling compelled by some as yet unknown force to join Dr. Heda and the other post-docs to run across the deck and leap into a boat hanging from the starboard side. All the while, he wondered: how did they know to do this? How did he even know it was the starboard side?

The tall bearded man also clambered aboard the small boat, albeit awkwardly. For the first time, Taborgas noticed one of his legs wasn't a leg at all, but a wooden peg. Taborgas stared at it as they dropped to the sea. When the boat smacked a wave, Taborgas looked away from the peg and at the device in his hand. It was a cylinder the length of his palm with a red button on one end and a strap on the other; the strap was around his wrist. He realized that this object was the only thing that attached him, the post-docs, and Dr. Heda to the lab in Tokyo, outside of themselves. He alone possessed a connection. Should he hit the button? He wanted Dr. Heda's advice.

But Dr. Heda was busy taking off his loose shirt. He displayed a surprisingly muscular chest for a scientist in his sixties. He hoisted a long harpoon like it was something he always knew how to do.

Three other boats lowered, and men in them rowed. A man in one shouted: "Captain Ahab?"

Ahab?

Taborgas raised his thumb to push the button, but was distracted by dead-eyed stares from his fellow post-docs. Each of them had their hands on an oar and were waiting for him to grab his. So instead of pushing the button, he took up the oar handle—something he had never touched in his life before—and he rowed. His fellow post-docs, too, rowed like trip-hammers, pulling the boat along in bursts. Dr. Heda raised the harpoon and stared out to the sea.

The tall bearded man yelled in Japanese to all the boat crews: "Spread yourselves! Give way, all four boats. Thou, Flask, pull out more to leeward!"

Ahab!

Taborgas, rowing, felt a sharp heat course through him. It wasn't the sun or the exertion; rather, he remembered a moment of feeling shame as a teen in the Philippines while reading what was supposed to be a classic American novel. The story described a group of mysterious Asians appearing like "phantoms" on the deck of a whaling boat and described them as "tiger-yellow" natives of "the Manilas." Taborgas whispered in Japanese to Dr. Heda, "Sensei!"

Dr. Heda turned, and, as if noticing the harpoon for the first time, jerked his head back in surprise or annoyance. He eyed Taborgas and spit out, "What is it?"

The fellow post-docs stopped rowing, as if that short exchange had taken them out of whatever had been holding them.

"The adjacency, Sensei," Taborgas said. "I think we've landed in 'Moby-Dick.'"

One of the other post-docs gasped. He was a systems engineer from Singapore named Nila who said, "The used book store upstairs! The owner this morning. I saw him reading it in Japanese!"

Dr. Heda's eyes narrowed, and he nodded at Taborgas, saying, "The button!"

Taborgas dropped the oar handle, but before he could swing the button mechanism into his hand, Captain Ahab shouted, "Look!"

He pointed with a brisk arm toward a spot in the ocean where the whale had been. His sharp movement rocked the boat, jerking Taborgas off balance. Without his hands on a oar to steady himself, Taborgas slid from his seat to the floor of the boat.

Meanwhile, Dr. Heda's gaze followed Ahab's arm out to the sea. He shouted: "The hunt is on!"

Taborgas tried to fight himself as he climbed back to his seat and again took hold of the oar, but he was egged on by the other post-docs' greedy growls, sounding more like pirates than engineers, as if all their lives they've waited for this moment to hunt a whale. All four started rowing again.

"The story," Taborgas said, rowing but thinking he had to grab the button. "Almost everyone dies."

The spot in the ocean where Ahab pointed burbled.

Something was rising.

Blood pounded in Taborgas's veins.

The vast and terrible ocean awaited, bracing and inviting.

Taborgas couldn't stop rowing. With each pull, though, his mind fought, thinking of the button, while at the same time his heart raced with the thrill of the chase. He told himself: "The moment I see a white whale, I'll hit the button."

Ahab pointed forward. Dr. Heda hefted the harpoon. The whalers in the other boats shouted instructions. And the post-docs, Taborgas included, bent their backs and rowed, locked in rising action.

✗

THEY DANCE IN ARSENIC
Ashley Dioses

Her headdress gleams ethereal in light
As eerily she dances in the night.
Her verdant ball-gown whirls and twirls, it seems,
Like a forbidden pleasure from one's dreams.
The emerald sheen of her fine dress of silk
Distracts the eye from skin like soured milk.
Her suitors trailed behind, across the floor,
Inhaling her perfume, like once before.
They dance together to eternal song;
Their poisoned flesh still holds, yet not for long.
And when their heartbeats lose their rhythmic dance,
They dance in arsenic, in Death's grim trance.

THE GOLDEN BOY
Aditya Deshmukh

This better not induce labor, thought Laura as she bent down to lift the Laughing Buddha. It'd lived in the dusty corner of her living room for a decade. Being the final gift from her mother, it had a special place in her heart. But now that the Buddha's jutting stomach was cracked because the statue fell last night, she had to replace it. Laura carried it to the storeroom. On pushing the door open, a cloud of dust attacked her. She wrinkled her nose, barely balancing the statue with one hand. "When was the last time I cleaned this mess?" She shuffled old things that had no use for her, but possessed sentimental value, and made a place for the Laughing Buddha. She shut the door on his smiling face, leaving him alone in the darkness and in dust and cobwebs. It disheartened her. She promised herself that she would have him repaired and installed in her living room soon.

The kettle whistled. Laura hurried to the kitchen. She put a tea-bag in a cup and poured steaming water over it, watching the water turn brown and black. Its aroma wafted through the air, teasing her nose, erasing her exhaustion. She carried the cup to her balcony and sat it down on her coffee table. She dusted the cushion on her chair, picked her cup and sat back staring out into the world.

It was evening, but the sky was black. A lightning cracked in the distance. Chirping of birds filled the air, in contrast to the sound of thunder, as flocks of ravens and sparrows rushed to seek shelter. "Looks like it will rain." Laura unconsciously placed her hand on her belly, as though talking to her unborn child. She felt a kick inside her womb. She giggled. *Chaisai should've been here*, she thought, circling her belly. She waited a couple of minutes for her baby to respond to her touch, but it seemed like it had fallen asleep.

She began humming a tune. Her lips curled into a faint smile. She imagined her child in her arms, looking into her eyes, playing with her nose with tiny fingers. She wondered whether he'll have green eyes like hers or brown like Chaisai's. And the name... She hadn't given it much thought. Maybe Kevin if boy, and Brianna if girl, after her grandparents. "What do you think, Chaisai?" She reached for her phone sitting on the coffee-table opposite to her chair. She called her husband. With every ring, her ears became desperate to hear his voice. He had been gone for a month, and their last call was a week ago. He didn't pick up. Of course, since it's evening here, there it must be midnight.

She wondered how Chaisai was doing. Was he broken and alone? He had shed no tear when his mother succumbed to old age, and had quickly returned to Thailand to pay his respects. But that was because he didn't want any sadness around his child. She wanted to go along with him, but Chaisai wouldn't allow her any unnecessary exertion. "Take care of our child," he'd said.

A raindrop fell on her nose before rolling down and dripping into the tea. Laura looked at the horizon, where a legion of dark clouds was gathering. She remembered her mother-in-law once telling her that a storm during pregnancy was an ill omen. A chill crawled down her spine. *No, I will not lose my child, not this time.* Gazing at the storm, she took a sip, then cursed and returned to the kitchen to fetch some sugar.

When she entered the living room, her telephone rang. Startled, Laura went to answer. As soon as she touched the receiver, the call died. Sighing, she sat on the couch. Her breathing had gotten heavy. Laura added a spoonful of sugar to her tea. She drank it all in one gulp. The cold tea felt strange to her tongue, but she had no desire to spend another ounce of energy making another cup of tea. Outside, the rain was growing stronger. Laura got up to shut the windows. Her door bell rang.

She walked to the door and peered through the magic-eye. All exhaustion left her and a sudden boost of pleasure shot through her. "Chaisai!" She pushed the door open and wrapped her hands around her husband. "I wasn't expecting you."

Chaisai kissed her forehead. "Phom kid theung khun."

"I missed you too." Laura guided his hand to her womb. "Perhaps not as much as our child did though."

Chaisai sat on his knees and gently lifted Laura's shirt up so that her stomach lay bare. She shivered when a cold breeze caressed her skin. Chaisai's kiss on her belly brought goosebumps on the back of her neck. "I did not want to leave you, Děk."

"You weren't supposed to return until next week."

"Are you not happy that I'm back?"

"I am. Of course, I am. I'm just surprised."

"Actually, I called you few minutes earlier. But I figured I wanted to see that surprise on your face, not just hear it in your voice." Chaisai moved a strand of hair off her cheek before placing his lips on hers.

"I missed you so much," Laura said with Chaisai's tongue exploring her mouth.

"I know." Chaisai loosened his tie and went to the couch. He took Laura's hand and pulled her towards him. With one hand behind her neck, another over her belly, he pressed her against him and kissed her hard. Laura bit his lip. "Looks like you really did, khon dii."

"You've no idea," Laura said. After making love, she was breathing heavily. "God, I missed this. I wish I had more stamina."

"We'll have plenty of time to work on that stamina after our child is born." Chaisai smiled.

"I don't think so. Baby stuff is hard. I watched these videos and—"

"We'll manage, khon dii." He kissed her hand. "Tell me, during my leave, how were your days?"

"Terrible. My sister ditched me last week, said something about her friends going to Vegas. And God, it's so hard to do anything when you're pregnant."

"Why didn't you tell me? I'd have come earlier."

"I didn't want to disturb you. Besides, our neighbour is helping me out. Anyway, tell me about you. Did everything go fine?"

"Yes." His speech had no hint of grief, but his eyes revealed the truth.

"I am sorry for what happened."

Chaisai looked out the window. "It was her time."

"Well, with the funeral rites going on for several weeks, I'm sure she must've found a place in heaven."

Chaisai laughed. "My mother never believed in heaven or hell, but yes, I hope she did. The funeral took only a couple of days, though."

"Then what were you doing this past month in Thailand?"

"This was my first visit home in fourteen years. I had to see some relatives and friends, and then there was the matter of selling the house."

"You're selling your house?" Laura's eyes widened.

Chaisai shrugged. "I don't know. I'm the only living member of the family and I don't see myself returning for good. My family is here now, with you, with our child." He stroked her cheek.

"But it's where you grew up. What about the memories of your childhood?"

"I've brought some stuff here. Not much, but it is all I need. Besides, the empty house reminds me of my Pôr Mâe. I need to let go."

"I understand." Laura placed her hand on his. "Will you show me your precious heirlooms?"

"They are not that special," Chaisai said, opening a box. "But this is something not all can procure. I remember my Pôr bringing it home for good luck just after my brother passed away."

"Oh God, I'm so sorry. How old was your brother when…"

"He was a stillborn." Chaisai said without looking at her. Laura felt tears welling her eyes. She had lost her first child because of miscarriage. And this news brought back the painful memory.

She touched her stomach unconsciously. She shook her head. *It won't happen again.* She wiped her tears and forced a comforting smile. "I'm sure your brother would be happy to see mom."

Chaisai sniffled. He laughed bitterly. "I guess it's only fair that now it's his turn to get mom's love. Anyway, remember what we promised? No sad talks around our child."

Laura nodded. "So you were talking about this good luck charm?"

"Yes," Chaisai began. "It was quite hard to bring it here. I had to have it shipped illegally."

"Illegally?" Laura asked, shocked.

"Don't worry about that, trust me, it was worth the trouble. And no, it's nothing dangerous. You'll see."

Chaisai pulled what looked like a statue wrapped in multiple layers of white cotton and paper from inside the box. "Kuman Thong, a Golden Boy," he announced excitedly and started unwrapping the statue. "It brings luck." He paused. "By the way, did you check out the links I messaged you the other day?"

"Oh, Golden Boy, yes, that's why the name seems familiar. Actually no, I forgot."

"Well, just try not to overreact."

"Wow, is it that expensive?" Laura asked. The Laughing Buddha came to her mind having a baby's features made of gold. But when Chaisai removed the final layer of cloth, a stench went straight to Laura's head. She covered her nose, and stared at the Golden Boy in horror.

There was *nothing* golden about the hideous thing Chaisai held in his hands. It was a shriveled, roasted and dried corpse of a baby. Laura's eyes widened. She screamed. "What the fuck is that?"

"Hey, there is no reason to be frightened, khon dii."

"It looks like a corpse, a baby's corpse! How dare you bring that thing here." Laura glanced at the Kuman Thong. It had no eyes, but she could feel its gaze, darker than anything she'd known. She felt its partially formed hands and legs reaching out for her, its tiny fingers prying open her flesh, tearing through her womb, its tiny disfigured mouth lusting after her child's blood. A shiver ran down her spine.

Chaisai kept the Kuman Thong back in the box, and put his arm around her shoulder. "It's alright, it's alright, I put him away."

Laura jumped away from him, her eyes singing with tears, her entire body trembling with fear. "Please tell me that…that thing is fake, that this is some kind of a prank."

"It is a corpse, yes, but khon dii, listen to me. It's not what you think."

"You brought home a corpse, Chaisai, a fucking corpse!"

Chaisai went to his wife, but Laura stepped back. "Don't come near me, not with those hands."

"You're getting it all wrong, Laura. Sit down, let me explain."

Laura kept staring at him with suspicion gleaming on her face. What devil had gotten into him? Was the man she knew as Chaisai still inside him? "You will get rid of it ASAP!"

"I…"

"You will," Laura insisted.

"Please just listen to me."

Laura sat down on the couch, wary of the box near her feet. Chaisai moved it away. "Sorry, I shouldn't have brought it here without taking your permission."

"You shouldn't have." Laura agreed.

"But it is a Thai tradition. My father called it my guardian angel. And I wanted our child to have him as a protector too."

"How can a corpse protect someone, Chaisai? It is a symbol of death and darkness. God knows whether by the act of merely bringing it here you summoned a vengeful spirit in this house."

"Kuman Thong is something more than a corpse. Yes, it is created in a cemetery, through a procedure that is as dark and twisted as he looks, but that doesn't make him dark. And yes, he is a spirit, but not an unkind one. We offer him food and clothes and toys, and in return he keeps the household safe and brings us luck. My mother took his care until her last day, and now it's my responsibility to look after him."

"This is a lot to take in, Chaisai." Outside, a lightning zigzagged in the black sky and the storm descended on them. Strong winds brought rain to their house that collided against the windows with the intensity of bullets. *What if Kuman Thong summoned this storm?*

"That's why I'd messaged those links, so that the experience wouldn't be this disturbing. But anyway, it doesn't matter. I'll send the Kuman Thong to my cousin, if it bothers you that much."

Laura nodded. "I never knew Thailand has such a creepy tradition," she said after a while.

"More appropriate term would be 'had'. The real Kuman Thong is illegal even there. Nowadays, they use wooden statues instead of baby corpses." He exhaled a long breath. "Anyway, I'm tired, khon dii. We should go to bed. I've craved to sleep beside my wife for a month. Torture me no more."

"First keep that box in the storeroom, and yes, place the Laughing Buddha in that corner." Damaged or not, she would like to see his stress-relieving smile for once. "And don't enter the bedroom unless you've showered and that thing's smell is off you."

"Yes, of course," Chaisai said. "I'm sorry, Laura. I never intended to ruin your mood, especially not when you're pregnant."

Just when Chaisai closed the lid of the box, Laura felt a pain in her stomach. Something wet trickled down her legs. Laura touched below. Her eyes widened as a nervous smile crept on her face. "Fuck!"

"Is something wrong?" Chaisai rushed to her aid.

"I think my water has broken."

* * * *

Laura encouraged her seven month old son to walk. He'd manage a step, but then again resort to crawling. He switched the direction, and headed towards the Laughing Buddha at a remarkable speed. He bumped into the statue, which fell on the floor. The old crack widened, and the statue split into pieces.

"Looks like now you're beyond repair, old man." Laura said. "Come here, you sporty." Laura encouraged Jesus to walk towards her.

She was so glad that he was growing stronger every day. There were complications in her pregnancy, and the baby had remained silent for twelve minutes. The doctors had tried all ways, modern and traditional, including twisting the baby's legs up to his face and back again several times, while sucking the mucus out of his mouth. And finally his cry had blessed her barely conscious ears. She had wanted to name him Kevin, but because of this miraculous resurrection, she and Chaisai decided there was no better name than Jesus.

Jesus stood up and looked at her with a finger in his mouth. His big eyes lit up. "Nóng-sà-pái," he said.

"Chaisai, he's doing it again."

"What?" Chaisai came out of the shower, wearing a towel around his waist. He kissed Laura's forehead and lifted Jesus in air. "What did my champ do?"

"It's time he called me mama, but he keeps calling me nong sa something."

"Nóng-sà-pái?" Chaisai raised his eyebrow.

"Yes, exactly."

"Strange. It is Thai for sister-in-law."

Laura placed her hands on her hips. "I urge him to say mama all day long and he won't do it. And sometimes he sees his father speak Thai on phone, and he's already picking up these long words? Not cool, Jesus."

Chaisai tapped his chin with a finger. "I don't think I have used nóng-sà-pái recently, Laura. I'm not sure from where he's learning Thai."

"Maybe he's talking in his own baby language and the gibberish just coincided with the Thai word."

"That's very unlikely." Chaisai scratched his head.

"Nóng chaai." Jesus said.

"Does that mean something?" Laura held her breath. She had no issue that her son was learning his father's language before hers, but the fact that he was learning all this by himself was a bit unnerving.

"Yes, it means brother. Why is he calling you sister-in-law and why would he call me bro—?" Colour left Chaisai's face. "Oh no!" He stared at Jesus as if he was something otherworldly. He kept the baby on the couch. "Laura, remember when I brought the Kuman Thong home? My Pôr never told me where he got it. What if he created it himself?"

"Why would he, and anyway what does that have to do with Jesus?"

"You know I had a brother…a stillborn." Chaisai swallowed because of fear as his and Jesus' eyes met. "Father brought the Kuman Thong home the day my brother was buried. He told me then that my brother will watch over me every day."

Laura looked at her son. The innocence on his face was gone and an ocean of darkness swirled in his eyes.

"Our baby didn't breathe for twelve minutes. What were the odds of him coming back to life?" Beads of sweat formed on Chaisai's forehead. "What if he was struggling against my brother's spirit. What if the Kuman Thong killed our son the moment he was born, to punish us because we refused to take his care. Mother had warned me about that…yes, she had." Tears rolled down Chaisai's face.

"I'll not lose my son, not again!" Laura screamed. She stared into her son's eyes, but he was not her son anymore. Somewhere deep in his eyes, bathing in the ocean of darkness, smiled the Kuman Thong.

THE PROPER STUDY OF MAN
Dave Truesdale

Alexander Pope proclaimed:
"The Proper study of Mankind is Man"

But he was drunk you know, his thoughts all a swirl
For as all good SF fans show

The proper study of Man
is galaxies and girls.

WHITE WAKE
John C. Hocking

"Earthquake? Well, it's not the Big One, but the tremor you may have felt last night around midnight might just be the beginning of something larger. Geologists at Stratton University place the little quake's epicenter on the ocean floor about 100 miles off our sandy shoreline. Johnny, what's it look like out there on the beach?"

"Well Bob, Dr. Anderson of Stratton University tells us that the quake was too small to produce a tsunami, but something tells me that these sun-bathers wouldn't be disturbed even if it had kicked one up. Everywhere you look you see tanned and smiling students bound and determined to make the most of yet another perfect summer day."

* * * *

The bar was dark, dirty, and filled with the pulsating din of lame rock music and too many people talking too loudly. Don let the door close behind him and squinted around, hoping for a familiar customer. As of late his goods were less than stellar and business was worse than slow. Hitting this bar rarely paid off, but he was behind on his student loans and needed a break.

Don fingered the lapel of his light sport coat and put on an easy grin. He took a stool at the bar, ordered a draught, and realized he was slumming. The place was definitely going downhill. He always felt like he was doing the proletariat a favor whenever he came here, gracing them with his collegiate presence and offering them his best blow, but damned if he wasn't starting to feel a little out of place. An aging biker in the corner spilled beer in his ragged beard. Two heavy-metal throwbacks in matching black leather jackets sneered sullenly at anyone who met their gaze. The table full of jump-suited factory rats alternately made drunken toasts and cursed each other. It just didn't seem like his kind of place anymore.

Don grimaced, tipped back his mug, and a heavy hand flopped onto his shoulder. He choked and spit a mouthful of beer onto the bar. The hand withdrew immediately, but Don spun around on the stool quickly enough to catch the offender's wrist.

"What's the deal?" Three trips to the university gym a week over the past four years had given him a solid grip. He used it now.

"Ahm, excuse me," said the fat man standing behind him. "I didn't mean to startle you, sir." The man's face was wide and jowled, and his round black eyes bulged darkly beneath a heavy brow. The wrist in Don's hand seemed cool and moist and soft. Although his wrist was being squeezed with considerable force, the fat man's face showed only a gentle concern.

"Well, what's the idea, then?" Don released the wrist, though whether from frustration at his inability to draw a reaction or revulsion at the man's clammy flesh, he couldn't say. Being addressed as 'sir' helped a little.

"Ahm, you're Don Lane?" The fat man's voice was deep and phlegmy, as if he suffered from a formidable case of post-nasal drip. He wore loose jeans and a baggy brown work-shirt buttoned all the way up to the folds of his neck. What little hair he had was black and combed straight back on his squat skull. The aroma of some particularly pungent aftershave came off him in waves.

"Yeah, I'm Lane. Who wants to know?" Don scrutinized the fat man and couldn't decide whether to be concerned or contemptuous. He noted the brown make-up caked on the fat man's collar and opted for the latter. What kind of pathetic old fruit was this?

"Ahm, I'm Mr. Lesko." The dark eyes blinked sleepily. "I understand that you are a dealer in certain goods."

Don's lips twisted in a crooked grin. There was no way this sleaze was a cop. He was a customer.

"Yeah, you could say that. You need something?"

"Ahm, no, sir. That is, I'm not seeking to buy, but rather to sell."

Leaning back against the bar, Don dug both hands casually into the pockets of his sport coat and touched the little bottle of pepper spray. Strangers didn't approach him in the bar and offer to sell him goods. Maybe this guy actually was a cop.

"Not interested," he said, keeping his smile. "I've got my own sources."

"Ahm, I'm sure you do, sir. But I assure you that you don't have anything remotely like what I have to offer."

"Heard that one before, Mr. Lesbo. Run along now and let me finish my beer." Don started to turn away and the limp hand fell on his shoulder once again. Instantly, he swung back around and his hands came out of his pockets as fists.

"Listen, asshole-" Don's eyes met the dark, intent gaze of the fat man and he fell silent.

"No, sir. You have never, ever heard an offer like mine. My goods have never been available in this part of the world before. Look." The man who called himself Mr. Lesko dug into a loose pocket of his baggy shirt and pulled out a rolled plastic bag full of whitish powder.

"Jesus!" snarled Don. He covered the proffered bag with both hands to hide it. "Do you want to land us both in jail?"

"Take it. Ahm, yes. Take it. Try it. Let others try it. As many as you can. They'll love it, Mr. Lane. And they'll come back to you for more." As he grew excited, the fat man's voice lowered even further, until it became a glottal croak.

Don sneaked a glance at the bag he had jammed between his thighs. Looked like a sizable bag of blow except that the powder appeared more dull in tone and more coarse in texture.

"Well," he said at last. "What the hell is it?"

"A delight from my homeland." The fat man's thick lips curled in a smug grin. "It's called White Wake, and it's made from deep water seaweed." The grin grew wider. "It's all natural, and better still, completely legal."

"No shit," mumbled Don, interested despite himself. "How do you take it? What's it do?"

"Eat it, drink it, inhale it, it matters not. It provides ease and comfort and fabulous dreams."

"Now wait, this isn't some goddamn herbal ginseng natural high crap, is it? That stuff never does jack shit. My customers are used to getting some bang for their buck."

The squat skull nodded briskly with attentive concern. "Ahm, oh no, sir. Oh no. It has a pronounced effect. None who use it are ever disappointed."

"Right." Don looked at the bag between his thighs skeptically. "And you say its legal."

"Ahm, for the time being at least. As I said, sir, it is new in this part of the world."

"Legal for now, huh? Like acid in the sixties, right? Sounds too good to be true." He pulled the bag from its hiding place and thrust it against Mr. Lesko's yielding paunch. "Your pretty stories aren't getting any of my cash."

"Ahm, but of course, sir." The fat man took a step back and lifted both hands to indicate that he wouldn't accept the return of the bag. "It is yours for no charge. Experiment with it. Let others try it. Your customers will be delighted, and when you want more, seek me here."

"Right. Sure. My ass." Seeing that the fat man wasn't going to take the package, Don thrust it back between his thighs. When he looked up Mr. Lesko was already halfway to the door. As Don watched, the man's bulky figure pushed out into the night.

Don stuffed the bag of powder into his jeans, finished his beer, and got out of there. The street outside was empty but for a chill wind. A night bird shrilled loudly somewhere overhead. He flipped on the Corvette's dome light and quickly examined his unwanted gift. It was about a quarter ounce of finely ground powder. Under the dome it looked off-white, perhaps even the palest shade of green. Don swore softly. One side of the baggie bore a smear of crusted pancake makeup. He shook his head. Jesus, what a fruit. He crotched the bag again and started the car.

* * * *

"Well that about wraps it up for Channel 17 Action News. I don't know about you, Johnny, but I'm going to step out in my back yard tonight to get a glimpse of that comet."

"You bet, Bob. Viewing this evening ought to be top notch. I hope all of our friends out there will take the time to say hello to a cosmic traveler whose last trip through these parts happened back when earth was just a little twinkle in God's eye."

"Thanks, Johnny. Goodnight."

"Goodnight, Bob."

* * * *

Don Lane's luck took a turn for the better. A chance stop at Slim Jim Wishbone's Watering Hole netted him a surprising quantity of business, as well as a lead to a supposedly monster party at the Badge of Virtue fraternity house. Many frats were averse to his merchandise, but Badge was different. As soon as he was in the door he was tagged for the last of his blow. Content, he visited the keg, hit on a couple of unresponsive sorority girls, and made ready to take his well-stuffed wallet home. He was almost to the door when he heard a voice call his name.

"Yo, Don!" A shaggy head bobbed in the crowd at the base of the wide stairway to the second floor. Don frowned, couldn't figure out who the guy was. "Hey, come on upstairs, man!"

Don was feeling good enough to make his way through the close-pressed crowd and up the stairs to the less stifling second floor. The shaggy-headed guy beckoned him into one of the bedrooms and shut the door.

"Long time no see, man." Shaggy took Don's hand in a limp grip, nodding and smiling. Don still didn't recognize him. Looked like some dim bulb sixties flashback hippie. There was someone else in the bedroom; another long-haired guy wearing a dashiki and sitting cross-legged on a bean bag chair. Don had to fight back the urge to either roll his eyes or laugh out loud. What a pair of losers.

"Hey, hey, Don. You carrying?"

"Sorry, boys. Fresh out. Catch me tomorrow, maybe."

"Aw no, man." The guy on the bean bag sounded heartbroken. "We've been saving all month for this party and we've come up dry all night. Are you going to let us down, too?"

"Like I said, I'm sorry, but it's been a busy evening."

"Shit!" The guy on the bean bag swore savagely. "I got no luck! I thought you said this guy was good, Mickey."

Beneath his overhanging fringe of hair Mickey's expression went sour with disappointment. "Yeah," he grumbled. "Yeah, I said that. Guess I was wrong."

Don felt a hot flare of anger, a quick pulse that made his guts clench and a flash of bright red flicker in front of his eyes. These total losers were disrespecting him.

"Okay," he said suddenly. "I guess I can't disappoint two gentlemen like yourselves." He dug a hand under his belt, and his two customers came toward him as if pulled by some supernatural magnet.

"What you got, man?"

"See? Y'see? Didn't I say Don wouldn't let us down?"

"It's called White Wake," said Don.

* * * *

"Well, this has to go down as one of the strangest ways to start the day I've ever heard. Dock workers and fishermen will be talking for some time about the rain of fish that came down on the beach and wharves around Stratton ferry at about six this morning."

"Did you say a rain of fish, Bob?"

"That's right, Johnny. Citizens on the scene report well over two dozen sizable, and very much alive, fish plunked down out of a clear blue sky. A number of graduate students from Stratton University were dispatched to the scene and collected several specimens of what they called abyssal fauna. They offered the tentative explanation that the fish were pulled from the depths by a waterspout, perhaps hundreds of miles away, then dropped on us here in Stratton."

"Amazing, Bob. Just when you think nothing can surprise you, along comes something nobody could have predicted."

* * * *

The phone was ringing two miles away under a lake. Don rolled over in bed and the morning sun slammed gold against his clenched lids. His stomach was queasy with old beer. The phone rang again, closer this time. Right next to the bed, in fact. Even so, if he hadn't left his window shade up to admit the brilliant morning sunshine, he might have just rolled over and slept through it. The vague trace of an unpleasant dream lingered at the back of his memory. He'd been drowning under an ocean of cold black water, but he was awake now. Don grabbed the shrilling phone.

"M'yeah. Hello." His voice was raw and the inside of his mouth tasted like road kill.

"Don? Is that you?"

"Yeah, this is Don. What's up?"

"Man! You got any more of the Wake? That stuff's bliss!"

"What? Who is this?" Don sat up and squinted at the clock. "It's only 7:35."

"It's Mickey. You know, the guy at Badge you sold that designer stuff to last night. White Wake? Remember?"

"Oh yeah, sorry Mickey. You woke me up."

"Did I? Sorry, man, I'm just so hyped on your new stuff. I tell you I was flying on it."

"Yeah?" Realization filtered into Don's drowsy skull. "No kidding? You liked it, huh?" He shook his head in mingled disbelief and contempt.

"Man, I was in the clouds. So, can I get some more? You only gave us half of what you had. Did you do it up? You can get more, right?"

"Yeah," said Don slowly. "I'm pretty sure I can get more. But the price has gone up."

* * * *

Well, Johnny, I'm sorry to say I've bad news on this outwardly perfect day. A typical summer night's party turned to terror for a group of teenagers on a secluded beach on the outskirts of Stratton last night. Seventeen-year-old Arthur Jamison reportedly fell asleep while his friends and fellow members of Stratton High's surfing club partied and drank beer. His friends claim that Jamison awoke with a shout and immediately attacked his friends in an unprovoked rage. Three youths suffered wounds and honor student Dave McDowell was slain with a cooking skewer taken from the party's campfire. Officer Charlie Erickson of the Stratton Police happened by in his squad car just as the terrified youths fled from the beach onto the highway. Arthur Jamison, still waving his bloody skewer and shouting incoherently, was reportedly shot more than once by Officer Erickson, yet ran back to the beach despite his wounds. Erickson claims that Jamison plunged into the surf and swam out to sea. As of this afternoon, his body has not been recovered.

* * * *

Don felt as if he'd been sitting at the table forever. The graying biker was at the same stool and still slopping back beer. Christ, it could have been the same bottle for all Don knew. Of fat Mr. Lesko there was no sign. Don stared at his flat beer, then at his watch. Nine o'clock, and he'd been here since six. He reminded himself that it would all be worth it to keep from disappointing his customers.

And they would have been disappointed, too, no doubt about it. Don almost had to hang up on Mickey just to get him to stop telling him how much he liked the new product.

"Ahm, good evening, Mr. Lane."

Don flinched and slid around in his chair. It was Lesko, bent over with his chubby hands clasped together like an ugly but attentive waiter.

"Whoa, you startled me. I've been waiting for hours." Don tried not to sound too unhappy. After all, he was fairly certain he wanted to do real business with Lesko. Even if the slob seemed to be wearing the exact same clothes he'd had on the day before.

"I'm sorry if I inconvenienced you." The fat man lowered his bulk into the seat across the table from Don, who fancied he could hear the chair groan in protest. "I prefer to conduct business after dark." His wide mouth bent in a conspiratorial grin. "I trust that my goods were all that I promised they would be?"

"Well, I guess." Don slouched back in his chair and played it cool. "Didn't do any myself. Managed to move a little to some customers who were interested in more, though."

Mr. Lesko leaned across the table. "How many?" His dark eyes seemed to bulge in the half light.

"How many?" Don didn't understand for a moment. "Oh, just a few." Lesko slumped back in what might have been disappointment. "Well, it's new product," continued Don defensively. "Nobody knows it from Drano. Today's buyer is cautious."

"Yes," said the fat man slowly. "I suppose so. Still, I should very much like to, ahm, acquire a distribution network and a sizable array of good customers in short order. You want more product, do you not?"

Don tapped both thumbs on his chest. "I'm your man. Whatever you've got, I can move."

"Ahm, an admirable attitude, sir. Please follow me." Lesko painstakingly hoisted himself from the chair. The fat man waddled to the bar's door with Don following in the vapor-trail of his cologne. The door swung out into the night and Don felt an unexpected flicker of uncertainty.

They were alone on the empty street. Don looked around, nervous without knowing why. There were no pedestrians and the stars seemed to hang right above the rooftops. Don couldn't remember ever hearing so many crickets inside the city before. The noise was distracting. "Where we going?"

"Not too far, Mr. Lane. Just to my car."

At the rear of an almost empty parking lot, beneath a lonely, overhanging tree, was Mr. Lesko's vehicle. Don smiled in discreet amusement. It was a huge pick-up truck with every bit of chrome trim the manufacturer could cram onto it. It sat low on its shocks, as though it carried a heavy load. When Lesko climbed onto the padded rear bumper, Don noted a bumper sticker that read 'Wharf Workers Local 309'. He frowned as the fat man pulled a tarp off something in the pick-up's bed. Lesko didn't look like a dock worker. Never heard a guy who owned a truck like this call it a car, either.

The tarp was tar-smeared canvas and where Lesko pulled it aside Don glimpsed a square block of dark and weathered stone with what looked to be hugely taloned feet carved into it. The grotesque feet rose into legs that were hidden by the tarp. Don bit back an exclamation. What was Lesko doing driving around with a statue? Was he some kind of antiques smuggler?

With a croaking wheeze, Lesko produced a small box, and flipped the tarp back over the prone statue. Then he turned and hopped from the bumper with surprising agility.

"Ahm, here you are, Mr. Lane. I trust this will meet your needs?"

Don held out his hands and took the little wooden crate Lesko offered him. The fat man turned away.

"Whoa, that's heavier than it looks." Suspicion crept into its accustomed place in Don's mind. "Hey, I'm not buying you out, am I? How much cash are we talking about here?"

The truck's door slammed and Lesko leaned out the window smiling. "No charge, Mr. Lane. Our firm is trying to acquire customers. Spread it around. When you want more, meet me at the bar. Ahm, we'll discuss money then. I'm there every night." The truck engine roared to life.

"Well, sure." Don was at a loss for words, unable to believe his luck. The fat man was either out of his mind or overloaded with the drug and determined to build a city-wide clientele. Don hoped fervently it was the latter. "You bet, Mr. Lesko."

"Ahm, Mr. Lane?"

"Yeah?"

"You should try some of the product yourself. A worthy businessman knows his goods."

* * * *

"Police have nabbed the culprits responsible for the ritual-style slaying of some two dozen local dogs and cats. An outwardly pleasant beachhouse proved to be the gathering place of a cult-like group that apparently included at least one prominent citizen."

"That's right, Johnny. Police are close-mouthed about it now, but rumors have it that a high-ranking official in the mayor's office was apprehended inside the death-house. Channel 17's exclusive sources within the police department have revealed that the bizarre cult believed the recent appearance of Comet Thurston was sign of a coming apocalypse and that the souls of the sacrificed pets were an offering that would please their god so that he might protect them from the cataclysm."

"Well, Bob, it does seem that these days people are feeling a greater need than ever to get in touch with their spiritual side."

"You said it, Johnny. The sad thing is how misguided some folks get about it."

* * * *

Don leaned against the head of the bed, propped up on pillows and feeling fine. The blonde next to him stirred and cooed in her sleep. He stroked her satin shoulder and tried to remember the details of the most financially successful evening of his life.

Mickey and his dashiki-clad friend had all but ambushed him when he returned to Badge of Virtue. And they'd brought friends. Don found it hard to believe that the two losers could have so many friends. It seemed that everyone in Badge had done little that day but listen to Mickey sing the praises of Don and his amazing new party weapon. And everybody, but everybody, wanted to try it.

Don was in his element. He cracked the little crate open and revealed a plastic-wrapped brick of powder bound with a band of white parchment. There were black, hand-drawn symbols on the paper strip, which Don cut loose and passed around. While everybody puzzled over the symbols, he decided to sell the powder by the teaspoonful. Ten bucks, no, the hell with it, twenty bucks each. And the stuff flew. People kept coming in, most of them ended up buying, and Don barely had to lift a finger. One kid even understood the marks on the band of parchment. He said it was in Tongan, a language from somewhere in the South Pacific around Fiji.

"White wake, black wave," read the kid.

"Isn't that backwards?" Don said. "I mean, first you get the wave, then the wake, right?"

"I guess. But that's what it says."

Then Don was scraping the spoon on the little crate's bottom. It was all gone, and his pockets were crammed with enough twenty-dollar bills to pay off his Corvette, and for less than four hours work. He could live with that.

He'd said good-bye to his happy customers and headed back to his apartment. Now, with dawn still hours away, Don leaned into the warm pillows and eyed the woman sleeping beside him. Even though Mary, or Cherry or whatever the hell her name was, wouldn't drink a glass of wine much less touch the White Wake, she had followed him home. Everybody loves a successful guy.

He felt like just savoring it all. He'd find Mr. Lesko tomorrow and see how much he could get in one lump quantity. He'd use today's profits and empty his bank account if he had to. Whatever it took, he'd do. Lesko's White Wake was the magic that was going to change his life. He suddenly remembered the fat man's last words to him and sat up in bed. Half of the original baggie was still stuffed into a pocket of his jeans. Don slipped naked out of bed and padded to the closet. He groped in the darkness until his fingers found crinkled plastic. When he crawled back into bed the woman sighed and shifted, but didn't wake. He re-established his position against the pillows and contemplated the half-full baggie in the gloom. The white powder gleamed dully on the dark blankets, like luminous froth on a black swell. He dug a finger into the bag. Outside, he could hear crickets singing.

Mr. Lesko said that a worthy businessman knew his goods. Don felt obliged to admit he had a point.

* * * *

"So with a low of close to sixty degrees, we've finally got some good sleeping weather tonight."

"Sleep? Who can sleep with all the racket, Bob?"

"Good question, Johnny. Scientists at Stratton University are still trying to explain the absolutely outlandish level of noise made by our local night life. As you've no doubt noticed, over the past few evenings crickets, frogs, and night birds have been doing their level best to keep all of us in Stratton from our rest. Some suggest that a change of climate, the unseasonably warm temperatures, or even an undetected toxic spill may be to blame, but the fact is, nobody really knows what's bothering our animal friends."

"Think they know something we don't, Bob?"

"Could be, Johnny, could be."

* * * *

Don Lane was floating. He felt so good he had to concentrate just to remain aware of his surroundings. There was a blissful quaver deep in his breast, as if he had learned a wonderful secret and could scarcely contain it. The dim outlines of his bedroom had slowly faded away, replaced by a vast cloudscape. He looked about, every cell purring with ecstasy, and saw that he was suspended at a measureless height, floating among fleecy clouds struck gold and crimson against a sky of translucent blue. Far off, at the limits of his vision, scattered golden flecks glistened against the limitless sky. Above him, the firmament seemed to rise forever, perhaps to paradise.

Below him, he could see no ground, just more clouds and sky and a tiny black spot that might have been the earth. He marveled at his own body, for he was naked and radiating a golden luminescence. Tears came to his eyes at the pleasure that pulsed and flowed through him. He didn't deserve this. It was too good. The air itself seemed charged with anticipation. As magnificent as all this was, something even more wonderful was going to happen. Don Lane spun in an endless sky, crying out with a pleasure that was too great to bear.

And then awoke in his own bed.

Don sat up in confusion. The morning sun was just peering through his window. He was astonished to find that, not only did he have no hangover, but he felt better than he had in months. Every muscle seemed relaxed, and his head was clear and sharp.

"Well, I'll be damned," he muttered. The woman beside him stirred uneasily. He shook his head. Mickey and his pals might be losers, but they knew a good thing when they tried it.

The phone rang, as sudden and unexpected as a slap. Don reached for it and the woman beside him sat up and screamed.

"I'm drowning!" Her hands flailed into his face. "It's awake! Get it away!" She fell over the side of the bed and was instantly on her feet, knees bent and fists clenched.

The phone rang again.

"Jesus Christ!" said Don, half amused. "It's just a dream, baby. Calm-"

"It's so hungry!" Her words twisted off into a throat-tearing shriek that stripped the smile from Don's face. He slid off the mattress, holding his hands out to calm her.

"Hey," he said. "Hey, it's okay."

"The wave!" she screamed. "It takes everything! It takes it all!" She leapt across the bed at Don and grabbed his throat in both hands. The phone kept ringing.

"It's time!" The woman's voice hurt his ears and her nails tore the skin of his neck, but Don outweighed her by more than one hundred pounds. His left forearm knocked her hands from his throat, then his right fist drove into her face. Her head snapped back, blood starting from her lips and nose. She took two unsteady steps backward and sat down on the carpet.

"Crazy bitch," panted Don. "What the hell is the matter with you?" Her eyes rolled, met Don's gaze, and a chill flooded his guts. There was no recognition there, just empty, bestial rage and fear. Don turned to grab his robe and she came up off the floor with a scream.

"It wants out! It wants in!" Don grabbed her by the shoulders and threw her bodily into the living room. She writhed on the floor, then scrambled to her feet as he stalked to the front door.

"This the way you want it?" he asked. She lunged at him and he jerked the door open and shoved her naked into the hall. He slammed the door and locked it with a grunt of satisfaction. He waited for her embarrassed pleas to come through the door.

"Eats us all." It sounded as though she was sobbing. "All gone and drowned."

The phone had stopped ringing. Don waited through a long moment of indecision. He took a step toward the phone, almost deciding to call the police, then he cursed and went to gather up her clothes. It was very quiet.

When he opened the door again she was gone.

The phone rang.

* * * *

"Law officers from four counties have been summoned to contain what's been described as the worst prison riot in 30 years."

"That's right, Bob. Authorities are still trying to explain what inspired a diverse collection of prisoners to throw themselves at their guards in a ferocious assault that rocked San Matthias Correctional Institute starting last night around midnight. Twelve are known dead at this time, and the prison is burning in at least three locations. Recaptured prisoners are said to be violent and incoherent, while rioters are reportedly shouting gibberish and fighting amongst themselves. Officials insist that conditions in the minimum-security facility are among the best in the nation, so it's difficult to see what could have turned the model prison into a scene of such destruction."

"And in a grim parallel to that story, Johnny, we have news of a disturbance at the much-respected Prinn Sanitarium. Preliminary reports indicate that at least two are dead in unprecedented violence at the upscale facility."

"Not to worry, viewers, as state and local police have both situations contained and under control."

* * * *

"I trust you didn't have long to wait, Mr. Lane?"

"Oh no. I'm getting used to doing business with you, Mr. Lesko." Don looked up at the fat man's bloated body silhouetted against the gaudy lights of the juke box and realized that Lesko was still in the same clothes. He stood over Don and made no move to sit down.

"How was business, Mr. Lane? Ahm, I trust you are not overcharging our customers?"

"Oh no. It's all gone. I moved it all."

The thick lips pulled into a broad grin, peeling back from the fat man's teeth. Don blinked. Lesko had at least one extra set of incisors; thick, pointed teeth that made his wide mouth look crowded.

"To a sizable clientele?"

"Dozens of people, Mr. Lesko. News of White Wake spread quickly, and the word of mouth was the best I've ever heard." Don paused and looked squarely into the fat man's dark eyes. "I'm confident I can move as much product as you can provide."

"Splendid, Mr. Lane, just splendid! Another crate awaits you in my truck."

"Maybe you didn't hear me, Mr. Lesko. I said I can move as much as I'm given. That little box didn't last me the night."

The fat man threw his head back and liquid laughter bubbled from his thick throat. He wiped a hand across his mouth and it came away wet. "Ahm, Mr. Lane, you are an impetuous character."

"No offense intended, Mr. Lesko. I just think I can do better for both of us."

"No offense taken, sir. I assure you there is nothing that could please both myself and my employer more than to have White Wake given as wide a distribution as possible in as short a time frame as possible."

"Your employer is serious about business."

Lesko laughed softly, and for a second Don thought he was being mocked. "My employer is serious about acquiring customers."

"Well, customers mean money."

"More than that, Mr. Lane. Much more than that. With enough customers my employer will change the world. Please follow me and we'll see what I can do to allow you to pursue your admirable ambitions."

Lesko's truck was in the same place, still riding low on its shocks beneath the shadow of the parking lot's only tree. Don kept thinking about the fat man's comment about changing the world and wondered if he were helping fund a political movement somewhere in the South Pacific. Not that it mattered.

"You got more in the truck?" The crickets were so loud that Don had to talk over them.

"Not enough to satisfy you, sir. Ahm, if you'll accompany me, I shall drive you to where we can obtain a more substantial quantity."

The passenger door was unlocked. Don slid into the seat with an odd tremor of trepidation. The floor was sticky under his shoes. Mr. Lesko gunned the motor, then threw the truck into reverse so hard the vehicle jolted and bounced on its overburdened shocks. An air freshener swung wildly beneath the rear-view mirror. Don squinted at it in disbelief. It was fashioned to resemble a marijuana leaf. Don almost asked Lesko whose truck it was, but the fat man's driving seized his full attention. Lesko didn't drive too fast and he seemed aware of other cars on the road, but he slowed at a stop sign or red light just long enough to be certain that there was no oncoming traffic before charging right through.

The truck moved swiftly from downtown into the less populous wharf district of the waterfront. As traffic thinned, Don breathed a sigh of relief and immediately noted that Mr. Lesko's cologne had lost much of its power. The once pungent aura of aftershave had faded enough so that he could smell what had to be Mr. Lesko's body odor. Don cracked the window and began to breathe through his mouth. No wonder the fat bastard used so much cologne. He smelled like a dead fish.

The truck lurched to a stop in front of a huge old warehouse with gray paint peeling from it like scabrous skin. A fresh fog blew inland, sent questing streamers around the warehouse's silent bulk.

"Ahm, wait here. I'll not be long." Lesko slid out of the cab and waddled off around the corner of the building. Don popped the door open and stood on the blacktop getting his breath back.

The night air was cool and moist with fog. He could hear the ocean, a vast and pervasive susurration like the ceaseless breathing of a restless creature as big as the world. Don circled the truck nervously, shrugging off an impulse to look at the statue beneath the tarp. A glimpse of those hideous clawed feet alone had been enough for him.

A strange trilling sound rose and floated on the clammy air for a moment, then faded. Don was sure it wasn't a bird but couldn't identify it. He strode surreptitiously to the corner around which Lesko had disappeared. He saw a darkly cluttered alley that stretched along the warehouse's flank and emptied onto a section of beach shadowed by sagging docks. Don peered hard down the alleyway. There was an open door on the warehouse's wall, and movement on the beach. A wave crashed hollowly and, in the pallid highlight of its dying foam, he saw figures emerging from the surf and Mr. Lesko standing on the beach to greet them.

Don withdrew suddenly, walked back to the truck and got in. His mind whirled. Was Lesko bringing the stuff in by ship, or even submarine? Maybe his drug didn't come from the Pacific, maybe it came from Russia. Who else would have submarines?

A moment later Mr. Lesko came staggering around the corner carrying a dripping crate the size of a small trunk. Don thought to help him, but the fat man quickly climbed onto the back bumper and dropped the weighty crate into the pick-up's bed without assistance.

The driver's door was jerked open and Mr. Lesko slid in beside him.

"Ahm, that, my friend, ought to be enough for even a salesman of your caliber."

"What's the price tag?" Don hadn't meant to say it like that. It was bad business to be so blunt about cash.

"Would five hundred dollars be agreeable?"

"Five-" Don choked. He'd made eight times that off a package a quarter the size of the crate in the back of the truck. "You've got yourself a deal, Mr. Lesko."

"Excellent, Mr. Lane."

* * * *

"Are you sleeping well out there? If you are you should count yourself lucky. Doctors and specialists across the state are reporting a dramatic upsurge in the number of cases of insomnia and troubled sleep, with a surprising emphasis on night terrors."

"Nightmares, Johnny?"

"That's right, Bob. It seems the stress of everyday life is really taking its toll."

"Whoa! Hey, Johnny, did you feel that?"

"I sure did, Bob. And I'm hoping all of you in our viewing audience found that earth tremor to be as minor and inoffensive as we did."

"Whew! That's my first televised tremor!"

"Maybe it'll help our ratings, eh Bob?"

"Could be, Johnny. Anyway, no harm done."

* * * *

The earth shuddered beneath his prone body. The gentle tremor triggered an apprehension that drew him back to the waking world. Don rolled over and felt something dig into his back. His head hammered with pain and when he put his hand to the sore spot above his right ear, he touched warm wetness. He dragged his eyes open. God, where was he?

Bushes. He was lying on the ground under some bushes. Don stood up unsteadily, dirt and dead leaves clinging to his sport coat. Crickets sent up a constant din around him. He saw where he was, and his memory returned with sick clarity. A few feet behind him was the brick exterior of the Badge of Virtue fraternity house. It was very late; all the windows were dark. Lesko had dropped him off at his car with the crate, and he'd gone directly to the frat and done good business. He'd been drinking far too much, and suddenly it seemed like everybody's cash had dried up. Shaggy-headed Mickey had made him promise to visit the big beach party that everybody was talking about. Don had waved good-bye, stepped out onto the porch, and something hard had slammed into his skull just above the right ear. Sudden shock flooded his belly with adrenaline. Where was the crate?

It was gone, along with his wallet and all the money he'd shoved into it over the course of the evening. He'd been rolled like an old wino. Don began cursing in a low monotone. Someone had waited for him to leave the frat, then jumped him, robbed him, and dumped him in the bushes. A wash of helpless rage weakened his limbs. He knew he shouldn't have brought the whole crate into the frat, knew he shouldn't have been drinking so much, but he'd wanted to be the center of attention, to dole out his bounty and be the life of the party. Don cursed himself with drunken bitterness. The crate had been nearly full. He felt the pain of losing a sizable sum of money, but was somewhat surprised to feel a deeper, more unsettling, sense of loss.

He'd lost all of the drug, and with it his chance to feel the ecstasy of being suspended in its endless cloudscape. It wasn't right. It wasn't fair. Don wiped his bloody hand on a handkerchief, then daubed it at the lump above his right ear. His other hand quickly dusted the dirt and leaves from his clothes. His face hardened with determination. Nobody was going to deprive him of what was justly his. In time he would find out who had robbed him and have his revenge, but now he just wanted more White Wake. More to sell and more to use. He'd earned it. He had a right to more. He shook his head and realized that this wasn't much of a problem, really.

He knew just where to get it.

* * * *

"This just in. A maintenance man at central Stratton's world-famous Grace Cathedral called police about an event that saddens all of us here at Channel 17 Action News more than I can say. It seems that vandals somehow removed the cross from its place in the altar's apse, destroying a work of art commissioned for the church back in February 1928."

"And that's not all, Bob. Although authorities have closed the church for an in-depth investigation, we've learned that the cross was replaced by what one police officer described as a 'a pagan statue with horrible claws', and that the walls and furnishings were defaced with filth and draped with long strands of sea kelp."

"Jeez, Johnny. It makes you wonder how much worse it can get."

* * * *

Don parked the Corvette in an alley and made his way toward the warehouse with one hand on his pepper spray. His steps were unsteady, but there was no one to see. His drunken gaze scanned the sky and alighted on a strange star. It seemed to throw a slim path of bubbling light across the night's black ocean. It was the comet, of course. He'd seen it on the news.

Don thought he heard a distant bass rhythm, a thrumming of drums, but his head still throbbed so cruelly that it was difficult to tell if the sound originated inside or outside of his battered skull. The alley opened for him, but the door into the warehouse was closed. Don stopped in front of it and dusted himself off again. The drumming was loud enough that it had to be coming from within the warehouse, and now it was joined by an odd chant. He'd never heard music like that before. But someone was here, he reasoned; they were playing the radio, probably having a party. The heavy door came open under his hand.

Inside was a vaulting emptiness, a green-lit darkness. He had a moment before he was noticed, and his eyes dilated to take in the scene. A meager handful of emerald tapers lit the vast hollow of the warehouse, and that which they illuminated seemed less significant than that which remained in shadow.

Naked figures leapt and capered before a mottled and worn statue, a colossus of aged and pitted stone. Two tapers were set at its feet, and Don knew he had seen a smaller version of those terrible stone talons before. Its body was one with the smoky darkness, slouching and reptilian. Its face was a drooping smear of streaked stone, a collection of ropy columns surrounding a black disc of a mouth and surmounted by slash-like eyes that burned his retinas with a color like none he had ever known.

The drums and the dance, the chanting and the moans, all ceased. Don felt the thrust of their gaze as a physical force, like branding irons on his skin.

He opened his mouth to speak and they fell upon him. The pepper spray was knocked from his feeble grip. Wet hands seized his limbs and bore him to the dirty concrete. Someone laughing held his shoulders down and drooled into his screaming face. Don looked up into the bloated features of Mr. Lesko and saw the purple gills that pulsed on his ridged throat.

"Want more?" Mr. Lesko was laughing, his scaled and flabby flesh shaking with glee. "Want more?"

Don could answer only by screaming, which he did until the thing that had called itself Mr. Lesko shoved a fist-sized clump of powder down his throat.

He choked and tried to crawl away, but the celebrants withdrew from tormenting him. The music began again and the dance as well, even more frenzied than before, but Don couldn't concentrate on it. He was aware of his body lying on the concrete as he might be aware of one of his better shirts lying on the floor of his apartment. It seemed regrettable, a less than ideal place for it to be, but it didn't really bear worrying about. He was trying to remember why he wanted to stand up, when the walls fell away into a boundless sky.

The brilliant clouds seemed almost blinding after the darkness of the warehouse, but Don didn't think of that for long. His glowing golden body was humming with keen pleasure and a heightened sense of glorious anticipation.

He looked around and saw that the black spot below had grown into an ebony disc, and that the golden flecks he had seen in the distance were much more numerous. Don wished he might see the shining motes more closely and was delighted to find himself soaring toward them effortlessly. He stared with stunned wonder at the dozens, perhaps hundreds, of golden figures hanging suspended in the air. They were nude and glowing, and they waved and smiled beatifically at him. It was as though he was airborne with a flight of luminous angels. The sense of expectation seemed almost palpable, and Don was achingly content simply to hover with his brethren in this airy paradise.

But the figure next to him was trying to get his attention. Don saw that it was the shaggy-headed fellow from Badge of Virtue, Mickey. How wonderful it was to see a friend here! But Mickey wasn't smiling, he was gesturing oddly. Don couldn't concentrate on him.

Don looked down and saw that the black disc had grown like a storm cloud. It was as black as an eye of night in the daylit cloudscape.

Now the floating figures were being drawn together, pulled by some force into a shining cluster, like a galaxy of golden stars. Don watched the beautiful process with detached admiration. Mickey caught his eye again. His face was contorted with an unfathomable urgency, and he was pointing downward while his lips worked silently.

Don felt a frozen wind blow through his skull, and suddenly vertigo wrenched at his belly. He was falling; they all were falling. The pleasure was gone, and in its place was an all-encompassing terror. All around him golden faces twisted into soundless screams. He looked down.

The black disc expanded until they were like skydivers plunging toward a nighted planet. Its edges grew ragged, stretched into ropy, reaching tendrils.

Don stared down in wordless horror. Here it comes. It's not a storm cloud. It's not a planet.

It's a mouth.

* * * *

"Ladies and gentlemen, I am profoundly disturbed by what may be the most tragic story Channel 17 Action News has ever covered. A midnight beach-gathering of some of Stratton University's best and brightest ended in death for more than forty young people, many of them affiliated with the Badge of Virtue fraternity house. Authorities are blaming the tragedy on an unknown designer drug. Here's our own Bob Rowland at the scene."

"Thanks, Johnny. I hope you'll forgive me if I'm somewhat at a loss for words. As you can see, the police have covered the bodies with sheets, but I can tell you I've never seen such terrible faces."

"You're guessing it's a side effect of this mysterious drug, Bob?"

"I don't know, Johnny, but these people died without a mark on their bodies and from the expressions on their faces you'd think they'd been tortured to death. Hey, what? What was that?"

"Bob, the camera's not steady. What's going on out there?"

"The sand's jumping. Oh!"

"It's another earth tremor, Bob! Hang on out there. Whoa! We've lost your visual. Jesus, what a jolt!"

"John! John! It felt like the whole damn world just dropped ten feet! The ground fell away right under my shoes. I can hear people screaming and-and-and-oh my God!"

"Bob, your camera is down, what's going on out there?"

"I can see it! One horizon to the other! Must be a fucking half mile high."

"What is it? What is it, Bob?"

"It's coming! I can see things moving in it."

"What's that roar? I repeat, we have no visual. Bob, what is it?"

"A black wave…"